Send Him Victorious

The dawn of disaster—a violent rebellion in Chelsea Barracks . . .

Harvey reached for the receiver. The voice at the other end was unnecessarily loud, even allowing for the distortion of the scrambler.

'Prime Minister, is that you?' Michael Critten was a bully, popular with the generals.

'Yes, Michael, what is it?'

Critten spoke rapidly for perhaps a minute. The Private Secretary watched his master for a reaction, but the well-trained face showed nothing. After a moment's thought the Prime Minister spoke. He was choosing his words carefully, trying to lower the temperature.

'Well, Michael, it's bad news, I admit. I know how you feel, but I don't think we can take this as evidence of general discontent.' There was a gabble of protest through the receiver, cut short with authority. 'Well, hush it up, man. It's perfectly explicable as a local incident, without political implications. The Press will be satisfied with that.'

Later, as he took his seat at the lunch table, Patrick Harvey had the momentary but unpleasant sensation that neither the chair nor the floor were there and he was falling through the air.

DOUGLAS HURD AND
ANDREW OSMOND

Send Him Victorious

COLLINS Fontana Books

First published 1968
First issued in Fontana Books 1969
Second Impression February 1971

For Stuart and Tatiana

© *Douglas Hurd and Andrew Osmond 1968*
Printed in Great Britain
Collins Clear-Type Press London and Glasgow

Monday, August 4th

12 noon

Like many older people, Mrs. Steele was reminded of the year the war began. Now, as then, there was something unreal about the heat, something forced about the general gaiety. People said the weather was caused by the Russian moonshot, and she thought with a shudder of the four cosmonauts stranded on the cold white planet. The papers were full of the African business—and who could tell where that would end? Something new seemed to happen every minute. As she crossed the King's Road she found herself wondering what would become of the young, with their long hair and crazy clothes. It was hard to believe they were made of the same stuff as her own generation. Sometimes she was amazed to think how long she had lived.

Skirting the crowd outside the Minoa Boutique, she turned into the Six Bells for her usual Mackeson before catching the bus to Battersea. It was soon after twelve and Mrs. Kemble had just come on.

'Mrs. Livingstone, I presume. Welcome to the Dark Continent, dear!' said Mrs. Kemble, who had spent some time thinking up this line, subtly referring to politics and the weather, and had used it twice already.

But Mrs. Steele was still thinking of the Blitz, and nodded as if she had received a serious piece of news. It had taken them six hours to dig her father out; her brother had stepped on a mine in Burma, and Harry's father had died in Korea before the boy was born. She had never married again. 'Yes,' she said, 'it's too hot to last. There'll be a storm tonight.'

Mrs. Kemble was quick to find a cause of mutual suffering. 'All these demonstrations, they get me down. Did you see those young idiots on the telly?' She dropped her voice. 'If you ask me, we should leave the blacks to settle their own problems. Why should that UNO tell us where to send our army?'

'I'll not hear a word against the Tories,' said a fat man in the corner. 'They scrapped the licensing hours, and that's enough for me.'

'Well, they had to think of something, didn't they?' someone else said.

But Mrs. Steele was not to be drawn. Finishing up her drink she said to no one in particular: 'It'll break tonight. You see. Then we'll all feel better.'

Back in the fierce sunlight she decided to walk home, passing by Chelsea Barracks in case she should get a glimpse of Harry. His leave had been cancelled three days before, and she had heard nothing since.

As soon as she reached the gate in Chelsea Bridge Road she could see that something unusual was happening. The whole battalion was on parade, every man in denims and full battle order and carrying a kit-bag. (Harry had taught her something about military matters.) No tin hats, she noticed. There was a long line of trucks drawn up on the inside of the railings.

She drew level with a small crowd on the pavement. A woman turned and said: 'They've been like that for an hour, you know. Poor boys, in this heat. I think it's a shame.' The battalion was standing easy and there was a lot of low excited talk, periodically quelled by the Company Sergeant-Majors. She saw Harry now, standing by a tall, upper-class-looking boy with fair hair. Why were there no officers on parade? She decided to wait.

Ten minutes later she was the only spectator left. As the clocks struck 12.45 a short figure in battledress, brasses flashing, strode from a door on the far side of the parade-ground. She recognised Sergeant-Major Reith. Enemy Number One Harry called him, and now that she could see the comic swagger, the tight-lipped face half hidden below the peaked cap, she was not surprised. Her son had the sort of independent spirit that the likes of Reith would need to crush. Her father had always refused to go to the shelter. Such things run in the blood.

Reith stopped, and turned away from the street.

A fierce shriek, a long note, then another shriek, and the mass of slack green-clad bodies crashed to attention: rigid, identity extinct. Somewhere a clock was still striking, and above the trees Battersea Power Station belched its pure white smoke into the sky. Mrs. Steele blinked tears of pride. In a world of change the perfection of this disciplined machine was a comforting thing.

Reith was speaking.

'Now listen to me, carefully. Colonel Rogers and the other officers have been detained for a special briefing, so we shall be moving without them—clear? The Commanding Officer has asked me to say a few words about our destination, before you all read it in the papers. The battalion is being transferred to R.A.F. Transport Command, Brize Norton—which is near Oxford, for those that haven't heard of it—and temporary accommodation will be provided there. When we get to Brize Norton, the battalion will be on six-hour call. There'll be no leave and every man will be confined to barracks—clear? Tropical kit, grenades and full ammunition will be issued later. That's all. Now I want to see this move carried out in an orderly fashion. No talking till we're outside the gate. Company Sergeant-Majors, carry on.'

The C.S.M.s had started to march forward from behind their companies, when an extraordinary thing happened. From somewhere in the ranks came a hoarse, high-pitched shout.

'We'll not fight for bloody niggers!'

N.C.O.s descended on the offender from all directions, but were deflected by other shouts, from the left and right.

'Get lost, Reith!'

'Up the Whites!'

From the centre again: 'Stuff the United Nations!'

'Shoot the blacks!'

The isolated protests were drowned by a yell of support from perhaps fifty, perhaps a hundred throats; as the noise died, the original voice could be heard chanting 'Hands off Rhodesia!' several times; there was a chatter of rifles flung to the ground, then silence.

Nobody moved. The N.C.O.s, uncertain where to begin,

waited for a word from Reith, but Reith was silent. Faced with the unthinkable, he searched in vain for a prescribed course of action. For the first time in his life the Sergeant-Major did not know what to do.

The Second Battalion, the Welsh Guards were also in the barracks—he could send for their senior officers; but would his own C.O. ever forgive such a humiliation? He could arrest the offenders and drill the rest into submission, trusting in habit and the power of his lungs; but how many offenders would there be? He could play it soft—gather them round him at the back of the square, talk to them as an equal, joke, sympathise, shame them with history—then carry on as if nothing had happened, collecting the names later; but that was a most unusual way for a Sergeant-Major to behave. . . .

The stunned mind struggled to a decision. Gathering his strength, Reith began to bark his orders.

Outside the railings Mrs. Steele stood still and unobserved. She began to feel faint in the heat, and clutched at the iron bars for support. 'I am the only person to have seen this happen', she thought; but she was wrong. Behind her two men in a Ford Zodiac were following events on the parade-ground with interest.

12.50 pm

At 10 Downing Street Patrick Harvey was alone in his study. A man of regular habits, he traditionally reserved the hour before lunch for going through official papers, and the top of the wide mahogany desk was littered with red despatch boxes. He worked fast, amending, signing, adding a crisp marginal comment here and there, occasionally dictating a rapid minute into a tape recorder. He had a reputation as an administrator, and this was the part of the job he liked best. Papers were easier than people; the dispassionate civil service prose reduced the worst problems to manageable proportions. As he tidied up the small affairs of state, he could almost forget that he had a national crisis on his hands.

8

Reluctantly he turned to the F.O. Box and started to read the telegram from the Ambassador in Pretoria.

'. . . The Prime Minister sent for me today. Dr. Langer said that the situation in Rhodesia was becoming intolerably dangerous for South Africa. He could tell me privately that the South African Government had done all in its power to prevent the Rhodesian White Brotherhood from overthrowing Smith and the Settlement of 1968. The South Africans had criticised the Settlement at the time, but it had brought law and order to Rhodesia, and they had wanted it to continue. But it was no good harking back to that. The White Brotherhood had broken the Settlement and seized power; the alternative to Brotherhood rule in Rhodesia was now a black nationalist régime. It was already clear that this régime would not be of the moderate type existing in Zambia, Malawi and the Congo. The black nationalists were receiving arms, finance and training from China; once in power, they would inevitably become the agents of rebellion in South Africa. He wished you to know that South Africa would use "every means without exception" to prevent this situation arising. The vital security of South Africa itself was at stake.

'2. This conversation was obviously a last minute attempt to influence H.M.G's policy towards Rhodesia. But I am satisfied that Dr. Langer was not bluffing. As already reported, I believe that the South Africans have decided in principle to intervene by force on behalf of the Brotherhood in Rhodesia. My attachés report that preparations are far advanced and that the operation could begin with paratroop drops on Salisbury and the Kariba Dam as early as Saturday, August 9. The South African Government would obviously prefer to avoid a military collision with British troops, but are not deterred by this prospect. They believe that any British or U.N. intervention will be too little and too late.'

Harvey glanced at the calendar, then threw the telegram in the out-tray. There was not much time. The Security Council was to meet that night and the British Delegation would need instructions. He had called the Cabinet for 3 p.m., but a decision that afternoon was unlikely. The

9

two factions seemed about evenly balanced for and against sending British troops into Rhodesia. They must be given time to argue themselves out, then he could step in and suggest a consensus. But that was an outside chance; more likely there would be resignations. Either way it would be a tough battle—in the Cabinet, in the country, in the Commons (if they had to be called from recess), in the U.N., in Africa. Endless meetings, speeches, decisions. . . .

He walked to the window. Two small boys were chasing a dog across Horse Guards' Parade. One tripped, fell, howled for a few seconds over a grazed knee, then rejoined the chase. The Prime Minister felt alone with the two boys, detached from the telegrams and boxes. He recognised without emotion that the political deathwish had been growing in him for some time.

His reverie was interrupted by simultaneous knocks on two of the study doors. One opened to reveal the butler, announcing lunch, the other a Private Secretary with the news that the Minister of Defence was on the line with an urgent message. Waving the butler from the room, Harvey reached for the green receiver. The voice at the other end was unnecessarily loud, even allowing for the distortion of the scrambler.

'Prime Minister, is that you?' Michael Critten was a bully, popular with the generals. There was no member of his cabinet for whom Harvey felt less inclined to delay his lunch.

'Yes, Michael, what is it?'

Critten spoke rapidly for perhaps a minute. The Private Secretary watched his master for a reaction, but the well-trained face showed nothing. After a moment's thought the Prime Minister spoke. He was choosing his words carefully, trying to lower the temperature.

'Well, Michael, it's bad news, I admit. I know how you feel, but I don't think we can take this as evidence of general discontent.' There was a gabble of protest through the receiver, cut short with authority. 'Well hush it up, man. It's perfectly explicable as a local incident, without political implications. The Press will be satisfied with that. And Michael—kindly remember you don't work for the C.I.G.S., he works for us. I'll see you here at three.'

Moments later the Private Secretaries' office was noisy with speculation. Like birds they fluttered and chirped, small men in the presence of big events.

'What was all that about, John?'

'God knows. Nothing much probably. Just Critten stirring it up again.'

'What a bonehead that man is. Now if I were Minister of Defence. . . .'

As he took his seat at the lunch table, Patrick Harvey had the momentary but unpleasant sensation that neither the chair nor the floor were there and he was falling through the air.

1 pm

Shortly after Jack Kemble had joined the *Sun* in 1968, it had been merged with *The Guardian* into a new middle-brow, middle-of-the-road daily—the *Globe*. Kemble had done well on the new paper and was acknowledged to be a more than usually competent Assistant Defence Correspondent, destined for higher things; but recently, for a reason he could not define, his ambition had deserted him. The enthusiasm of his early days on the *Sun* was a dimly remembered joke, like adolescence, and expertise had brought less than the expected satisfaction. 'Jack's a real professional', said the men in the newsroom, by which they meant he could drink and lie better than most. Perhaps it was meeting Anne Downes that had made him suspect the existence of a few hairline flaws in this ideal.

Elbowing his way through a crowd of demonstrators outside Number Ten, he walked up Whitehall. That morning's special briefing at the F.O. had been ludicrously bare of fact. Obviously the Cabinet had not yet decided whether to move against the new white régime in Rhodesia, and we should have to go through the usual humiliating prevarications at the U.N. Still, it was difficult to see what a Tory P.M. like Harvey could do, with four rightwingers in the Cabinet and anything up to a hundred rebels in the party. . . . Slotting the facts together, he wrote an anodyne column in his head.

He reached the top of Whitehall and crossed to the right. Northumberland Avenue had always seemed to Kemble the dimmest street in London—a canyon of pigeon droppings, draughty home of forgotten sub-sections of the public service—but that morning it was seething with violent activity. Rows of police were holding back a 'Hands off Rhodesia' march from Trafalgar Square, where Edgar Zimmermann, leader of the Labour Left and the 'Africa for the Africans' movement, was addressing a lunch-time rally. Whoever was winning, it was not the police. Clutching his Polaroid glasses and collapsible umbrella, Kemble fought through the mob to the other side.

It was strange how unmoved he was by this crisis that divided his countrymen so fiercely. There was a day when he would have been in there waving a banner with the best; but he had dropped his lukewarm university communism along with his student friends, and now wore no label. Close observations of politics had stripped him of political passions. When threatened with serious argument he was fond of describing his position as 'Extreme Centre,' and had been heard to defend the Bantu and the white supremacists with equal witty eloquence. There was no doubt that he was admirably qualified to work for the *Globe*, and to join the clientele at El Vino's—which he then did.

Anne was waiting by the door. Tall, dark, verging on the skinny, dressed with the kooky but expensive style you would expect from a girl who had just got a second in psychology at Oxford and whose father was British Ambassador in Rome.

'Your beauty astounds me,' he said, reaching to kiss the powderless cheek.

'You're late, fatso—and to add injury to insult, you pick the only bar in London that refuses to admit single women.'

'It's a historical monument.'

'So are you, mate.'

After five minutes they found a table and Kemble ordered a large Scotch and a Campari soda. Placing his whisky carefully between *The History of the Left in Europe* and the little glass of red liquid, he lowered himself into a wheel-back chair. A retort was needed.

'If your daddy's colleagues could be a mite more crisp in explaining their minds, I'd have been here half an hour ago.'

'Your tie is loose.'

'That is because I have just fought my way through several thousand maniacs who aim to settle British foreign policy with a pitched battle in Trafalgar Square.'

'Well I hope you struck a blow for the Africans.'

'My concern was with my own skin, and that is a rather delicate shade of yellow, which absolves me from taking sides in such matters.'

'Funny as ever. It really amazes me that a man of your intelligence should have reached the advanced age of thirty without taking a decision about anything. Did your father dominate you?'

The conversation was interrupted by the *Daily Telegraph* Motoring Correspondent, who fell across their table. He appeared to have tripped over Anne's umbrella. A fresh round was called for, but before it could arrive Kemble was summoned to the telephone. It was the *Globe* switchboard to say that he was wanted urgently by the Assistant Editor. Waving goodbye more to his drink than to his girl, Kemble ran for the *Globe* building. He climbed to the third floor and crossed the littered waste-land of the newsroom to the glass-walled office in the corner.

Joe Hollis, the Assistant Editor for politics and defence, was a red-haired Scot, and like all red-haired Scots went pale when cross. Today Joe was very pale.

'Well done, Kemble. We should have had you in Munich —the nation's gold medal boozer. You were supposed to look in before lunch. You didn't. Once more, laddie, and you'll be on Gardening Notes.'

'Sorry, Joe. There was nothing—'

'Kemble, my office is paved with your excuses. Here I sit, the only link with the outside world for millions of decent hard-working Conservatives, and not a ruddy corres-pondent in sight. . . .'

Kemble recovered his breath and sat down. Hollis was a taciturn man, with all the dispassionate caution of his race; he would not indulge in these theatricals unless there was a punch line.

'All right, Joe, what is it?'

'Anonymous call. Could be a joker, but I think not. Sounded like an official on the sneak. Said there's been trouble at Chelsea Barracks. I want you there in ten minutes.'

'Me? But why the hell can't—'

'Because it could be big, it could have a political angle. I should like to run this story myself, and you're the only man I've got.'

Kemble sighed. 'You're the boss. What happened at the barracks?'

'The Grenadiers have killed their R.S.M.'

4 pm (5 pm Italy)

'Will Signor Brunswick be taking tea this afternoon, Sir Courthope?'

'Yes, Francesco, but later; I will have mine now, with lemon.'

Sir James Courthope, Private Secretary, sat in a chair which the shadow of late afternoon had just reached. From the hotel terrace he could see down the folds of rocky hillside to the roofs of Amalfi and the harbour where a large white yacht lay at anchor. It was the best moment of the day for the Private Secretary; the heat was relaxing its grip, but the King still slept. Everyone in Ravello knew that Signor Brunswick was the King of England; the incognito was no disguise but a simple device for making unnecessary any official calls by the Mayor, Bishop and Prefect. Sir James Courthope had as usual entered himself in the hotel register as Mr. Dunn; the head waiter, after some indecision at the first visit three years ago, never called him anything but Sir Courthope. As he sipped his tea and watched the breeze stir the cypresses he thought that this was much the most enjoyable of the regular royal holidays.

The head waiter crossed the terrace fast and apologetically: 'His Excellency the Ambassador calling from Rome.'

The telephone was in the manager's office, the line was bad. The fluster in the Ambassador's voice conveyed itself in feverish crackles as he wrestled unhappily with the simple security rules for this kind of conversation. 'That you, Dunn? Got through at last. Look, there's a personal message for Mr. Brunswick from Number One in London. Very urgent and very, er, extraordinary. Came through an hour ago. You've met Raikes, my Head of Chancery. I've sent him down with it in my Jaguar. Less obvious than the Rolls, don't you think? He should reach you in about two hours from now.'

'I see. Does the message ask for a reply?'

'Well, no—at least, not in so many words, but it's so, er, extraordinary . . .' The Ambassador tailed off unhappily, and Courthope walked back to his chair by the bougainvillaea.

Odd, he thought, that a man so experienced as the Ambassador should let himself become flurried by a message from the Prime Minister.

He called for a gin and tonic. There would be time for three chapters of Gide before the King woke up.

Three hours later Raikes toiled round the last of the bends up to Ravello. He was hot, dirty and apprehensive. The Ambassador had refused to let him drive his own car (as being too humble) or to take an official driver (as being insecure). He had come perforce in the Ambassador's own Jaguar, long notorious throughout Italy for its scrapes and collisions. The fan belt had broken on the *autostrada*. There was a spare, but Raikes had not known how to fit it, and his hands and Aquascutum suit were spattered richly with grease before a patrol car came to his help. He had turned on the car radio to find the news and typically the knob had stuck at maximum volume so that the last half of his journey had been made miserable by the blaring of the kind of music which he least admired. He drove into the dignified hotel court-yard with a message for his sovereign in his pocket and the din of 'slow down, baby, I'm losing my grip' in his ears.

15

Courthope was hardly the older man, but his pale good looks and light suit gave him an easy victory over Raikes, grubby and rumpled by the struggle with the Jaguar.

'You have the message?'

'Yes, here'—pale blue envelope, dark blue crest—'the Ambassador thought perhaps I should myself . . .'

'No, that will not be necessary, the King asked me to receive it; but perhaps you could wait in case there is an answer. Sit down and have a drink.'

Half an hour later Courthope returned with another envelope, even stiffer than the first, white with black crest. Raikes thought he detected a trace of bad temper behind the normal quiet insolence.

'This is top secret and cannot be telephoned. It should go by telegraph tonight of course, and please tell the Ambassador that he must make himself personally responsible for its despatch, and warn Downing Street by telephone to wait up for it.'

Raikes began to fumble in his pockets for money to pay for his Carpano.

'Leave it. I'll pay, you've no time to waste.'

The courtyard in front of the hotel was cooler now but the Jaguar in the corner was still radiating heat. It was slow to start, and as two reluctant waiters pushed Raikes down the slope he saw Courthope smile unkindly and turn away.

'£3,500 a year,' Raikes thought, not for the first time, 'and the public school fees—but can it, can it be worth it?'

Rome Telegram No. 356 of 4th August to the Foreign Office

FLASH   Dispatched 11.58 p.m.

Following Strictly Personal for Prime Minister from
H.M. The King.
Begins

Thank you for your message about the affair at Chelsea I approve your action in checking publicity, which might encourage similar outbreaks elsewhere. I consider it essential that the authority of my Ministers over the armed services of the Crown should not be impaired. I trust therefore that the

16

necessary firm measures of discipline will be taken and that the Cabinet will now without further delay decide its policy towards Rhodesia on its merits, without being influenced by any political opinions supposed to be held in the Army. In my judgment delay and vacillation are now the chief dangers.

You have discretion to show this telegram to your colleagues and to the Chiefs of Staff. I am writing to the widow of the Sergeant-Major I am ready to return to London at once if you so advise.

Good wishes. Ends.

Shortly after Raikes had gone, Sir James Courthope also descended the winding road from Ravello.

The evening tide of tourists was flowing strongly through the narrow streets of Amalfi and at the post office there was still a queue clasping postcards. Courthope, who knew Italy well, went straight to the office marked Direttore. He had a telegram of his own to send. The Postmaster, a gross Sicilian, protested that he could not send a telegram to London in code without authority from the regional office in Naples. Courthope made him call the local Carabinieri. After the call the Postmaster bustled to fetch two dusty glasses and a bottle of sticky white vermouth, and the telegram was soon on its way.

4.10 pm

Mrs. Kemble looked up from drying glasses to see her son come through the door.

'Hallo, love. You look tired. Where've you been?'

You're the one that looks tired, Kemble thought. She was due to retire at the end of the year. 'The barracks,' he said. 'They've had a riot.'

'A riot? I don't believe it.' Kemble smiled; the disbelief was partly natural optimism, partly an invitation to the harbinger of doom to step it up a bit. But the tea, he thought, would come first, and sure enough she said: 'Got time for a cup of tea? I've got a kettle on in the back.'

'Just ten minutes then,' he said, and followed her into the little room at the back of the pub. She looked forward to his afternoon visits and he tried to make them as regular as he could. They sat down together by the gas stove. She made the tea good and strong, and poured it into the two cups which had been set out ready with the milk and sugar. 'Now then,' she said, sitting back, 'what's this nonsense about a riot?'

'No nonsense, Mother. It was a nasty business. They broke the skulls of two sergeants and knifed their R.S.M.'

'Knifed—what—killed him, you mean?'

'Killed him.'

'Oh my lor, how dreadful; But it's the Grenadiers, isn't it?'

'It's the Grenadiers.'

'Fancy, a fine regiment like that. Whatever is the country coming to? Why did they do it, Jack?'

'That's what I've spent the last three hours trying to find out. They're putting out some story about a brawl with a couple of trouble-makers, but I think there's more to it. They've locked up seventeen men. The battalion was on the move, you know—they're probably going to Rhodesia —and if that had anything to do with it, we really would have a story. But nobody wants to talk to little Jack, so he's come to have tea with Mum.'

'Poor Mrs. Steele, she'll be worried.'

'Who?'

'Mrs. Steele—her boy's in the regiment. She was in here this morning, left just before lunch. Said she was going to walk home by the barracks. Oh Jack, do you think—I mean, she might have seen it all.'

'Mother!' Kemble seized his mother by the arm and turned her sharply towards him. 'Say that again. You know a Mrs. Steele, who has a son in the Grenadiers, and who left this pub this morning to walk by Chelsea Barracks?'

'Yes, that's right,' said Mrs. Kemble happily. It was a long time since she had been useful to her son. 'She cleans at the fire station.'

'What time did she leave?'

18

'Soon after twelve. About quarter past it would be. I remember—'

'Do you know this woman's address?'

'No, dear. But they'll tell you at the fire station.'

'So they will, so they will.' He leaned forward and kissed her violently on the cheek. 'Genius!' he said, and ran for the door.

'What about your tea?' she said.

8 pm

Lord Thorganby, who distrusted the telephone, sent his Private Secretary, Alan Selkirk, to his house to warn his wife and guests that the Cabinet was still sitting and that they should start without him.

The traffic was heavy because the police had shut off Trafalgar Square, expecting a new demonstration, and it took Selkirk almost half an hour to change and drive his Sunbeam to Eaton Place. Lucky he kept a second dinner jacket at the office, but pity his electric razor worked so feebly; he felt bristly and unwashed, and in the hot traffic his clean shirt turned sad. In Eaton Place two or three policemen had cleared a parking space outside Thorganby's house. Most of it was filled by a Bentley covered by posters in red, white and blue: 'True Britons say HANDS OFF RHODESIA.' Selkirk parked gloomily behind the Bentley. Lady Thorganby had sent out the cards herself, and Selkirk did not know who was coming. But the Bentley was unmistakable, and the harsh voice in the passageway as he went in confirmed that Barnett Coper was a guest.

Coper had sat in a Conservative midland seat for twenty years without achieving more than an occasional raucous supplementary question. Governments had come, gone and been reshuffled, honours lists devised and published; Coper's name had appeared in none of them. Beneath the surface Coper's disappointment grew and had suddenly exploded two months earlier. He owned two farms near Bulawayo, but everyone had been surprised at the

19

energy with which he took up the white Rhodesian cause as soon as the Multiracial Settlement of 1968 collapsed. He had refused the Government Whip and set up the 'Hands off Rhodesia' movement, the most successful mass political campaign since C.N.D. Already everyone called it simply 'The Movement.' Night after night Coper addressed packed crowds in London or other cities, or led with his Bentley long motor-cades through the streets. The cars honked long-long-short-short-long ('Hands-off-Rhodee-SYAA!') and blared 'Hearts of Oak,' the Movement's signature tune. Lately there had been more violence at Coper's meetings, and the Labour Party had suggested that he be expelled from the House.

It was a bad sign that tonight Coper should dine at Eaton Place. Selkirk had been trying all day to find out whether Thorganby would resign if the Cabinet decided to send troops to Rhodesia. Coper had a Wolverhampton accent and snuffled as he ate. If Thorganby was ready to hobnob over dinner with so unlikely a man it looked as if he already regarded him as an ally.

As the front door opened for Selkirk, Coper was noisily planting on his hostess a vast bunch of pink roses, crackling in Cellophane, while Mrs. Coper lingered in the background. She did not share her husband's public life, and Selkirk was surprised by her youth and elegance.

'A Continental habit, I know, Lady T., but I hope you'll forgive me, it's a special occasion.'

Lady Thorganby was dowdy in green satin with sparse frizzy hair; a politician's daughter and a politician's wife, she had dealt with the Copers of the world for nearly half a century now. 'They're charming, Mr. Coper, what a kind thought. Good evening, Mrs. Coper, won't you leave your coat? I'm afraid David's still in Cabinet, so we must just carry on as best we can without him.'

'Here's young Selkirk, he'll tell us the latest,' said Coper, turning to see the new arrival.

'Lord Thorganby asked me to say that he thought the Cabinet would sit till about nine, and he hoped we would start.'

Selkirk followed the Copers into the drawing-room. On the sofa sat Lady Molly Downes, wife of the Ambassador in Rome, pudgy in a short pink dress and ready to be bored. From the other side of the room a girl said: 'Alan! Come and explain why you look so derelict.'

Selkirk turned sharply. He had known Anne Downes all his life as a neighbour in Scotland. Birthday parties in the nursery, tennis during the holidays, two or three dances at Oxford, and most recently the Anglo-Italian Society. Each stage had been a degree less intimate than the one before. He realised suddenly that he did not know her very well, and that this was a mistake. She was a beauty, with her mother's grey eyes and high voice, her father's black silky hair and slim figure. She was making hesitant conversation to a bulky man in a white dinner-jacket with red carnation. His face, beginning to puff out slightly into middle age, carried the smooth tan which comes from a sun-lamp; by contrast the hand which he held out was pale.

'Good evening, Selkirk, I'm delighted to see you. Have you come straight from Lord Thorganby?'

The polite formality with which Dennis Ralston habitually spoke and the care he took with his appearance always struck Selkirk as very slightly un-English, and none the worse for that. Chairman of Herakles Aviation, which had two years before emerged as Britain's largest aircraft manufacturer, director of the National and Scottish Bank and a dozen companies, Trustee of the Tate, owner of a perfect Georgian house near Arundel, quiet contributor to many charities and the Conservative Party—there were still magic circles and Ralston was in them; energetic, superbly competent, but without a trace of arrogance. His friendship with Thorganby had started when the Labour victory of 1964 and the Labour budgets of the late 'sixties had taken from Thorganby first his ministerial salary and then uncomfortable slices of his private income. Ralston had helped to find him two or three uncomplicated director-ships and an American tenant to shoot his not quite first-class grouse. Now that Thorganby was back in office, the directorships and the American had been disposed of, but the friendship with Ralston remained. The two busy men usually contrived to see seach other once a fortnight. Selkirk

21

by now shared his master's liking and admiration for the industrialist, and in particular for the detached calm with which he ran a collection of interests far more exacting than a government department. Selkirk never failed to be impressed by the quiet, air-conditioned luxury of the office in Herakles House—Bacon and Jackson Pollock on the walls, never a paper on the desk.

Coper bustled over to join them, and Ralston greeted him politely, asking if he had any news. Coper had a drink under his belt already and a cheerful sweat on his forehead. 'You mean the by-election, I take it. You should have heard the din in Newbury market place last night. Eve of poll, and our chap really had them hotted up. D'you know, I think the Movement's won, romped home. I never had a better meeting.'

Lady Thorganby handed them all Martinis from a tray held by the butler. 'I must say, Mr. Coper, I think it's disgraceful of you to put one of your noisy Movement people up against Tony Chivers. Such a nice man, son of the Lord Lieutenant and a County Councillor for fifteen years. Newbury has always been Conservative, and your butting in will just hand it to Labour.'

'Now, Lady T., you're speaking without the book, and I'm not sure your lord and master would agree with you. I'll tell you one thing about Chivers, he's got no chin, and another, he can't be heard at the back of the hall. He's a born loser, that chap. Anyway we'll know the answer soon enough. Declaration's first thing tomorrow.'

'When I asked you for news, I was thinking of the Cabinet, not the by-election,' said Ralston quietly.

'The Cabinet, eh? Still at it, young what's-'is-name says. But they can't send the troops in, the country wouldn't stand it, the Army wouldn't stand it. Even Harvey, wet though he is, must realise that.'

'I know nothing of politics,' said Ralston in his careful voice, 'but I should have thought the decision was a good deal more complicated than you describe. How long are you spending in London, Miss Downes?' He turned back to Anne, and Lady Thorganby, who did not like her guests to talk politics before dinner, seized the chance to steer Coper to

22

the sofa where Lady Molly was giving Mrs. Coper a servant-by-servant account of the trials of embassy life.

'Just for a few days,' Anne said. 'It's my mother's annual descent on Marks and Spencers, and I was allowed to come too. Lady Thorganby is my aunt.'

'If you are going back tomorrow evening we shall be seeing each other. There is no reason why you should know it, but your father has asked me to stay this week. It's the week of the Rome Air Show and on Thursday your father is very kindly giving a party for me at the Embassy. We are keen to sell our executive four-seater to the Italian Army and your father has promised to collect the generals and technicians to come and hear about it. He has been most helpful and taken a great deal of trouble.'

Anne was silent, and Selkirk felt he must say something. 'Not a very good time of year, surely, sir? The top brass will be out of Rome, up in the hills or at Fregene.'

'You may be right, you may be right. I am waiting for a telegram tonight from our business agent there to tell me exactly what the prospects are. But if we pull it off, the order will be a really big one, so we have thought it worth the effort.'

A tall, heavy man with pink outdoor cheeks came quietly into the room. The fourth Earl of Thorganby, Lord President of the Council, knew there would be a special decanter of malt whisky by the drinks tray, and he helped himself before interrupting the conversation of his guests. He shook hands with each one with exactly the same smile and apology.

Coper cut in with: 'What's happened, Thorganby, what's happened?'

Lord Thornganby did not like the familiarity and anyway enjoyed the suspense. 'I saw on the news-stand at the corner that England were 228 for 4, but at this rate there'll be a thunderstorm tomorrow.'

'I mean the Cabinet, of course,' said Coper. 'Are you in or out?'

'In, still in, but scoring fewer runs than England, I fear. No decision yet, and we go on tomorrow.'

'But there can't be any doubt, surely! Haven't you told

them you'll resign if they agree to send troops? What can Harvey think he's at?'

Thorganby despite himself was nettled by the man's crudity. 'Don't you think we'd better leave this boring crisis of ours till after dinner? I've hardly spoken a word to your wife yet.'

Alan Selkirk sat next to Anne at dinner. She held herself straight in her chair and twisted her wine glass. Opposite, oblivious of her gaze, Coper launched noisily into his soup. Selkirk liked Anne and liked dinner parties, but saw that this was going to be uphill. Small talk would get him nowhere.

'What's on your mind, Anne?' he said. 'Why are you looking at the member for South Staffordshire down the sights of a rifle?'

She turned on him sharply.

'Because one of his thugs stamped on my foot in Trafalgar Square last night. I can hardly walk today. And tonight I was coward enough to shake hands with him.'

'For God's sake, what were you doing? You know there's trouble there every night now.'

'If you want to know, I was helping make trouble. Carrying a banner—"Clean up Rhodesia now"—red on white, we were very proud of it. But tell me is Coper serious? He's unspeakable of course, but tonight he seems just too awful to be dangerous.'

'I don't know. He behaves like a clown, he *is* a clown, but he's a born organiser too. He must be, to have got the Movement where it is. Mussolini was three parts clown after all, and I expect Hitler slobbered in his soup. But do you mean to say you've come from Rome just to get stamped into the gutter over Rhodesia? You must be out of your mind.'

Anne, an honest girl, blushed. 'There were other reasons —but why not, anyway? Don't be so dim and bureaucratic. If you go on like this you'll be just like my father. He's waited so long for someone to ask his opinion that now he hasn't got one. Oh, how I hate you smug civil servants!' Selkirk tried to smile as if he did not mind the remark. Without much success; it was too near the truth. Before he could

24

reply, an apologetic hand was on his arm. 'I'm sorry, Alan, I'm having a bad day. Don't take any notice. Who is this tycoon on my left?'

'Not so loud,' Selkirk said. 'That's Ralston, the aircraft king. He's nice, you know, as well as clever. I thought you were a bit short with him.'

'So that's Ralston is it? He's better than I expected. Daddy admires him so much I thought he'd be hell. Quite good-looking too, in a capitalist sort of way. Married?'

'No, but I've heard talk of a flat in Canonbury, and I expect you'd rate a little place of your own if you were interested.'

'No, thanks. Other fish to fry.' For the first time she laughed and relaxed. 'I was short with him because he's going to stay with us at the Embassy. I hate living in a sort of bogus hotel always full of strangers. Do you know, the Papal Nuncio tipped me once in Chile—seriously—and in Rome I found an Air Force General in my bedroom. He said he wanted to kiss me, but he was really looking for somewhere to be sick.'

'Well, that's something you must have got used to at Oxford.' Selkirk realised his soup had gone cold. 'Why are you having a bad day? Don't tell me if you don't want to.'

'Oh, it's partly the other fish, and not knowing what I want to do with myself, and now this Africa thing—but you wouldn't understand that. You couldn't hold a banner if you tried . . .'

She was talking easily now, and as he watched her face move, and the candlelight catch the colour of her hair, Alan Selkirk let his mind drift far from politics.

10.30 pm

In Witney the pubs were closing, and the peace of a summer evening was disturbed by raucous laughter. Doors banged, and behind the post office a motorcycle roared to life. From the door of the police station Sergeant Fairbrother watched for the usual offenders, but there was seldom trouble on a Monday night. He wondered whether the missing soldiers had been tempted to wet their throats. Every publican in the district had been warned, and there were three patrol cars out. A lot of fuss just because two army trucks had taken the wrong turning.

Like the rest of the village, he missed the Americans. Their money had been a great help to the trades-people, and the social evenings up at the base had been popular with the girls. Several had got married and gone 'State-side,' as the airmen used to say. After the Americans had gone the airfield had become a transport base for the British Army and for most of the year there was not much activity. The Belfasts and converted V.C.10s could not compare with the B-52s.

The telephone rang behind him and he turned inside.

'Police. Sergeant Fairbrother speaking.'

A girl's voice said: 'Just a moment, I'm putting you through,' and after a pause a young man with a cultivated accent came on the line and wanted to know to whom he was speaking. Sergeant Fairbrother felt the chill wind of higher officialdom. 'Sergeant Fairbrother, sir, Witney police,' he said.

'Good evening, Sergeant,' said the young man. 'Ministry of Defence here, Army Movement Section. I'm sorry to bother you at a time like this but I was wondering whether you had any information yet about our missing guardsmen.'

Sergeant Fairbrother could hear machinery in the back-ground; it sounded like the Telex he had seen on last year's course at the Yard. 'No, sir,' he said, 'nothing's come in yet. We've got the cars out. It's just a question of time.'

'So you think they are on the road?'

'Well, we haven't found the trucks yet, so it's probable, shall we say?'

'Ah yes, the trucks. How many is it now? Three, if I remember right.'

'Two, sir.'

'Two. Correct. And what time did they leave the base?' Sergeant Fairbrother, whose son was at Reading University, wondered if this young man had a degree. He seemed remarkably off the ball. 'The base, sir?' he said. 'They never got there.'

There was a moment's silence at the other end, then: 'Of course they didn't—how stupid of me! I'm afraid things have been pretty hectic up here. We're all feeling the pace a bit. I expect you are too. Well, Sergeant, thank you very much for your help. Good night and good hunting!'

'Good night, sir.'

Sergeant Fairbrother reached for his pipe and turned back to the door. Cheeky young pup, he thought.

Midnight

Extract from the diary of Alan Selkirk   AUGUST 4

. . . Must see her before she goes. Who's the other fish? Must be a professional protester. Takes two to hold a banner.

Back to politics. Ladies hardly through door before Coper launched in. Shrewder than he looks. New Coper scheme: King to use old power of the Monarchy to dismiss Harvey, install Thorganby as head of National Government to stop operation against Rhodesia. Coper wanted to push this at Oxford rally tomorrow. No reaction from T. and Ralston, so I said: preposterous, royal prerogative couldn't be revived, clear majority in Commons for U.N. and military operation, no Labour men would join that kind of National Government, King would never sack Harvey, etc. May have overdone it (result of Anne). Coper had done his homework: cited 1834 (William IV sacked Melbourne), said Commons so out of touch with public opinion that H.M. would be justified in acting in national interest. Parliament would have to stay in recess for a few months to give new Government time to act; no difficulty, as budget already through. Some older Labour men would join. And so on. Another pause; T. busy cutting cigar. Ralston asks T. what he thinks. T. fiddles with matches, then says that normally my constitutional doctrine would be right; 1834 precedent too far off and anyway a fiasco. But present situation was

27

exceptional, and tougher than we knew. Hints at some bad trouble today (must have picked up something in Cabinet), says worst humiliation would be if Government gave Army orders which were disobeyed. King still had prerogative under constitution and might reasonably act if he thought national disaster imminent and present Government wholly out of touch with responsible opinion. Ralston asks if T. knows what King actually feels. T. twiddles again with cigar—pause—then says he thinks H.M. close to Harvey and respects his judgment. Coper blows up, detonated by three glasses port, says: H.M. no right to let country slip into chaos while he sits in Italian sun; he is C.-in-C. (untrue) and particularly responsible for armed forces; how many innocent lives will be lost if Army goes into Rhodesia? etc., etc. Ralston stays on fence, but doubts whether moment is ripe for Coper to launch his idea. Coper tries to draw T. further, but T. firmly joins ladies. Anne and mother left early.

A worrying evening. Does T. see Coper as ally after resignation? He might even fall for National Government idea, if King came round. What do I do if T. resigns? (Take leave in Italy!)

Tuesday, August 5th

3 am

The cells of the guardroom at Chelsea Barracks are of two types. The detention cell is a large, well-lit room with beds for six men; the overflow from this cell can be put in the guard's sleeping quarters, a similar room with a door which bolts on the outside. In the corridor beyond is a row of four smaller and more austere cells. These are the close arrest cells, and each is designed to accommodate one man.

The previous day the number of offenders had exceeded the number of beds, and men had been forced to double up in the close arrest cells. When late in the afternoon the Army Special Investigation Branch had narrowed the suspects for Reith's murder to six, twelve minor offenders of the Grenadier Guards had been sent to join their battalion at Brize Norton, and the problem of accommodation had eased. But Cell 3 still contained two men: Guardsman Steele and Meredith, chief suspects for the crime. Neither had confessed under interrogation, but their guilt was almost beyond doubt. Meredith's bayonet had been missing from his belt, and the toecap of Steele's right boot had been matted with hair and blood. The bayonet found in Reith's chest was now in the Fingerprint Department at Scotland Yard, and Steele's boot had been taken to the Scotland Yard Forensic Laboratory in Gray's Inn Road. Formal charges were expected in the morning.

The cell was lit by a single bulb bracketed to the ceiling, which produced just enough light to reveal the state of the inmates to an observer using the small hole in the solid iron door. Meredith was asleep, limbs sprawled over a mattress set against the far wall. He was an ugly man, in a peculiarly English way; a collection of fleshless bones, covered in acne and topped with pale wavy hair. He was also a man without friends; intimacy of any kind seemed to disgust him. The most he asked for was respect, and this he had got without much trouble in the Grenadiers, being cleverer than most of them (he had been at Charterhouse for two years), proficient in every military skill and the best centre-forward the battalion had had for years. In January he had abandoned a job with the Midland Bank for reasons which no one could establish and after four months in the Guards Depot at Pirbright, had joined the battalion in June. In two months at Chelsea Barracks a clique of wary admirers had formed around him, and when he had shouted out on parade they had provided the support which swelled the protest to the point where law-abiding soldiers could join in, just for the hell of it, and not be identified. Later in the day some of his platoon had offered statements saying Reith hit Meredith first.

He slept with his mouth open, snoring slightly. If his conscience was troubled it did not show. The difference between Meredith and most of his fellow-soldiers was that he had strong political opinions, especially where Africa was concerned. Lately he had made no secret of these, and had collected an audience in the N.A.A.F.I. A rumour had spread that the Mau Mau had killed his mother, and two men had come back from a seventy-two to say that they had seen him at a Movement rally in Birmingham. He had acquired a reputation for being in the know. When the movement orders had been issued that morning, every-one had assumed that Meredith would have some information, and he had not disappointed them. Helmets, he had pointed out, were being left behind because troops fighting for the United Nations wore blue headgear.

Steele lay on the wooden bed fixed to the floor of the cell, staring at the ventilation shaft in the roof through which occasional drops of rain splashed on to his face. The bottom half of the walls was red and the top cream, and ten feet up on the outside wall the only window was a rectangle of opaque glass bricks, which reduced the lightning to a dull flicker. Years of bull had kept the place in lovely condition. In his three years with the Grenadiers Steele had never seen the inside of a close arrest cell, but now it seemed inevitable, part of the order of things, that he

should be where he was. He felt neither anger nor remorse.
The Major from the S.I.B. said he had kicked Reith's head
in, and because he was used to believing what he was told, he
supposed that it was true. But he remembered nothing
—only Reith getting nowhere with his little speech; cat-
calls and laughter; tempers rising in the heat; then Reith
jumping off the Land-Rover to get Meredith, and everyone suddenly lashing out. He tried to think about his
mother but could not, he wondered what would happen
next but could not imagine. He wanted only to sleep.

Meredith had not spoken since they were locked up—
except about an hour before, when he had turned over and
seen Steele still awake, and said: 'What's the matter, Harry?
Conscience troubling you? Try reading this. It'll make you
feel better.' He had thrown a folded sheet of paper across the
cell: it was the famous pamphlet.

'So that was your work, was it?' Steele had said.
'Thanks. I've read it, and it's stupid muck.'

Meredith had looked at him for a moment in a bored
but indefinably dangerous way, then said: 'You're a stupid
ignorant git, Steele, but you're on the right side.'

The pamphlets had been found all over the barracks
early on Sunday morning. After reveille fatigue parties
had been detailed to clear them up. In a personal address
the Colonel had promised twenty-one days C.B. for any
man found in possession of one, but copies were still in
circulation. For lack of anything better to do, Steele
took the crumpled paper from his pocket and began to
read.

SOLDIERS OF THE KING!

You are about to betray your country.

You will shortly be sent to Rhodesia by the Tory
government under the orders of the United Nations. This
evil organisation has become the instrument of foreign
powers hostile to the British people. It is the means where-
by the black nations of Africa, to whom Britain so generously
granted independence, seek to drive the white man from their
continent.

Prime Minister Harvey will order you to do this in the

name of 'international law' and 'racial equality.' He may even claim that he is sending you 'to protect world peace.' Do you know what these words mean? Be honest! Of course you don't. Nor does Harvey, who is trying to hide the fact that he and his Government are too chicken to stand up for Britain. Winston Churchill must turn in his grave to hear such lies.

WHAT IS THE TRUTH?

The truth is that Rhodesia was discovered by the British when it was a wilderness. Thousands of our people went to live there, and have worked to turn the wilderness into a prosperous country—with churches, schools, roads, peaceful farms and thriving industries. It is now their home. All they ever asked was to be left in peace, to live and work in the land which is theirs.

After years of neglect by British Governments, who were too lazy or too scared to help them, they had no choice but to take their independence in 1965. After three years of bitter struggle they were then forced by Harold Wilson and his friends at the United Nations to sign the so-called 'Multiracial Settlement,' under which the black Rhodesians were to inherit power after a period of a few years.

AND WHAT HAPPENED?

The Negroes could not wait for the power they had been promised. Armed by their Communist friends, they began to burn the schools and destroy the crops. Innocent British people were brutally murdered.

The picture on the front page was taken by the Rhodesian police. It shows a white farmer and his family, attacked in their own home.

THIS IS WHAT YOU WILL BE ASKED TO DO—KILL AND MAIM BRITISH PEOPLE LIKE YOURSELVES—MEN, WOMEN, CHILDREN—TO HELP A BLACK RABBLE TAKE OVER THEIR COUNTRY.

Never in all our history was the British Army called to perform such a shameful task.

Your orders will come from the Prime Minister, Patrick Harvey. But Harvey is alone. The overwhelming majority of the British people are against him. Many M.P.s, of both parties, are against him. The members of his own cabinet are against him. The King is against him—but can do nothing.

ONLY THE BRITISH ARMY CAN STOP THIS MAN. WHEN THE ORDER COMES, REFUSE! LAY DOWN YOUR ARMS! YOU WILL HAVE THE THANKS OF THE BRITISH NATION.

GOD SAVE THE KING!

The lines of imperfect print blurred together, and Harry Steele drifted into sleep at last. Images of horror receded, and he was sitting in the front room of the house in Battersea. There was a fire going, and the only sound was the clanking of the poker as his mother tried to stir a flame from the coals. Clank, clank. He was a small boy back from school and the room was warm and secure. Clank, clank, crash. The poker in the grate became the bolt of an iron door.

'On your feet!'

It was the Sergeant of the Guard with a captain from the Military Police. A tall, thin man with a blond moustache and protruding eyes, whose uniform hung on him badly. He came past the Sergeant and stood in the centre of the cell, tapping the side of his knee with a leather swagger stick and examining everything around him, as if he were about to perform some acrobatics and was not sure there was enough space. 'Who's this, Sergeant?' he said, tapping Steele's chest.

'Guardsman Steele, sir.'

'What's he done?'

'Guardsmen Steele and Meredith are suspected of the same offence, sir.'

'I see.' The Captain was bouncing the swagger stick in the palm of his gloved hand. 'Evidence?' he said.

'Sir?' bellowed the Sergeant, and only a trained ear could have detected a question in the monosyllable.

'Evidence, Sergeant. What is the evidence against this guardsman?'

'Blood, sir. On the boot.'

Steele's eyes bored into space as the Captain came up close and looked him up and down, like a man buying a piece of furniture. 'The boot, eh? My, my, that must have hurt the Sergeant-Major.' The man had a faint northern accent, and Steele noted with surprise there was no hostility in the voice. 'Yes, I can see we have a dangerous customer here!' It sounded almost like approval. 'Now, Sergeant, as I said, I have a few further questions to put to Guardsman Meredith. Steele can stay where he is. I should like the Lance-Corporal in here, if you don't mind. I think you'll find him in the washroom.'

'Sir!'

'You can leave the door for the moment.'

Steele's gaze, which until then had maintained a steady ninety degrees from the line of his shoulders, shifted to follow the Sergeant out of the cell. When it returned to the front, the view had altered to incorporate the barrel of an Enfield revolver held three inches from his head.

The Captain spoke rapidly in a low voice.

'No tricks, Steele. You're coming with me, just as you are.'

'But, Major—' it was Meredith, pulling on a sweater —'He knows nothing. He's not even—'

'Belt up, Jake; he's coming. You stay here. Colonel's in the washroom with the rifle—ammo was just where you said it was. Know what to do? We've got the other one.'

'Yes.'

'All right, Steele, let's go.'

As he walked from the cell in his stocking feet Steele was wondering why Meredith called the Captain 'Major'.

They had reached the end of the corridor before the washroom door opened. Steele heard the Sergeant's pace quicken, then stop; other feet, rubber-soled, moved fast across the concrete; a grunt of pain, and the Sergeant said: 'What the hell's going on?' Steele turned and had time to see a man in civilian clothes put the Sergeant in a half-nelson before the Captain jabbed the revolver into his neck and said: 'Eyes front, Steele, and not a sound.'

They had reached the front of the guardroom and the Captain was peering through the plate-glass window overlooking the gate. The glare of the floodlights revealed only rain, beating on the pavement in a mist of spray. The Captain reached for a switch by the door and the floodlights died in a fading orange glow. 'All right,' he shouted over his shoulder.

In that enclosed space of brick and concrete the shot was like the crack of doom. It was followed by a single continuous yell of pain, silenced by a second shot.

'Come on, Steele—move!'

They were running out of the gate, left down Chelsea Bridge Road. A Ford Zodiac braked sharply ten yards ahead of them. The Captain clawed at the back door handle. 'Inside, Steele,' he said, 'quick.' Meredith ran up, grinning excitedly, and the Captain pushed the revolver into his hand. 'Take this, Jake, and sit in the back, in case your friend gets uppity.'

The man in civilian clothes climbed in beside the driver, and stared solemnly over the back of the seat at Steele. He wore a black eye-patch. The Captain leapt in after him and said: 'Drive.'

The car accelerated towards the Embankment, jumped the lights and turned right.

When they reached Albert Bridge, the Captain said: 'The other one's in the boot, Jake. The Colonel was a bit unorthodox with him, so we had to get him off the scene. Must keep things tidy. The law will think he bolted. When we get to H.Q. you can do the honours; I'll show you where.'

'Wilco,' Meredith said, then: 'I still don't see why we had to bring this cretin.'

'Didn't expect to find him there, I must say. Thought I handled it rather neatly. He might be useful to us.'

'I wouldn't count on it.'

'You know what the alternative is.' The Captain twisted to face the back of the car and raised a quivering finger in Meredith's face. 'And that would suit you fine, wouldn't it? You're a cold-blooded bastard, Meredith, and that's why I picked you. But remember, I give the orders. No one gets hurt unless I say so.' The Lancashire accent was stronger than before. He turned forwards again and stared out of the window, then added after a pause: 'I spent twenty good years of my life in the British Army.'

Steele fought to control his shaking limbs. There were

only two thoughts in his head: he had never known Meredith's Christian name, and Fords should have more room in the back. Slowly a third began to formulate: he must remember the route.

'Blindfold him,' the Captain said to Meredith.

5 am (11 pm, Monday, New York)

Sir Charles Melton wiped his forehead with the purple silk handkerchief from his breast pocket. An unnecessary gesture; the Security Council was ruthlessly air-conditioned, but the air felt stale. Several hundred people had sat in the room for five hours at a stretch. No windows, unending talk, and the clock near midnight.

Talking now was Tanzania. The alphabet put him two away from the United Kingdom round the horse-shoe table: beautifully pressed light grey suit, an inch of spotless cuff, two of handkerchief. Melton through his exhaustion half-heard the soft pleasing voice accusing Britain of skul-duggery and deception. Prize scholar from a missionary school, Secretary of the Oxford Union eight years back, tipped to be Foreign Minister within months. The voice stopped and the drone of the consecutive translation into French began. The TV cameramen in the glass boxes in the gallery veered their lenses towards Melton, knowing he would speak next, and he automatically put on the spectacles with the dark-horned rims. He knew he looked the part: grey-white hair swept back, long nose, strong grey eyes, good chin. The cameras could not see the weight of sleep on his eyes and sandwiches on his stomach. He had not had a decent meal for days.

The translation ended, Melton raised his pencil and the President said: 'Delegate of the United Kingdom.' Melton reached for the microphone.

'Mr. President, I must again, I fear, ask for the under-standing of the Council. I have, of course, reported to His Majesty's Government the terms of the draft resolution on Rhodesia before us and the fact that it is supported with different degrees of enthusiasm by all the distinguished

36

delegates who have spoken. I regret, however, that I have not yet received instructions which will enable me to vote on the draft. I must ask, therefore, for an adjournment of at least twenty-four hours.'

Tanzania objected volubly. There had been too much delay already, the issues were clear, the vote must be that night.

The American Representative, Rosletter, leaned across to Melton from the chair on his left. 'Charles,' he said, 'if we vote tonight, will you veto?'

'Yes. Can you get me twelve hours?'

'God save us all. Mr. President.'

'The Delegate of the United States.'

'Mr. President, I think we all understand the sincere emotion with which the Honourable Delegate from Tanzania has spoken. We are all anxious to bring this long debate to a constructive conclusion and naturally impatient of any delay. On the other hand the draft resolution before us calls for particular action by the United Kingdom, that is, intervention by British armed forces in Rhodesia, which we recognise presents great difficulties for our British friends. I suggest, Mr. President, that we adjourn until 10 a.m. tomorrow morning and meanwhile urge the Distinguished Delegate from the United Kingdom to inform his Government that the Council will certainly wish to reach a decision at that meeting.'

The President of the Council was tired and mindful of his mistress waiting in Sutton Place. He glanced round the chamber, muttered: 'Agreed, adjourned until 10 a.m. tomorrow,' and banged the gavel.

The African delegates gathered excitedly in one corner. The rest of the room emptied, and Melton walked down the corridor to the bar in the Delegates' Lounge, kept open for the late session. The barman gave him a whisky and water without being asked. Melton looked round the room. The babble of journalists and delegates among the shiny dark green potted plants deepened his gloom. Each one thought he was the hunter, but they were all hunted game. He had cultivated a reputation for aloofness and no one approached him until a young man hurried past on his way to a telephone. John Spriggs—scruffy, ill-educated, intelligent—represented the *New Statesman*; he had nothing in common with Melton and Melton liked him a lot. 'Not so fast!' Melton said. 'What's the news, John?'

'Cabinet ended around nine they say, but no talk outside Number Ten as they left. What's that mean, Sir Charles?'

'God knows. It's five in the morning in London now. If the Cabinet still haven't decided they must be in real trouble.'

'Do you think they'll really agree to send in troops against the whites?'

'You tell me. I'm just a diplomat; it got past our stage long ago.'

'Poor bloody Tories, sods the lot of them, but I'm sorry for them tonight. They'll have to do it, there's no real choice, but it'll dish them, and we'll be lucky if it doesn't dish us all. Did you hear the Guards mutinied today at Chelsea Barracks? Good night now. Must ring Jane. I'll give her your love.'

How like Spriggs to assume that one knew who Jane was; and to invent that crack about the Guards just because he saw Melton's tie. Melton lingered over his whisky, trying hard not to think of Hooper. Hooper was his Minister-Counsellor, his second-in-command. Hooper was ambitious and quick, and despised the Ambassador's mind. Hooper was now frustrated because it was August, and he would have been leading the Delegation if the Foreign Office had not recalled Melton from his summer leave for this debate. Before Hooper's eyes undoubtedly danced those concise admirable telegrams which might have gone out over Hooper's name. Hooper thought that Melton himself had wanted to come back from leave and had engineered his own recall to cut Hooper out. Damned fool, Melton thought, emptying his glass and trying to forget the clean sea and air at his cottage on Cape Cod, the thickets of slowly ripening blackberries, the white sands on which his grandchildren played each day. Hooper was waiting for him in the little office.

5.30 am

The first grey light struggled through the steamed-up windows of the penthouse flat in Chalcot Square. Jack Kemble did not like what it showed: the stained William Morris chair-covers and the whole clutter of art nouveau he had collected in the sixties, the stacks of old magazines, the blown-up photographs, the black metal spotlights and the shelves of jazz records (he had once been jazz critic for the *Sunday Telegraph*, until the Sunday he reviewed a Duke Ellington concert five days before it happened). He looked at Anne asleep beside him and thought of the girls who had been there before—the pretty divorcée from press cuttings section, the R.A.D.A. student who was now a star, others whose names he had forgotten. A tap was dripping in the kitchen. It was no place for an Ambassador's daughter.

Meditation required a cigarette, but the packet was out of reach. He tried to think when he had last seen the dawn and was reminded of commemoration balls and airports. There was no doubt about it, those who had seen the dawn had the edge over ordinary folk; they surprised the waking world with decisions taken in the intimate moment of self-communion. This would be his morning of decision . . . Marry Anne and start again; something honest and worthwhile; live in the country, children and dogs, long walks across the moors. . . . His eyes were closing on the vision as the telephone rang.

'Kemble?' It was Joe Hollis. 'Kemble, is that you?' Joseph infuriating Hollis. Kemble held the receiver away from his ear to mute the high-pitched bark. There was no justice in a world where poets and lovers must bow to the demands of Scottish bureaucrats. 'Kemble, can you hear me?'

'Yes, Joe, I hear you. Jack the Hack at your service, night and day.'

'Did you give anyone my private number?'

'For shame.'

'Well, someone's got it. And whoever it is, it's the same

chappie that tipped us off about the mutiny. He's just called me again.'

Kemble sat up. Anne was awake, searching for her pyjamas.

'What did he say?'

'They've had more trouble at Chelsea Barracks. A break-out from the guardroom. There's been some shooting. He said the M.O.D. would cover it up, but the police aren't ready to move the evidence. We may get something if we're quick.'

'How will I get in?'

'You won't. Just sniff around and keep your eyes open. Call me at the office as soon as you can. I'm relying on you, Kemble.'

'You do that, Joe.'

Kemble replaced the receiver and lay back. Anne was sitting cross-legged on the bed, having failed to find both halves of the pyjamas. Her dark, thick hair tumbled on to her pale shoulders. Amazing, thought Kemble, that such pale skin could be so warm. He reached for her hand. She climbed between the sheets and laid her head on his chest.

'Do you have to go?' she said.

Kemble said nothing, pulled her closer. Her hand was playing affectionately on his ribs and stroking the soft folds of his stomach. The sunlight had turned to pink and the room was warm. This was J. Kemble Decision Morning, of which he would not be cheated.

'No,' he said, 'there's no rush.'

6 am (Midnight, New York)

In the office of the British Delegation on the seventeenth floor of the U.N. building Hooper was waiting, impatient, and then cross when he smelt the whisky on Melton's breath. Old fool, he thought, drinking himself silly at the bar, when there were telegrams to be sent.

'Oh, there you are, sir,' he said. 'Nothing in from the F.O. yet. I've dictated a summary of the debate for them, and perhaps we should send an emergency telegram on these lines to make sure we get the right instructions.'

Melton glanced at the sheet of blue draft paper with the red 'immediate' label already pinned on. 'From the point of view of this post,' he read, 'I must again urge most strongly against a negative vote . . . most undesirable repercussions among all sections of opinion at the U.N. . . . grave doubts as to whether we can secure a further postponement. . . .'

Hooper's look assumed approval, but it was not forthcoming.

'It's no good, Ronald,' Melton said. 'We're past the stage of telegrams now. They know all this stuff.' Then to a tired girl with dank hair bent over a typewriter: 'Get London on the phone and tell the switchboard I must speak at once to the Secretary of State, wherever he is.' And to Hooper: 'He'll have a scrambler by his bed, if he's got as far as bed. Politicians like staying up all night, it makes them feel important.'

It makes Hooper feel important too, he thought, noting the glint behind the rimless glasses, but I'm fifty-eight and it makes me tired.

The telephone rang and Hooper leapt for it, but it was not the Foreign Secretary. Hooper listened, grimaced, then held his hand over the mouthpiece.

'It's the President of the Security Council. He sounds upset and says the Africans are insisting on the Council meeting again in two hours. They've heard some report of the South Africans being about to move into Rhodesia.'

Melton took the phone. 'Melton here, Señor Presidente. I'm afraid I cannot agree to this suggestion. Meetings in the small hours are always a mistake. Tell them it's six o'clock in London and only the milkman stirring. Tell them I've nothing more to say and I hope and believe my Ministers are fast asleep. Tell 'em if they insist on another meeting tonight I shall send a Third Secretary with instructions to say nothing and veto all resolutions. They'd much better go to bed and hope I've got the answer they want in the morning . . . I'm sure you can put it to them tactfully,

41

Señor Presidente. We all need a few hours' sleep. Good night.'

He had hardly put the receiver down when the telephone rang again. 'Is Sir Charles Melton there to speak to the Foreign Secretary?'

Melton motioned the girl beside him to stop typing. 'Charles Melton here, Secretary of State. Sorry to get you out of bed.'

'Bed, Charles, bed? What are you talking about? No one's doing much sleeping around these parts. I was going to call you anyway. The P.M. and I read your stuff on the tape and we wanted to say you're doing excellently. First-class speech—we're all very pleased. The Chief Whip's full of your praises.'

Melton groaned inwardly; this kind of cheery talk from a politician to a civil servant meant things were very bad. Chief Whip indeed. 'Thank you very much. We've held the position for a few hours here, Secretary of State, but I should warn you that in the morning the Security Council will certainly tell us to send in troops unless we veto the resolution. Even a veto will only save us a couple of days while they whip up a special Assembly . . .'

'I know, Charles, I know. Believe me, we all understand your difficulties. But they aren't the only ones, you know. The Chiefs of Staff are being more than cagey and there was a bust-up at one of the Guards barracks yesterday which has them scared. Then there's the "Hands off Rhodesia" boys in Trafalgar Square night after night, and a by-election yesterday with a lot of Rhodesia in it—we won't know the result for an hour or two yet. Some of the colleagues are still kicking and screaming. But don't worry, Charles, it'll turn out all right, and you can be sure of one thing: we'll back you to the hilt.'

'If I may say so, Secretary of State, it's not backing I need, it's instructions. Do I take it then, that the Cabinet has still reached no decision as to the use of force?'

'Don't rush us, Charles, don't rush us. We're almost at the end of the road, but there's still some fight left on the other side and the P.M. thought it better to adjourn.

Awkward if there were too many resignations, you know. But don't worry, we'll get you something before the day's out. Your telegrams have been a great help. Just make another of your long speeches to spin it along. We'll support anything you do. Go to bed now, and my regards to Cynthia.'

Melton put down the receiver and looked out of the curtainless window on to the black East River and the lights of Queens beyond. He knew and liked Ryder Bennett, His Majesty's Principal Secretary of State for Foreign Affairs, and was not deceived by the bluff good cheer. Behind him Hooper's irritation boiled over.

'Do you mean to say they've still not made up their blasted minds? Surely they see we must send in troops if we're to keep any kind of position with international opinion. Why do politicians never see what's in front of their noses?'

A tug hooted in the East River below. Melton realised he was desperate for sleep. 'No more to do tonight, Ronald. Don't fret too much. United Nations opinion is not the Voice of God. The Cabinet is worrying about the Chiefs of Staff and the backbenchers, and whatever happened at Chelsea, and whether Thorganby will resign, and a by-election in Berkshire. Funnily enough I think they may also be worrying a bit about what is the right thing to do. Can I give you a lift?'

6.30 am

The door slammed and was briskly locked. Harry Steele was a prisoner once more; but his new cell was quite an improvement on the old. He was now in a large carpeted bedroom, pink and white, with a sunken marble bath. A film star's room. Not for the first time that day he had the sensation that he was dreaming. He walked to the window and was surprised to find that it opened. The room was on the second floor of an old house surrounded by lawns, and beyond the lawns, trees, and beyond the trees, just visible in the early morning mist, a high stone wall topped with broken glass. Parked in the drive about fifty yards to the left was the mud-spattered Ford in which he had been a passenger.

Like all guardsmen Steele had been trained to accept orders, however strange. Such was the strength of his training that he still searched for an official explanation of the night's events, and now his exhausted brain came up with a new and beautifully convincing explanation: the whole escape from the barracks had been an experiment, laid on to test his reactions; no one had really been shot at all. They were probably watching him now, waiting to see if he behaved like a killer. He was in a nuthouse.

A door opened below the window and two men approached the Ford. One was Meredith, the other he did not know. They opened the boot and took out a cover, then began to heave at a large brown object. Grunting with the effort, they lifted it out and dumped it on the gravel to rearrange their hold, at which point it became recognisable to Steele as the Lance-Corporal of the Guard, Tommy Evans of King's Company. The battalion had left him behind as escort for any further prisoners released by the S.I.B. It was clear from the angle of his head that his neck was broken.

They carried him to a walled garden at the back of the house, then came back for spades.

Steele used the shower to wash his vomit from the bath, and lay down on the bed. So it was not a dream, not a medical experiment, not a situation covered by the Pirbright curriculum. He would have to think for himself. Clearing his stomach seemed to have cleared his mind.

He recited the facts aloud to himself to make them seem more real: 'I have been kidnapped by an armed gang, who have killed two men in my battalion, including my mate Tommy Evans. Meredith is with them. He was the leader on the parade-ground, set the whole thing up, and they came to get him out. They took me because I was in the same cell, which they weren't expecting. There is something they want me to do, and if I refuse, they will kill me. I must play along with them until I get a chance to skip.'

Ten minutes later the door opened to reveal the M.P.

Captain, now in civilian dress. From long-ingrained habit Steele leapt to attention by the bed. The Captain waved him to sit down and pulled up a gilt chair from the dressing table.

'Relax, Steele,' he said. 'There's none of that here. Discipline, yes; bull, no.' He sat down. 'Cigarette?'

'No, thank you, sir. I don't.'

'Good thing. I need fit men in this outfit. We may have to run fast.' He laughed, and Steele forced his face into what he hoped was a conspiratorial smile. 'Well,' the Captain continued, 'bit better than the place you came from, isn't it? Tried the bath yet?'

'No, sir.' This time Steele managed a genuine smile.

'Kinky, eh? She must have enjoyed herself in that.' His eyes clouded over at some lascivious memory. 'Yes, Steele, you're better off all right. You'd have gone inside for ten years, you know.' The soft, friendly voice suddenly became a violent shout. 'Ten years, boy—think about it!' Then to the bedpost: 'Bugger me, we kill two good men to get him out and the little devil can't even say thank you.'

'Thank you, sir.'

'That's better.' The voice softened again. 'Now I expect you're wondering why, aren't you?'

'Sir.'

'I'll tell you. One: Reith was a bastard, and had it coming to him, so we were on your side. Two: we have a job for you.'

'What makes you think I did it?'

'I was watching. Steele—just me and the Colonel and one old lady. We stood there and saw you put the boot in. They had to pull you off. Nasty.'

'You weren't so sure of that in the guardroom.'

'That was a bit of acting, for the Sergeant's benefit.'

'I don't remember—'

'I dare say you don't, but others do.' The voice had risen to a shout again. 'Make no mistake, Steele, you're a marked man. There's nowhere you can run, so either you help us or we hand you back. Take your pick.' The bulge in the Captain's jacket pocket indicated a third alternative.

Steele worked to recover a respectful attitude. 'What's the job, sir?' he said.

'You'll find out. But first a couple of questions. You may have to kill again. What would you say to that?'

This was the test, thought Steele. Every muscle of his face, every movement of his eyes was under observation. A quick 'yes' would be unconvincing. He tried a sly smile. 'So that's it,' he said. 'Well, let's see: if you hand me over now, I'm no worse off, am I? But if I go killing again ... there should be a price for that.'

'There is. Two thousand quid, false passport and an airline ticket to where you like.'

Steele brightened. 'That's very reasonable, I must say.'

After a pause the Captain said: 'Good'; but the word was on a rising note, so there was no finality about it. He was still tipping the little chair on to its front legs and peering at Steele intently. 'It's in a good cause, mind you,' he continued '—which brings me to the second point. Did you read this?' It was the pamphlet again.

'Yes.'

'What did you think of it?'

This was easier. 'I think it was bloody right,' Steele said.

'Ever known any blacks?'

'No, and I don't want to.'

'What do you think of them?'

'They're scum.'

'And this country's going soft on the blacks, right?'

'Right.'

'And it's the job of decent men like you and me to stop it, right?'

'Right. Look, sir—I don't know what you're after, but if all you want to know is whether I'll knock off a nigger, there's no problem.'

'Not so simple. We're after the others too, the whites, who are helping them.'

'Same thing, isn't it?'

'In my view, yes.' The Captain leaned back, then walked to the window and stared at the trees. After two draws on his cigarette he stubbed it, half-smoked, on the sill and turned back into the room.

'You'll do, Steele,' he said. 'I told them you were all right, and I'm not often wrong about such things. In every good soldier there's a born killer.'

Steele laughed—the genuine, too-easy laughter of relief. 'It's what we're paid for.'

'It's what you're paid for now, boy-o. Come downstairs and have some breakfast, then we must find you some new clothes. Briefing's at eight. And by the way—'

'Sir.'

'Drop the "sir." This isn't the Grenadiers. "Yes" or "no" will do nicely. People call me "Major" here and the Frenchman "Colonel," the rest use Christian names. No point in knowing what you don't need to.'

'Right, Major.'

They went downstairs.

6.30 am

It is rare for the Assistant Editor of a national daily to be out of bed before ten; for him to be making notes in a steamy café off Sloane Square shortly after dawn borders on the incredible. But Joe Hollis was an unusually dedicated man. Since he had lost his young wife to the I.T.N. newscaster his relationship with the Globe had come to resemble the eleventh-hour love affair of two middle-aged people. The paper, which was ineluctably descending the charts of the Audit Bureau of Circulations, needed him as much as he needed it. Not that this morning's escapade was all dedication. He was a chronic insomniac, and the stranger's phone call in the early hours had ended his hopes of sleep. He also, rightly in this case as it happened, distrusted his subordinates.

He was rather pleased with his foray into reporting: the old hands could still teach the young ones a thing or two. There had been no other press at the barracks and though there was no chance of an exclusive, the Globe were now assured of more background than the rest. He had been lucky of course. The Detective Superintendent on the case was a member of Hampstead Golf Club, and they had played together twice; Hollis's card and a note about the tip-off had been enough to get him past the gate.

The sight of violent death in that most orderly of settings had been particularly shocking—viewed from his glass-walled office it would have had no impact whatever —but what had interested Hollis most was the evident tension between the police and the military. The S.I.B., prodded by the Adjutant of the Welsh Guards and encouraged by two officers and one civilian official from the Ministry of Defence, had shown an almost obsessive interest in his early-morning caller, questioning him closely on the time and the voice. The Ministry wanted to believe that the release of Reith's murderers was the work of outsiders and were determined to make the facts fit the theory; the Superintendent, who distinguished clearly between justice and politics, was unconvinced.

Escorting Hollis from the guardroom, the portly official from the Ministry had pressed his fingers together as if in prayer, pursed his lips, and said: 'Mr. Hollis, we have seen the late edition of your paper. Your allegations of mutiny are without foundation. The Army is loyal. A full statement on this appalling incident will of course be issued later by the Ministry, but I would not like you to leave without knowing that we see a pattern in all this. In our view these two guardsmen were abducted by outside accomplices, who have made it their business to penetrate this battalion and to obtain the maximum publicity for seemingly mutinous events which they have themselves organised. If this is so, I need hardly point out that their best ally appears to be the *Globe*. Direct allegations are difficult at this stage; but I would be grateful if when you come to write further on this subject, you would bear in mind what I have said.' Good will had had nothing at all to do with the smile on the scrupulously shaven face. A limp handshake, and Hollis had been in the street.

Two minutes later, as he walked up Lower Sloane Street, a black Austin had pulled up beside him. 'Joe,' the Superintendent had said, 'if your untutored head is going to be filled with theories, you'd better hear some good ones. Come and have a cup of tea.'

The Superintendent could not have chosen a more faithful agent of the truth. His precise reconstruction of events was now recorded with equal precision in Joe Hollis's notebook.

The police suspected Evans, the Lance-Corporal of the Guard, for whose disappearance there was no explanation. Motive and opportunity were there. Evans was known to be a close friend of Steele; he was also an excitable man, who had twice lost his stripe for violent behaviour and had no reason to be fond of Reith. It seemed likely that at some point during the night he decided to release Steele and Meredith. His opportunity came at 3 a.m., when the Sergeant of the Guard was doing a tour of the barracks and the rest (a driver and a drummer) were asleep. The latter were easily disposed of. The door of their sleeping quarters had a bolt on the outside, so Evans was able to lock them in without waking them. He then armed himself with a rifle and broke into the locked ammunition box. Having cut the telephone wires, he waited for the return of the Sergeant, who carried the cell keys on his belt. The Sergeant was forced at gunpoint to release Steele and Meredith; after opening the cell, he tried to recover control of the situation and was shot twice at point-blank range, once in the stomach and once in the face. The three offenders then doused the lights and fled from the barracks, leaving the rifle in the guardroom. It was not until 4 a.m., when five bandsmen returning from a late engagement could get no reply on the gate and telephoned the Orderly Officer, that the crime was discovered.

The Ministry argued that Evans could in all innocence have opened the gate to a third party—particularly if the latter were wearing uniform—and then been removed from the scene. Their theory was based on the hypothesis that Evans would not have behaved as he did, and that if Evans alone had threatened him, the Sergeant would have risked action earlier. There were only two pieces of evidence in their favour: the rifle appeared to have been fired by a man wearing gloves and Hollis's caller could not have been any of the three, since the same person had told him of Reith's death. But the rifle could still have been fired by Evans, and the call, which was made almost two hours after their escape, proved only that they had sympathetic company.

'So you see, Joe,' the Superintendent had concluded, 'theories are dangerous things. I recommend you to stick to the facts. We'll never know what happened unless we can find a witness, and by the way—' the baleful eyes had been lit by a mischievous gleam—'if the guardsmen didn't do it, nothing would bring them to the surface quicker than a story which put the finger on them. Eh? Would it? I'll leave you to think about that.'

Thrust and parry. Hollis was fascinated. He would not have thought the Super had it in him: his golf certainly wasn't up to much. He closed his notebook and paid for his tea.

One could only feel sympathy for the Ministry. Reith's death, the missing trucks in Oxfordshire, now this—three scandalous incidents in one day in the nation's most famous infantry regiment. That was bad enough, but if they were allowed to look like related acts of mutiny, the position was really serious. The battalion had clearly been selected to spearhead an operation against Rhodesia because its loyalty was thought to be unshakable. If it was seen to have rebelled, how would the rest of the army react?

There were two things the Government could do. The first was to pretend that politics had nothing to do with it. The *Globe*'s front page had blown that one wide open. To avoid imitation by rivals the story had been held to the late edition and obviously the Superintendent had been too busy to see it, but it had scared the Ministry stiff and set them on their second interpretation: mutiny, a put-up job, chief protagonists rescued, two three-tonners hi-jacked —yes, they might even try that. It was shaky, but better than nothing.

He walked into the street and headed for the taxi rank in Sloane Square. The rain had stopped and the sun was breaking through. The air was full of the noise of water, soaking into the earth, and for the first time in two months the city had a fresh, washed look. A lot of people seemed to be whistling. But the cheerful moment passed; the blood on the floor of the cell and the frightened faces of the soldiers were not so easily forgotten.

The trucks—that was the oddest business of all. Two large military vehicles lost without trace in rural England—it was unbelievable. Kemble said he had got the story from a contact in the Oxfordshire Police, but it was years since he had been on the *Oxford Mail* and since when had he been a friend of the law? On the inspired hunch that some of the mutinous soldiers would make a run for it he rings up this country copper; old-time friendship triumphs over police security and hey presto. It was too good to be true. Hollis had advised against using the story, at least in its raw form. But to check it would have invited official suppression and the Editor, for whom the white Rhodesians were God's gift to Africa, had decided to go ahead. Since finding Mrs. Steele Kemble could do no wrong. No wrong? He'd stayed in bed that morning, hadn't he? For that, Hollis determined, he would have young Kemble's head.

7.30 am

Patrick Harvey was not a great Prime Minister but he had learnt one secret of the profession: not to let bad news upset his routine. Good and bad days alike began with orange juice, porridge, and a four-minute egg on a tray at half past seven, with the newspapers, without any official telegrams or letters. But this morning propped against the egg was a Foreign Office envelope. Harvey looked at it resentfully and nearly rang for its removal, then realised what it must be. He swiftly worked out a compromise: first orange juice and porridge, then the King's reply to his message, then the egg and the newspapers. He smiled irritably at the reply: lucky constitutional monarch, sitting on the terrace at Ravello, exhorting his Ministers to brisk decisiveness! No, that was unfair, the King was doing his best to help and it might have been disastrous if he had come down on the other side. It would be amusing to show Thorganby the royal message; Thorganby probably believed that the King thought as he did on Rhodesia. The message might even as the King hinted be used as a weapon of last resort to get the Cabinet to approve Operation Constable.

Harvey tackled the egg. It was overdone and cooling fast, but his annoyance was diverted to the *Globe*'s banner headline. 'MUTINY AT CHELSEA,' and underneath: 'Guards refuse Rhodesia orders. R.S.M. killed.' Harvey swore aloud. Critten had promised to stop the papers. This meant he had been even crasser than usual or in his crude way he had given the story to the *Globe* to frighten the Cabinet off Constable. Either way it stank.

His eye was caught by a sub-headline half-way down the page—'Trucks missing'—and he reached for his glasses. '. . . On arrival at Brize Norton,' he read, 'it was discovered that two of the battalion's vehicles had disappeared from the column. Patrol cars of the Oxfordshire police have been searching for the missing 3-ton vehicles, so far without success. It is believed that the drivers of the trucks may have lost the rest of the convoy, but in the absence of official comment, the possibility of mass desertion cannot be ruled out . . .'

Harvey flung the paper to the floor. He did not need to read the leader; he could imagine every thundering, self-righteous word. He reached for the telephone. 'Tell the Press Secretary I want him here as soon as he comes in.' This was bad. Again he felt defeatism mounting inside him but to his surprise suppressed it more easily than before.

Rulers of nations need one faculty above all others—that of avoiding obsession, of switching their concentration completely from one subject to another and turning it off at will. Harvey was developing the faculty fast. He lay back on the pillows, and for five minutes forced himself to concentrate on the pleasures of good coffee and early morning sunshine. His sense of proportion returned.

The Grenadiers, Critten, Coper's monster meetings—these were side-issues. The way ahead seemed suddenly simple. He must get the Cabinet to agree to Constable and bring the date forward. The troops should go in on Thursday morning. Critten would bluster that it was impossible, but everything had been ready for weeks. Thursday—that was right; no time for more mutinies, no time for Critten and Thorganby to rouse the Party against him, no time for Coper's campaign to get out of hand. Once Constable had actually started the noise at home would soon die down. Just forty-eight hours to wait. As he kicked off the blankets Harvey felt that he didn't deserve to be Prime Minister if he couldn't get through two bad days and come out on top. Suddenly he was enjoying himself.

His shave was interrupted by Ryder Bennett, the Foreign Secretary, submerged in the gloom which Harvey had just shaken off.

'Sorry to break in so early, Patrick, but there's bad news.'

'You amaze me. Sit down, Ryder, take some toast. Why are you up so early?'

'Melton woke me up two hours ago. Doing his best, I think, but getting edgy and says he can't get the vote postponed beyond today. But that's not the trouble. The C.G.S. rang me up an hour ago. Those thugs of mutineers who knifed their R.S.M. yesterday—they shot their way out of the glasshouse last night and vanished.'

'Wait a minute. Why did the C.G.S. ring you? It's nothing to do with the F.O.'

'Of course it's not, but Roger Dunphee was in my house at Wellington. I know him well—and he's out of his depth about the politics of it.'

'Politics? Do you mean to tell me he phoned you and not Critten?'

'Certainly he rang Critten, but that was one of the odd things. Critten, who was screaming so loudly about the mutiny yesterday, didn't seem to worry much about the mutineers getting away. The C.G.S. said there's a strong suspicion that the Grenadiers have been got at by some kind of political outfit, but Critten took it very coolly and wouldn't ask the Home Office for a watch on ports and airfields. Now it seems to me . . .'

Harvey cut in: 'Look, Ryder, Critten's a fool, we both know that, and with luck he'll resign before I shave tomorrow morning. But he's right over this. The Chelsea business at a normal time would have us screaming; but now it's not the main point. The main point is the Cabinet this morning. If we win, everything else will fall into place. So for God's sake go as you said you would and get your side mobilised. And don't wast time on the mutineers. There are lots of lunatics on the fringe of Coper's set-up, and I wouldn't wonder if some of those thought up the rescue as a stunt. Off you go, and don't be late for Cabinet. And tell my duty officer as you go out that I want the Newbury result as soon as Central Office gets it.'

Ryder Bennett was followed by the Press Secretary. Joynson was an old Fleet Street hand—quick, irreverent, loyal —and was generally considered one of Harvey's best appointments.

'Good morning, Bill, come in. You've seen the *Globe*, I suppose?' Knowing it was unfair, Harvey could never help behaving as if every piece of adverse publicity was the fault of his Press Secretary. But Joynson was well prepared.

'Yes. I know what you're thinking, but there was no leak. They found an eye-witness to the Chelsea business—an old woman. It's the luck of the game. We'll play it down as hard as we can, say her report was exaggerated.'

'I would prefer you to deny it completely.'

'That would be difficult.'

'What about the trucks? Why wasn't I told about that?'

'That's much more serious. Until an hour ago the Ministry genuinely believed it was a balls-up. Now they've found the trucks hidden in a wood. They were empty. Twenty-three men are missing. The *Globe* were wrong about the convoy. The trucks were unaccompanied, and left Chelsea about 6.30. The first contained a final batch of men from the barracks, including a dozen detainees. The second was carrying ammunition and grenades. Some of that's gone too.'

'I don't believe it was desertion.'

'No, nor do the Ministry. There's too much of a pattern. The pamphlets in the barracks—that must have been the work of an insider. The escape from the guardroom last night—they could have had help. The *Globe* are getting tip-offs.'

'That's how they knew about the trucks?'

54

'No. They're protecting their source there. We think it must have been the police. That's being investigated now.'

'If there was any irregularity, I want the heads of those responsible. You can threaten the *Globe* with what you like —no further access to confidential briefing, the lot. I'm quite prepared to speak to the Editor personally.'

'The danger is that if we over-react they will believe the worst. There's no chance of suppressing the trucks story now, but we can make it work for us. There is strong evidence here of outside intervention. It's unlikely that twenty-three guardsmen would decide to desert at the same time, still less likely that they would be able to vanish without trace. The police found tracks of a third large vehicle in the wood: it seems that no one left the scene on foot.'

'This is beginning to sound like Chicago.'

'Right. That is the sort of comment the Press will make. I suggest you allow me to reveal all the facts and make the strongest case I can for outside interference. It's a risk. On the evidence we have they won't all swallow it, but some will, and there's a chance that we'll then see a reaction against the pro-Rhodesians—among the public and the army. If, of course, that's what you want?'

Harvey smiled. Blood from the stones. Half an hour with Joynson, and even the Pope would commit suicide.

'Yes, Bill, that is what I want. Do as you suggest.'

'One more thing.'

'Yes?'

'I should like to try and persuade the evening papers to hold the trucks story. If we rob the kidnappers or whoever they are of the publicity they're after, they may overreach themselves. With any luck we shall have more evidence by tonight. If they are holding loyal guardsmen, one of them may get free.'

'All right,' Harvey said. 'Let's hope so.' Hope was becoming his staple diet.

8 am

'Silence, gentlemen, please!'

The Major was in his element.

Since he had been cashiered from the Parachute Regiment, life had held few pleasures for Major Horace Rackstraw. Apart from a brief, lucrative spell with President Tshombe's mercenaries, the years had gone by in a seedy round of second-rate jobs, cheerless commercial hotels and hired women. When he tried to emigrate, he found he had neither the money nor the credentials. In an effort to resist the anonymity closing over his head, he had joined the National Socialist Party. The hysterical talk was little to his taste. He was a man of action, and membership of the partly merely fretted his tether to breaking point and provided an object for his violence. It could have been a little girl in a wood; as things turned out, it was a young West Indian, buying milk from a machine in Birmingham on a wet Sunday afternoon.

Six months ago it seemed that Rackstraw had reached the end of the road: from officer of the British Army to penniless ex-convict, frying hamburgers in Wimbledon. But then he had found a benefactor. Suddenly there was money in his pocket and a purpose in his life. They had been busy months. He had tracked down and vetted, one by one, his ex-comrades from the Congo, scoured the underworld, explored the ranks of the British Nazis to the last man. Finally he had been able to report to his open-handed chief that the team was ready. Throughout a long night in a remote country inn Horace Rackstraw had received his orders, precise and detailed as they should be. A base was selected, the Frenchman had arrived and the team was assembled. The waiting on Sunday had been a strain; the audacity of the plan had unnerved him once or twice. But now the operation was in full swing and the thrill of command was racing through his veins. Yes, the Major was in his element.

'Gentlemen, if I could have your attention.' The appeal was unnecessary. No one was talking, and the ten pairs of eyes around the dining table were fixed on the speaker. The Frenchman was leaning against the mantelpiece, picking his teeth. At the end of the table Steele was smiling. (Rackstraw assumed it was the love of a battle; in fact it was his own often-repeated 'gentlemen.' Never, Steele was thinking, had a nastier-looking bunch answered to the name.)

Rackstraw unveiled a blackboard.

'This is the scene of today's operations. Oxford. About twenty miles from here down the A40. This open space you see here is Saint Giles, a pedestrian precinct in the centre of town. This is the Randolph Hotel. We have reserved a room here, on the corner, in the name of Johnson. Across the street is Balliol College, where some of you might have gone if you'd had the brains . . .' He paused for laughter but there was none. 'The students are on holiday, but the college is being used for a conference of school teachers. Some of them are billeted in these rooms overlooking the street. The teachers are wearing yellow name-cards. I'm glad to say we have an artist among us, and he has done me a couple of cards—' he held them up for inspection—'so we shall have access to those rooms.'

There was a rustle of approval from the listeners round the table. Whatever was intended, it had been well planned. Steele noticed that Meredith was watching him.

The Major continued: 'The cross in the centre of the street—here—is a monument. It's called the Martyrs' Memorial. It seems that some worthy gents were burnt at the stake on that spot, which I think is very appropriate.' Pause. No laughter. 'At 1800 hours this evening the "Hands off Rhodesia" movement will be holding a rally there. They've built a wooden platform in front of the monument and Mr. Barnett Coper, M.P., will be speaking. Now here—' he chopped the air above the blackboard—'is a park. The anti-Rhodesia boys have decided they're going to have a counter-rally in that park at the same time. The students are coming back in bus-loads for it. Every bloody weirdie in the land will be there. It's odds on that at about 1830 hours they will decide to march down this street—Banbury Road, or this one—Broad Street, to have

57

a crack at the others. In case they don't think of it themselves, some of you will be there to help them along. So at 1900 hours at the latest, we can expect a fair old collision in Saint Giles. Gentlemen, it's our job to hot that collision up until it's a full-scale riot, and to hot that up until it's a bloody massacre.'

Rackstraw paused to examine the effect of this announcement on his audience. If there were any weak ones this was when it would show. It was easier to nobble guardsmen than to lob a grenade into a crowd of students. But the eyes round the table were steady: he had chosen well. Only the cawing of rooks disturbed the silence. 'Right,' he continued, 'if everybody's with me so far, I'll tell you how we go about it. I shall be here, in a second-floor room of the college . . .'

Steele was seized by an urge to laugh. Like little boys playing soldiers. How to start a riot, 'in six easy movements,' as if it were making a bed-pack . . . One, provoke the other side by shouting the foulest thing that comes into your head; two, pick a fight with anybody you like; three, when the fighting gets going cause the maximum injury to as many people as possible; four, lob thunderflashes in all directions, add one grenade and a petrol bomb for flavour; five, fire half a dozen shots into the crowd with a silenced weapon from an overlooking window; six, drop smoke-bombs and as the crowd scatters leave amateur-looking weapons lying in the road. It was when you thought of the results that it was not so funny . . .

Suddenly Steele was the centre of attention. The Major had worked down to the end of the table.

'. . . Steele, you will be in the graveyard.' This time the Major got his laugh. When Meredith's mouth was in this unusual position it appeared that most of his molars were metal. The Major turned to the blackboard. 'This space here, behind the monument, is a graveyard. Plenty of cover. You'll be supplied with a few little gadgets to throw over the fence—we'll have a look at those later. Remember, Jake and I will be covering you from our window positions, so you'll be well protected.'

That, thought Steele, is the sort of protection I could do without.

Rackstraw's peroration was interrupted by the telephone. The change in his manner was extraordinary: the jocular commander had become a hushed subordinate.

'Yes, sir. Briefing them now. . . . The Strand? From here? About three hours, I should think. . . . Of Mr. Rhodes himself, is it? That's good, very good! I like that, oh yes . . .' The obsequious laughter rattled round the room. Rackstraw slipped a degree in the estimation of his hirelings. '. . . Well, sir, I need them this morning to rehearse the Oxford op. The Colonel? Yes, I'm sure he would enjoy it. I'll put him on.'

The silent figure with the eye-patch stood on his foul-smelling yellow cigarette and detached himself from the fireplace. When he finally spoke, Steele did not understand a word. He thought it must be French.

11 am

The crowd had been waiting outside the Corn Exchange in Newbury since early morning, and in the last hour or so had grown as the news spread that there had been a recount. Mostly comfortable unpolitical people with shopping baskets and muddy farm cars; but immediately in front of the Corn Exchange steps was drawn up in rough order a squad of young men and girls in leather jackets. To begin with they had shouted a few Movement slogans but now they were smoking and some had taken off their jackets in the warm sun. Their placards read: 'Bishop says, we all say, HANDS OFF RHODESIA.' Police stood between them and the steps.

Just before eleven the doors opened. The Returning Officer was a bull-like man. While they brought the microphone he mopped his brow. On either side of him stood the candidates and their wives, smiling fixedly.

'I, Leonard Willis, by virtue of the authority to me entrusted, do hereby declare the result of the election held in the southern division of the County of Berkshire on the 4th of August to fill the seat formerly held by Sir Walter Fisk, Knight Bachelor, lately deceased. The number of valid votes cast was 54,483. The candidates received the following votes. I shall list them in alphabetical order. Albert Bishop, Esquire, 21,360; the honourable Anthony Robert Chivers, 21,815; Ronald Sims, Esquire, 11,308. I hereby declare the Honourable Anthony Robert Chivers duly elected Member of Parliament for the said division.'

There was a roar of surprise and anger from the leather jackets, which swamped the unorganised cheers from the other parts of the crowd. The squad broke order and surged towards the steps. The police managed to hold them back during the ceremony of thanking the Returning Officer, and then advised the newly elected member to leave by a side door.

11 am

In 1969 a generous sculptor with a bent for politics had presented Rhodesia House with a large bronze of Cecil Rhodes affectionately clasping a laughing Negro. Without being obvious about it, the statue suggested that the Negro was doing Mr. Rhodes a favour; but if you were determined enough to see it differently, you could. It was therefore the perfect piece to celebrate the previous year's somewhat ambiguous settlement, and the entrance to Rhodesia House on the corner of Agar Street and the Strand had been duly modified, at great expense to the impoverished Rhodesian state, to accommodate it.

The statue was now surrounded by about fifty people. The fringe of the crowd consisted mostly of those Londoners who will stop and watch anything, particularly if someone else is already watching it. Around the base of the statue was a cluster of Movement people, doing verbal battle with some students from the L.S.E. A woman was attempting to mount the plinth and was being gently restrained by one of the two policemen on the door. A few press-photographers were about, and they were joined by the Assistant Defence Correspondent of the *Globe*, who explained that he was in hot water and hoping for a story to soothe his superiors. The press-photographers laughed: they had spent a lifetime at such political gatherings, waiting in vain for the least hint of drama.

The Movement were hoping for good news from Newbury, and someone had brought a transistor radio. A hush fell as the by-election results came through. '. . . Anthony Robert Chivers, 21,815 . . .' There was a shout of triumph from the L.S.E. students, and in the excitement the wild-eyed lady from the Movement succeeded at last in climbing the plinth. Clutching the bronze knees of Cecil Rhodes, an exasperated constable tugging at her feet, she began to harangue the crowd.

Nobody had noticed the small suitcase at the base of the statue or the man with the eye-patch who had left it there five minutes before, and when it exploded, killing the woman and the policeman, there was a moment of shocked disbelief. It was not so much the unfamiliar sight of corpses in the Strand as the thought that someone had broken the rules.

As the dead and injured were carried into Charing Cross Hospital, the moment of suspended reaction passed and each side started to blame the other. The crowd grew and a vicious fight began. Clutching their cameras like mothers protecting their babies, the photographers ran to expose their film and Jack Kemble, who was nursing a bleeding ear, searched for a taxi in the mounting chaos.

12 noon

*Extract from Minutes of Cabinet Meeting
held at 10.30 a.m. on Tuesday, 5th August*

. . . After the Chiefs of Staff had withdrawn the *Prime Minister* said that the military and diplomatic position as illustrated by the Chiefs of Staff and the Foreign Secretary showed that an immediate decision was required from the Cabinet. He still hoped that this could be unanimous but he would if necessary hold a vote. Before doing this he would briefly explain his own views. The Multiracial Settlement of 1968 in Rhodesia had been consistently supported by all parties in the House of Commons and in the country, and welcomed by the world at large as a striking triumph of British statesmanship. That settlement had now been overthrown by force, and unless it was restored Rhodesia would quickly relapse into racial violence and anarchy. The United Nations considered that the practical responsibility for doing this lay with Britain; so, he believed, did a large majority in the Commons and the country. A military plan had been prepared which he judged would be quickly successful; it should be put into effect without delay. The present uncertainty damaged every interest which the Government was committed to protect and if prolonged might be disastrous.

The Minister of Defence said that in his view the Prime Minister had over-simplified the situation. Violent demonstrations were taking place every evening in London and other cities. There had been a revulsion of popular feeling against the Government as a result of their Rhodesian policy. This revulsion had spread to the armed forces, as the mutiny at Chelsea the previous day had shown. It was his duty to warn the Cabinet that in his estimation there was a serious risk of Operation Constable failing because of disaffection in all ranks of the Army. He could no longer guarantee that orders would be obyed. A situation without parallel would be created if the Cabinet authorised the operation.

The Foreign Secretary informed the Cabinet of the result of the Newbury by-election which had just been received. He said that the victory of the Conservative candidate despite unprecedented propaganda and intimidation by the Rhodesia Movement showed that the violence in the streets was not a genuine expression of popular feeling. This was the moment to move strongly to restore public order in the cities and discipline within the armed services. He would like to know what measures the Home Secretary and the Minister of Defence proposed to take to that end. But the immediate step necessary was to endorse the proposals in the paper which he had circulated to the Cabinet and authorise Operation Constable.

The Lord President of the Council said that before coming to a vote the Cabinet must weigh the words of the Minister of Defence about the state of the Army. In his long Cabinet experience he had never heard so grave a statement. In his opinion it raised a constitutional question which could not be ignored. The loyalty of the armed services was to the Crown, and this was more than a formality. At a moment of crisis the Crown should still be a symbol of national unity, particularly to the Services. The King might well wish to exercise his undoubted right to warn his Minister of dangers which he might see in the action which they proposed. For these reasons he thought it essential that the King should now be advised to return from Italy, and that meanwhile no decision should be taken on the Foreign Secretary's proposals.

The Minister of Defence and the *Secretary of State for Scotland* concurred with the Lord President's suggestion.

The Prime Minister said that hitherto he had advised the King that a curtailment of his holiday would create unnecessary alarm. He now agreed with the Lord President that the time had come to advise His Majesty to return. There was however no need to delay a decision on Operation Constable meanwhile and indeed this would be entirely contrary to His Majesty's opinion. He had taken steps to discover this opinion, which he was at liberty to communicate to his colleagues. The Prime Minister then read to the Cabinet the text of Rome telegram No. 356 to the Foreign Office.

The Cabinet decided by a majority

(a) to approve the proposals in paper DP (104) 74 circulated by the Foreign Secretary;
(b) to instruct His Majesty's representative at the United Nations to vote in favour of the draft resolution now before the Security Council;
(c) to authorise the execution of Operation Constable at dawn on Thursday, 7 August.

The Cabinet adjourned at 12 noon.

12.10 p.m.

Ryder Bennett ignored the lift and ran up the main staircase of the Foreign Office with affection. Thank God they'd never let that crazy committee pull the building down. He felt young and full of bounce. Instead of going straight into his office he walked through the long ante-room, full as usual of Private Secretaries, men from the News Department and the curious or ambitious in search of gossip. They would almost all be on his side.

'Sir Charles Melton on the telephone please, as quickly as you can.'

He paused in the middle of the room. 'Gentlemen, the Cabinet has taken its decision. You will soon know what that is. We will now have about ten busy days. I hope you are feeling as energetic as I am.'

He heard the faint rustle of speculation as he passed into his own room. His senior Private Secretary followed at once.

'There's a telegram in already from Melton, sir, saying that the Africans at the U.N. are convinced that South Africa's about to send parachutists into Salisbury.'

'He's reported that before. There should be an up-to-date comment from Pretoria.'

'Nothing new yet, sir. The communications people are overrun with traffic and some of the priorities are getting mixed up. But I've just got this from the section across the way.'

The intelligence digest ran to three pages but a conclusion was typed in double-spacing at the top. 'While the indications are not complete, they strongly support the Ambassador's estimate that the South African Government has decided to intervene in Rhodesia and suggest that military action will begin on some date between the 9th and 13th August, directed towards Salisbury, Bulawayo and the main posts along the frontier with Zambia.'

'When's the 9th, Henry?'

'Saturday, sir.'

'Couldn't be better. We shall be comfortably in by then. Has a copy of this gone to Number Ten?'

'I wanted you to see it first.'

'Send it personal to the P.M., would you? This means we can't afford a slip in the time-table. What are you looking unhappy for, Henry?'

'Well, it's way outside my field, but the Minister of Defence, being so opposed to Constable . . .'

'But you didn't hear him, he's bound to resign at once; he committed himself too far in Cabinet, in fact he led the losing pack. Thorganby might just stay—the P.M. handled him magnificently—but I can't see how Critten could fail to resign.'

'You're probably right, sir—it's just that with the time-table of Constable so important, there is perhaps a risk that he might decide to stay on . . .'

'Yes, I see what you're driving at, yes . . . Henry, see what you can dig out of Critten's Private Secretary about his intentions and I'll scribble a line to the P.M. And send in some sandwiches and a whisky and soda, will you?'

Left to himself Ryder Bennett walked to the window. On the Horse Guards and round the lake in St. James's Park small knots of people moved aimlessly about in the hot afternoon sunshine, confused remnants of the morning's demonstration. Ryder Bennett thought about men in politics. He had worked closely with Thorganby and Critten for ten years in opposition and government, but he did not know what either was really like or what they would now do. Even Harvey, whom he knew much better, had amazed him that morning with his mastery of the meeting and the way he had kept back the message from the King for use as the ultimate weapon.

A messenger brought in the sandwiches and the lunch-time edition of the *Evening Standard*. 'RIOT—TWO KILLED IN STRAND. Police charge as Cabinet meets.'

'Nasty bust-up round Charing Cross this morning while you was talking, sir,' said the old man with relish.

Just in time, thought the Foreign Secretary, another postponement and Coper would have won.

12.30 pm

'Hold it there, lady—that's right—with the cup. Up a bit more . . . Lovely!' Click, leap, click, crouch, click, click. If only this young man would sit down, she thought, I could listen to what the lady is saying.

'Mrs. Steele, I don't think you've seen our magazine, so I've brought a copy along . . .' Big, shiny pages, a coloured woman on the front, dressed in silver paper. '. . . Lovely, isn't it? *Femina* is a completely new concept in journalism for women. We combine fashion and practical hints for the home with intellectually challenging features. The secret of our approach is that we recognise the housewife has a mind of her own.' The long, booted legs twined and untwined in the yellow plastic skirt. Surely that thing couldn't be comfortable. The room was full of smoke. '. . . Next month, Mrs. Steele, we are doing a feature on mothers. Mothers who have—how shall I put it?—who have been, er, *disappointed* in some way by their children. That is why we are so interested in your story. If you don't mind, I'll switch this little machine on—just so we get it right, you understand. Testing. One, two, three, four. Right. Now I want you to relax. I'm going to ask you some questions, and you just answer them in your own time, in your own way. A cosy little natter between mothers, O.K?'

'Have some of your own then, do you?'

'Oh yes. Caspar's a bit younger than Harry, but I'm sure we can understand each other's problems. Now the first thing I want to ask you is whether you think the lack of a father . . .'

Such questions. She wished she had never let them in. The woman had said there was £50 in it for her, and it seemed harmless enough; but now these questions—personal, embarrassing. Not at all like that nice boy from the *Globe*. In future she would talk only to him.

A tap on the window: it was George Belling from the Coach and Horses. Now what could he want? Gratefully she went to the door. She would ask George to show them out; he could handle this sort of thing.

'George, am I glad to see you!'

'Gwen—' He was out of breath; he looked queer, scared almost.

'What is it?' she said.

'It's the phone, for you.'

'Not more of these newspaper people. George, I can't. Tell them I'm not at home.'

'Gwen, you're confused, you're not thinking straight. It's the phone at the pub. There's only one person ever rings you there. I think it's Harry.'

She ran all the way, but when she got there the line was dead. Friendly hands helped her to a chair and George Belling poured a Mackeson, then went back to get the magazine people out of her house. She began to cry.

1.30 pm

The bedroom had a telephone. It was in a closed cabinet by the side of the bed, and the Major must have missed it.

It was not until late in the morning that the significance of this fact had dawned on Steele, and not until he had been instructed in throwing a petrol bomb and provided with a false moustache that he had found a chance to return there.

Burford 403. Burford? Twenty miles from Oxford, the Major had said; it would make sense to somebody. The police? The logical step had seemed the most difficult, and the number of the Coach and Horses was ready in his head. But before his mother could reach the phone he had heard footsteps on the stairs. He had had three seconds to get under the bed before the door opened. The feet prowling the room had been Meredith's.

That was an hour ago. He looked at his watch. ETD 1500 hours. He would be lucky to get another chance; better to wait till they reached Oxford. Now it was beer and sandwiches (the Major had thought of everything) and they were all crowded round the television, laughing their heads off. Someone had blown up a statue in the Strand, people lying all over the place. What was so funny about that?

An *Evening Standard* was lying on the floor. Steele stooped to pick it up and suddenly he was looking in a mirror. They had used his new army photograph, taken at the barracks three weeks before. 'GUARDSMEN ESCAPE— SERGEANT KILLED . . . two shots at point-blank range, in the lower abdomen and the face.'

Steele dropped the paper and looked up. The Frenchman was watching him and laughing, the scar behind the patch turning pink.

Who was he?

If Guardsman Steele had had access to the synoptic index in S Department of the International Criminal Records Office of Interpol in Paris, a search among the tagged cards under 'Visible Scars' would soon have led him to the dossier of Robert Henri Poidatz, French citizen and ex-officer of the Tenth Parachute Division. Among other information the dossier contained the following English-language summary of the subject's personal history.

'Robert Poidatz was born at Nancy, in 1925, of French father and German mother. Commissioned into the French Army shortly after the Second War, he was wounded and decorated twice in Indo-China. Transferred to Algeria, in 1956 he was captured by the F.L.N. and tortured, losing the use of one eye (left eye socket, cheek and forehead still bear severe burn scars). Following the Settlers' Revolt in Algiers, January 1960, he deserted and joined the underground O.A.S. movement. He is known to have taken part in the assassination attempt on President de Gaulle at Petit-Clamart on 22 August 1962. Swiss police have evidence that he was responsible for the murder in Geneva in June 1963 of Gaston Biffaud and Léon Baumgartner, intermediaries in negotiations between the F.L.N. and a U.S. oil company in 1957. In 1962/63 he commanded a company of white mercenary troops in the Congo. He has contacts with Portuguese Intelligence: in June-December 1969 he is believed to have carried out a series of political assassinations in Dar es Salaam at their request, notably that of Fernando Inacio Catarino, Secretary-General of

FRELIMO (Front for the Liberation of Mozambique). In September 1972 he delivered a shipment of Italian automatic weapons through Beira to the White Rhodesian Brotherhood. Despite his age and heavy build, he is physically strong and mentally alert. An expert in the use of small arms and plastic explosive, he is also fully trained in techniques of unarmed combat (Baumgartner and Catarino were both killed by a blow to the neck). Last known address: 315 Calle de Baltasar Bachero, Madrid. Last seen: Marseille, January 1973. Usual alias: Colonel Claude Brochier. (He carries a forged French passport in this name, but due to his distinctive appearance prefers to cross frontiers by clandestine routes.) Preferred weapon: standard French Service pistol, 9 mm. Parabellum M.1950.'

3.30 pm

The polychrome heap of paper bags at Anne Downes's feet told the story of her morning: Bazaar, Susan Small, Annacat, Fenwicks, Elliotts, Gear, Simpsons and now Fortnums, not for a jar of Chinese ginger but to meet Jack Kemble in the ground-floor restaurant. Her feet ached and her suspender-belt had slipped and 1.3% of a Grade 2 Ambassador's salary had been disposed of (a reward for her degree), but she was full of the satisfaction that only a woman can derive from skilful expenditure. Anne was not a girl for whom a social conscience was incompatible with an appreciation of the good things in life. After the long months in the Radcliffe Library, smelling of dust and perspiring student flesh, and three years of Algerian wine in the Banbury Road, it was a joy to upstage the contessas in the Via Condotti and flirt with the bronzed young Fascists of Roman society. Jack was late again; she took off her shoes and ordered Chinese tea for one.

For most of her friends introspection was a ruling passion, for Anne it was more of a hobby; but today she felt that her affairs had reached a point where thought was necessary if confusion was to be avoided. What was, ultimately, the correct definition of her feelings towards

Jack Kemble? He was her lover of course, but was he only the third and best to date in a continuing series? It was a relief to be with an older man after two emotional university affairs; their relationship had stayed at the level of good-natured, disrespectful banter. Fun for a while, but now she was slightly tired of it. Kemble was such an *unserious* man. She wished somehow there was more purpose, more of a hard core in his life. What he did was so easy, she had never seen him under stress. How pompous that sounds, she thought, and was aware that the thought itself was infected with his cynicism. Lately he *had* become more serious, but over her, and that was not quite what she wanted. His devotion, she had noticed, waxed as his satisfaction in himself waned, and that was a sandy foundation for anything. Perhaps she should marry him. Perhaps she should drop him. Conclusion deferred.

Alan Selkirk—now there was an interesting character. So bright, so successful; prizes and scholarships all the way, captain of this and head of that, top of the Civil Service exam; the apple of every mother's eye from Hexham to the Highlands. They had not met for two years and last night she had been determined to dislike him. Civil servants came high in her list of hates: men who kept the Cellophane on the seats of their car, powdered under their armpits and never stuck their necks out, hiding in the safety of numbers. Alan had not said much to dispel the image; and yet she sensed that under the orthodox exterior was a soul tired of caution. Some day soon he was going to surprise somebody. The potential was intriguing and she was glad she had agreed to meet him that evening. For the first time in a year she sensed a hint, the merest hint, of a conflict in her affections.

'Sorry, love. Have you waited long?' The kiss on her cheek was oddly unexuberant. Kemble looked pale and the chair creaked at the strain of his collapse.

'What's wrong?' she said.

'I've been sacked.'

'Oh no. My poor Jack—why?'

'It's a long story.'

'I want to hear it.'

'No, you don't. Waitress. One tea please and some of that cake.'

'But I most definitely do.'

'Well, it's been coming for a long time. Yesterday was a bad day. I should have gone to the office before I met you at El Vino's but I couldn't be bothered. Then Hollis breaks up our lunch by sending me off on a reporter's job. I was furious of course, then I had a lucky break and picked up the mutiny story and I suppose it went to my head. Last night while you were at that dinner I overdid it in the boozer and had a wild idea. The hunch was right, but the way I checked it wasn't. I made a copper sing by impersonating someone else.'

'Is that so unprofessional?'

'Horribly; but it's worse than that, it may even be a crime. The editor had the P.M.'s office on the line, threatening fire and brimstone, Hollis was gunning for me anyway after this morning's effort, so out I had to go.'

'Just like that! But it's unfair. What about your union?'

'Not a hope. Anyway I don't want to go back. Fleet Street's been looking very jaded lately. I couldn't make a rational decision of it, but I knew I was hanging myself. Inspiring, isn't it? The ageing hack in search of his soul.'

'What will you do?'

'Freelance. Telly. A book. I don't know—my range is limited, isn't it? I need time to think.'

'Jack—'

'I know, don't tell me. You're glad, it's what you've wanted all along. I'm not serious enough. Well now I am going to be so serious that I doubt if I shall have time for a girl who spends her daddy's hard-earned cash in places like . . . Annacat—what's that, for God's sake?'

'A shop. I love you.'

'It's mutual.' No qualifying cracks; just a tired smile, and that pathetic 'hit me' look. They said nothing for a while, and Anne thought she might be going to cry, and then she had an idea.

'Jack—come to Rome. There's plenty of room in the

house, they'll be delighted to have you.' He looked un-convinced. 'We could have a marvellous time. The change of scene will help you think.' He was wavering. 'Come with me —tonight. There's always plenty of seats on these night flights. Please, Jack.' He was smiling.

'All right,' he said, 'I'll come.'

Had he really needed persuading?

4 pm (10 am New York)

The electric figures at the top of the hotel on the next block flickered to ten, and Hooper, sitting in the stationary Rolls-Royce on Fifth Avenue, began to fret. The cross-town traffic was thick, and even if Melton appeared at once they would be at least ten minutes late for the Security Council meeting. What could he be doing upstairs in his flat? Not reading the telegrams, for Hooper had them on his lap, neatly tagged together, with this morning's latest instructions on top still untyped. While Hooper waited he put in the commas with his Parker pen.

A ten-year-old Puerto Rican pressed his face against the side window and Hooper, always conscious of security, held the file up against his chest. The boy laughed at the prudish gesture and ran across the avenue into Central Park. Hooper's pen jabbed at the telegram. 'My colleagues and I have now decided. . . . You are therefore authorised . . . In casting this vote you may if you think fit explain . . .' Where the hell could Melton be? Surely not drinking at this hour.

Hooper saw the porter of the block of flats turn inward to greet someone coming out of the lift, and put his pen away. Leon the chauffeur opened the door of the Rolls and Sir Charles Melton clambered slowly in.

'Yes, to the U.N., Leon, that's right. Good morning, Ronald, sorry to keep you waiting. I thought I ought to wear a stiff collar today, historic occasion and so forth, but that fool Robinson had sent them all to the laundry. Found one at last, right at the back of the drawer. Is that

72

the latest telegram? Thank you . . . yes. I see. It doesn't add much to what the Secretary of State said on the phone two hours ago. It's more artistic to keep up the suspense, so let's say nothing about our vote until we've cast it, even to friends. No need to make another speech.'

The Rolls drawled to a halt before an amber light, and Hooper's irritation broke out. 'Get a move on, Leon, we're late already.' Leon gave a slight shrug and Melton pressed the button by his side which raised a glass screen between driver and passengers. 'No need to fret, Ronald, you've got the instructions you wanted, and Latin Americans are always late.'

In fact the President of the Council had entered the chamber five minutes before the British party, and been vexed to find that he was not the last. Journalists were still buzzing round the horseshoe table, fastening on each personality like flies on scattered lumps of sugar. They swarmed about Melton as he entered, but he waved them aside and without answering their questions took his seat, between the American and the Russian. The President banged his gavel and the journalists melted into the press gallery.

'The 2142nd meeting of the Security Council is called to order. I have no speakers on my list. Before we vote on the resolution in Document No. S/4568 I will, as is customary, read it to the Council. The resolution as it now stands reads as follows:

The Security Council,

Recalling its resolution of 20 December 1968 approving the Multiracial Settlement in Rhodesia;

Reaffirming the inalienable right of the people of Rhodesia to a genuine independence free from exploitation or discrimination of any kind;

Condemns the illegal seizure of power in Rhodesia by the White Brotherhood;

Decides that the resulting situation constitutes a threat to international peace and security;

Requests all member states to refrain from any dealings with the racist regime;

Calls upon the United Kingdom to employ all measures, including the use of force, to restore their rights to the Rhodesian people;

Requests the Secretary-General to report within ten days on the implementation of this resolution.'

The President glanced around the Chamber. 'I will now put the draft resolution to the vote—the distinguished delegate of Tanzania wishes to speak.' There was an audible groan round the galleries; the Tanzanian spoke too long and too often, especially at peak viewing hours. But this time he caught and held his audience—his three audiences: the fourteen other delegates round the Security Council table, the journalists and television men in the galleries, the millions of listening Americans from coast to coast. Melton, who was a connoisseur, surprised himself by detecting genuine emotion beneath the smooth missionary tones.

'Mr. President, I will be very brief. We now all have our instructions, but it is only the instructions of the distinguished delegate of the United Kingdom which matter, because his Government alone has the power to carry out this resolution immediately. Now I do not know what his instructions are. But I want to make him an offer. If his instructions are to vote against this draft resolution, that is, to veto it, then the sponsors of this resolution will accept yet another adjournment of two hours. During that time we would ask the distinguished delegate of the United Kingdom to speak again to his Government and say just two things from us, the Africans here at the U.N. First, we believe that unless the British act, within days, perhaps hours, there will be South African troops in Rhodesia. Second, we have argued with the British for days, months, years about Rhodesia. We have argued with them about Smith, Welensky, Whitehead—all of them. We are hoarse with argument, Mr. President. But now it is different. Now even Smith is in prison for opposing the Brotherhood. This Brotherhood that rules now in Salisbury is not a government, not even a dictatorship, but a gang of criminals. They will exploit the white farmer and the African farmer alike. They have thrown even Smith's laws and Smith's judges out of the window. And they are relying on the colour of their

74

skin to save them. They say: "Only the British can defeat us and they will not move because we are white. Most of us are not British, but we are white and that is enough." But we too, we Africans, know the British. We are not sentimental about them, we usually disagree with them, we think they are sometimes wrong, often lazy. They think the same of us. But we also remember men like Livingstone and Lugard. We remember the missionary schools and the universities where we were taught. And remembering these things, we do not believe that Britain will end this whole long imperial effort in Africa by leaving Rhodesia, perhaps the finest of her former colonies, to rot under the rule of a crew of unscrupulous adventurers.'

There was a ripple of handclapping from the public gallery quickly hushed by the tall blue-uniformed guards. The drone of the French translation began. Melton sat impassive in his chair, waiting for the vote. He was a civil servant; he could not match the man's rhetoric, it would be a mistake to try.

Hooper, sitting behind him, pressed forward a note: 'Could I see you urgently for a moment in Committee Room 12? Harold Walker.'

Melton turned round. 'But Walker's not been in his place this morning or yesterday,' he said. 'That young Donaldson's been sitting for Australia.'

'I know, but Walker's outside now, and very anxious to see you.'

Melton looked at the clock. 'No time; the French translation will be over in a couple of minutes. He'll want to know how we're voting. Go and tell him, but he's not to tell anyone else.' Hooper slipped out and Melton felt tired of the U.N. He supposed that the Australians had been instructed to vote the same way as the British. But Walker was running for chairmanship of the Political Committee next month, and it would not do for him personally to vote against the resolution; so he had put in Donaldson for the last day—just in case of trouble.

The translation ended, and sure enough Walker slipped into the Australian seat, bending his long rubbery neck towards Melton in a gesture of goodwill. As the President put the resolution to the vote, Melton felt almost as a physical sensation the gaze of the cameras upon him.

'Will those in favour of the draft resolution raise their hands?' Slowly Melton raised his hand. Fifteen hands—white, yellow, brown, black, unanimous in the air. 'I declare the resolution to be carried.'

A buzz of excitement and of journalists scrambling towards telephones. The American on his left nudged Melton: 'Well done, Charles, they wouldn't have gone that far without you. The White House will be very very pleased.' The Tanzanian was making another speech to the reporters in a corner of the Chamber. Hooper was already drafting in his mind the reporting telegram to the Foreign Office. Sir Charles Melton ran his finger round the inside of his stiff collar. That was history, he supposed. You raised your hand, and got your name in the index of some dull book. He saw Walker approaching, and slipped out in search of a drink.

4.15 pm

5 AUGUST
Office of the Lord President of the Council.
S.W.1.

Dear Prime Minister,

As you know I have consistently opposed the course of action approved by the Cabinet this morning. While deploring the breakdown in Rhodesia I have felt that any attempt to impose a new settlement by the use of force against the Rhodesians of European origin would be bound in the long run to fail and would be repugnant to the great mass of British opinion. In these last hours I have been convinced that it would also place an intolerable strain on the loyalty of the armed forces. I cannot in conscience remain a member of an administration pledged to what I believe to be a tragically mistaken step, and I must therefore ask you to accept my resignation. In doing so I would like to express my gratitude for your many kindnesses to me and for the privilege of having served under your leadership.

Yours sincerely,
Thorganby

PERSONAL AND CONFIDENTIAL

5 AUGUST *Ministry of Defence*

My dear Harvey,
I must write to you as a result of this morning's Cabinet. Although I was against what was decided I am sure that at this critical time the unity of the party and of the country should come first. I therefore take this chance to reaffirm my loyalty to your leadership, and my readiness to continue in my present position.

Yours ever,
Michael Critten

PERSONAL AND CONFIDENTIAL

5 AUGUST 10 *Downing Street*
*S.W.*1.

My dear Critten,
Many thanks for your letter for which I am most grateful.
I had assumed from your part in the disagreements of these days that you would not wish to remain a member of a Government which was committed to an action of which you so strongly disapproved. I am glad that I was wrong.
However, I feel that despite your magnanimous gesture you will inevitably find it repugnant to direct Operation Constable, and I am therefore making a small number of Cabinet changes. Knebworth has been pressing for some time to retire from the Chancellorship of the Duchy of Lancaster and I hope you will feel able to take this on. It carries, as you know, the responsibility for co-ordinating home transport services and I am sure you will find this a rewarding challenge.

Yours sincerely,
Patrick Harvey

Extract from Evening Standard
(*Late Night Final Edition*) 5 *August*
CRITTEN, THORGANBY QUIT
CRITTEN SLASHES P.M. ON RHODESIA

In a statement issued from his London home this
afternoon shortly after his resignation, Michael Critten,
Defence Minister since 1972, said: 'I have from the
outset opposed a policy of military intervention in Rhodesia
and the involvement of the United Nations in what I regard
as the domestic affairs of an independent nation. I therefore
felt unable, after this morning's decision by the Cabinet, to
continue . . .'

4.30 pm (5.30 pm Italy)

The humid air of a Roman summer lay like a blanket over the
city. In the study of the British Ambassador the heat had
reached sauna level and all present except H.E. himself
were mourning the siesta curtailed by this suddenly called
meeting. Sir Peter Downes sat behind the leather-topped desk
monopolising the infinitesimal breeze which came from the
garden window. He was handsome in a military way: square
chin, tidy moustache, straight blue eyes. His black hair was
beginning to thin, but he still looked younger than his
fifty-five years.

Sir Peter glanced with pleasure round the study. The
bookshelves were comfortably filled with traditional volumes
on the Risorgimento, and in one corner twenty years of
Stanley Gibbons catalogues, British Empire only. Sir Peter
believed that a testy manner helped him to keep discipline,
but underneath he was in a good mood; he enjoyed the
fluster of a crisis, and his daughter was coming home that
night.

'All here now, Raikes? I had to advance the time of
this meeting as I must go to the Ministry of Foreign Affairs
at six to talk to the Minister about Rhodesia. They're
still deciphering the telegram in Chancery, but it's clear
that the Cabinet have agreed to send troops in.' There was
a murmur of surprise and the Air Attaché lit his pipe

ferociously. 'This isn't the time to discuss our personal opinions. We must all of course support the Cabinet's decision when talking to Italians, but don't get drawn into comment or speculation. Stick to what's in the telegram, and when you've said that, shut up. Sidney,' turning to the Air Attaché, 'they want overflying rights for the troop transports. You'd better get the details down on a piece of paper and come along with me at six with plenty of maps. Another thing: Fogli's sure to ask me for an assurance about the safety of the Italian community, which of course I can't give. Raikes, will you look up the file and find out how many of them there are? And does their Consul-General in Salisbury have cipher facilities?'

No one knew, but luckily the Ambassador moved on. Raikes wondered why the Ambassador never called him by his Christian name and when the butler would bring the drinks. He wished the Air Attaché would spend a little more on his tobacco.

Sir Peter had changed his voice down one gear to discuss Royalty. 'Now, the King. So far as we know, he means to hold to his original plan and leave Ravello on Sunday. The Swanstar of the King's Flight will arrive the day before at Naples Airport, and the A.A. will be there to see that things go smoothly. I shall see the King off myself on Sunday, taking young Longden with me. The question arises whether the whole diplomatic staff should also attend. What do you say, Raikes?'

This was the sort of problem which Sir Peter loved to debate for hours, till the pros and cons were mountainous on either side, and no decision seemed possible. Raikes was not ambitious and had promised to take his wife and children to the sea on Sunday. 'It's a question of what you think best, sir,' he said, 'and I'm not sure there's a precedent either way; but the King is supposed to be incognito, so perhaps he might be embarrassed if we all went down. Sir James Courthope rather gave me the impression that . . .'

To Raikes's annoyance, the Ambassador cut him short. 'You're probably right, but I'll take the Press Counsellor, in case there are journalists snooping around.'

The opening of the door by the butler had raised general

hopes, but he carried no tray. 'Excuse me, sir, Mr. Longden is outside. He would like to see you urgently.'

'Of course, of course, don't waste time, tell him to come in.'

The newest and youngest member of the Embassy appeared, pink with suppressed excitement and carrying a long telegram. He tried to make his voice sound casual. 'I'm sorry to butt in, sir, but this has just come in and I thought you ought to see it.'

The Ambassador took the long sheet of paper and spread it flat on his desk. 'Another F.O. Guidance. Won't they ever stop sending us these things?' He began to read aloud the highlights of the message for the benefit of the meeting. 'Disturbance yesterday at Chelsea Barracks ... R.S.M. suffered injuries from which he subsequently died ... certain political overtones ... assailants arrested but escaped during the night ... you should play down sensational reports which may appear in the Press ... circumstances of escape being carefully investigated ... you should take the line that the general loyalty and discipline of the armed forces are beyond question ... for your own information there is some reason to suspect that a criminal organisation may have inspired ...'

With a sigh he handed the telegram back to the hovering Third Secretary. 'Good God, what are we coming to? Take this to the Military Attaché, will you, and say I want to discuss it with him when I get back from the Ministry. Now, where were we?' He glanced at the scribbled card on his desk. 'Yes, of course, the Air Show. I don't want to be difficult, but I really must ask to be kept fully informed. Here we are, Tuesday already, and the Air Show opens Thursday morning. I've got this fellow Ralston coming to stay this evening, and a reception here for a hundred people after the opening, and no one has bothered to tell me what it's about. I will be asked all kinds of questions, and will need a detailed briefing.'

The ambassadorial glare raked the sofa, passing from the Air Attaché to the Commercial Counsellor; both were veterans and sat unmoved. Sir Peter flowed on: 'I had another letter yesterday from Ralston. He's bringing what he calls a "valet-cum-guard," which is very inconvenient, but I suppose we can find room. Apparently he'll have some valuable blueprints with him. Seems to think we've never heard of security. But it's clear he has high hopes of selling his executive plane, the Witch, to the Italian services. Of course they've bought from Fiat or the Americans for years now, but Ralston's done his home-work. He had General di Sarto over to his factory and reckons that if the Air Show goes well, he'll sell thirty at least. Now I need hardly say that this would be a first-class breakthrough into a new Italian market—thirty planes at £150,000 each, plus spares, say £6 million straight off—and we in this Embassy must do everything we can to support him. Now as for the reception—'

The Commercial Counsellor broke in. A blunt, red-faced man, he had by some miracle been left in Rome long enough to learn his job. 'I think, sir, that Ralston is too confident. I sent you a brief yesterday, but you don't seem to have seen it. The trouble is, the Silvestri firm—you went over their factory at Naples last year—have produced the Cavaliere, a plane very like the Witch. They claim better performance but admit higher fuel consumption. They're naming no price, but I believe they would sell at a loss to keep Ralston out. The Italian press will take their usual patriotic attitude in these matters and give the Cavaliere maximum publicity at the show, and, of course, the Minister of Defence is a Neapolitan, which won't help.'

'Thank you,' said Sir Peter Downes. Most men would have been stopped by the irritation in his voice but the Commercial Counsellor was a thorough man and believed in finishing the job. He went on: 'There's one other thing, sir. The instruments and safety equipment of the Cavaliere are from Britain—a firm called Wolverhampton Precision Instruments. The Board of Trade wrote to me about it, usual sort of see-saw letter, warned that if we back Ralston the Wolverhampton people will be on their necks.'

'Well, that's wonderful, isn't it?' Sir Peter was now really cross. 'What am I supposed to do? Turn Ralston away? Tell him we hope the Cavaliere gets the contract? I remember Silvestri—he showed me round the factory. The Prefect told me he was a Fascist. His father shot four partisans with his own hand, and this one still keeps the local thugs in cash. A slimy bully, married to some run-down Sicilian countess. You'd better draft me a telegram. Say that though I understand there's a British element in the Cavaliere, I am totally committed to Ralston, and a contract for the Witch would be a major triumph. The Board of Trade are just feeble, want to please everyone. Anything else about these planes, before we go on to the reception itself?'

'There is one more complication, sir.' Raikes groaned inwardly. The meeting would go on for ever now. Why couldn't the Commercial Counsellor shut up? 'The F.O. have heard that the South Africans are sending a big delegation to the show. As you know, in the last few years they have been very successful at finding chinks in the U.N. ban on arms sales, and it usually starts with big delegations at shows like this. Most of the stuff exhibited here has a civil application but some of it could be adapted to military purposes. The F.O. smell a deal between the South Africans and persons unknown, and ask us to watch out.'

Sir Peter snorted. 'Typical nonsense. What are we meant to do, put microphones in their bedrooms? But that sounds like Silvestri—just his line of country. Can I drop a hint to Fogli tonight?'

'Better not, sir, I think. They say the source of the information is exceptionally delicate.'

'Which means they paid a lot for it. Now, Raikes, we must get on to the arrangements for the party itself. I thought we could have one bar on the terrace . . .'

Raikes's thirst became desperate.

5.50 pm

IN MEMORY OF
MAGDALENE CHARLOTTE COXE
WHO DIED 31ST OCTOBER 1843 AGED
2 YEARS AND 8 MONTHS

Harry Steele crouched beside the flaking headstone and

pondered the life expectancy of a twentieth-century guardsman. A huge crowd was jammed against the railings of the graveyard, shouting and singing and waving banners (the speeches had not yet begun), heads swaying in a haze of dust which fell slowly in a fine white powder on the ivy-covered graves. Behind the memorial, in the shadow of the wooden platform, St. John Ambulance were treating a woman on a stretcher and directly in front of Steele two journalists were fighting for possession of a telephone box. The one already inside finally got the worst of it, and folded downwards to the floor of the box.

Steele sat at the eye of the storm and searched the windows to left and right above the flimsy foliage for the long-barrelled Lugers which he knew were there. Ten minutes later he opened his satchel and disarmed the petrol bomb; then, lying flat beside the gravestone, he activated the fuses on the smoke bombs and after waiting for another minute, hand-kerchief pressed against his face, began to run, choking and weeping, stumbling through the gravestones in the dense, billowing fog.

6 pm (7 pm, Italy)

'I'm sure that's right, sir, and Harvey and the rest of them will be much relieved. Can I just run over it again before I telephone?'

The King's suite opened on to a roof garden laid out over the hotel dining-room. Massed pink and scarlet geraniums surrounded a contrived well-head in the centre. The bougainvillaea from the terrace below had climbed the partitions which screened the garden on two sides, and in one corner had formed an alcove where deck chairs and a table were set, looking down over the valley to Amalfi and the harbour. The evening sun on the mountain opposite picked out a small boy driving goats down the twisting path. It was so quiet that the faint noise of their bells reached the two men sitting in the alcove.

Sir James Courthope went on: 'I will ring Harvey at once and say that you have considered the message he sent after Cabinet this morning and propose to return to England tomorrow, Wednesday, afternoon. Further, that you wish, provided he sees no objection, to broadcast an appeal for national unity tomorrow evening, and would be glad if he could arrange this with the B.B.C. and I.T.V. for about 5 p.m. Then I'll ask Rome to send a message through the usual channel to Sharp and get him to send out a King's Flight plane to Naples to bring us back tomorrow. He'd better send it off at once, I think. The timing may be rather awkward; the Princess of course is in Thailand with two of the Flight's Swanstars, but Sharp will manage something. We should leave here about mid-morning, if you agree, sir; then we could be in London about three.'

The King agreed. There was a moment's silence, and the goatbells sounded closer as the boy rounded a corner. Courthope leant forward. 'I've just had another thought, sir. Harvey ought really to see the text of the broadcast; but there may not be time for that in the rush tomorrow afternoon. He may have changes to suggest, he may want to show it to other Ministers. I should have thought of this before. Your broadcast will be a big event for him. It's a legitimate weapon which you're putting in his hands, and he can reasonably expect to see it in advance. But you won't want to telephone or telegraph it. I suggest, sir, that I get Miss Simmons to type your manuscript now and I will take it back on a commercial flight tonight. I can get it to Harvey at once, and he'll have plenty of time to consider it. Then I can make the arrangements with the television people myself instead of leaving it to Number Ten, who on past form will make a hash of it. That would mean leaving you with John Perkins, Miss Simmons, and of course Walkers. The more I think about it, the more I feel that would be a better plan—as long as you don't mind my leaving you with Perkins. What do you say, sir?'

This plan too was approved, and Courthope left to do his telephoning. As he crossed the hotel landing, the flickering image of Lord Thorganby appeared on the television set which two old ladies were watching in the corner. '*Inghilterra-gravissimo crisi governativo*', said the announcer smugly. '*Due dei ministri piu importanti del governo*

*di Londra, Thornganby, Lord Presidente del Consiglio, e
Critten, Ministro della Difesa . . . il Primo Ministro, accettando
le dimissioni dei suoi colleghi, ha affermato . . .'* There was
Harvey, a photograph taken at least twenty years ago, and
a flash of Big Ben for good measure. *'Questa sera, alla sede
delle Nazioni Unite a New York . . .'* Courthope turned
quickly into his room and took up the telephone.

6.30 pm

In the anteroom of the Lord President's office Alan
Selkirk was still opening telegrams. A three-day march of
African students from the University of Kent, which had
started as a protest and was ending as a gesture of support
for the Government, was converging on Parliament Square
against increasing opposition, and on the advice of the
police riot control squads all Whitehall staffs had been
sent home at lunch time. Selkirk would have kept one of the
girls if he had foreseen the volume of incoming telegrams
which would be set off by Thorganby's resignation. They had
come first one or two at a time, then by the dozen, and in
the early evening by batches of almost a hundred. They
were differently worded, but the message was always the
same. 'Congratulations, you are the only honest one among
them. Stick at it. Don't let us down.' Again: 'Don't let us
down.' After the first few batches Selkirk had realised that
this must be a concerted action by the Movement, planned
days ago for just this turn of the crisis. Thorganby must
guess it too, but even so the telegrams were well worded to
touch him. 'You served under Churchill. What would he
think of this Munich? Don't let us down.' 'Ex-servicemen of
Linlithgow rely on you to stand fast. . . .'

The buzzer buzzed and Selkirk went into the main office
with a sheaf of telegrams. The large chair at the desk
under the antlers and the portrait of Sir Robert Peel was
empty. On the desk a portable radio was almost invisible
behind the mound of orange envelopes. Lord Thorganby stood
by the window, a glass of neat whisky in his hand, looking
down into Whitehall. He had changed after the Cabinet

from his short black coat and pinstripe into a heavy country suit.

Normally at this hour, as the evening sun caught the top of the Banqueting Hall, the last secretaries and civil servants would be hurrying home to mow lawns before the dew fell and read their children to sleep. No. 11 to Victoria, No. 15 to Paddington, then Esher or Henley and the trim, ordered unchanging English life. Now there was emptiness, except for the helmets and occasional horses of patrolling police. Grubby posters lay in the gutter. Selkirk watched Thorganby watch the scene, and wondered what was in his mind. The usual calm assurance seemed unshaken.

'Ah, Alan, more of those damn telegrams? Only time in my life people have taken much notice of what I've done. Put them over there with the others and pour yourself a drink. Then would you ring up King's Cross and cancel the two sleepers for tonight? Oh, of course, you didn't know about that. I booked them from the flat after Cabinet. It sounds odd, but for an hour or so I thought by resigning I would simply be rid of all this,' pointing out of the window, 'and I meant to go back to Hallkirk and have a rest. My wife was keen of course—and we always have a dinner for the gillies and keepers just before the Twelfth—I haven't managed to get to it for three years now . . . of course, you're not a shooting man.' Lord Thorganby tailed off, realising that he had drifted into something like self-revelation. 'Anyway, that's out of the question now. Not because of the telegrams, though they come into it. Did you hear the news? Coper's holding a vast meeting at Oxford—thousands of people in St. Giles, the whole road full. Just think of that—you were at Balliol, weren't you? Things are getting fierce. Then look at this letter by hand from Ralston; you brought it in with the last batch of telegrams.'

STRICTLY PRIVATE

Herakles House
5 AUGUST

Dear David,

First, to thank you for a most enjoyable evening last night. I am writing to Elizabeth.

Second, of course, to congratulate you on your resignation. Those who know you expected nothing less.

Third, to say this. As you know I am no politician, but years in business have given me a nose for opportunities. The ground is crumbling under Harvey's feet, faster perhaps than he realises. When he collapses it would be a disaster if you were not ready to pick up the bits. We rely on you.

Yours ever,

Dennis R.

Alan Selkirk read the letter through again, slowly, so that he had time to think before commenting. Was Thorganby playing with him? Why was he so impressed by Coper's demagogic stunts? The tweed suit, the sleepers from King's Cross, the gillies' party—were they just a feint to hide his determination to stay in London and help the Movement? Selkirk could not get out of his head the way Thorganby had gone half-way to accept Coper's preposterous notions over the port the night before. Ralston's letter was neither here nor there, little more than a friendly declaration of confidence, but Thorganby was fastening on it as another reason for not leaving London.

'I don't see what he means by Harvey collapsing, sir. After all the P.M.'s got a big majority in the House for what he wants.'

'But not in the country, Alan, and in the long run that's what counts. Coper has real talent, and he has reached a genuine vein in the country. Anyway, I've decided to stay. If you will cancel the sleepers, I'll scribble a note to Ralston. Then perhaps you'd take it across to Herakles House yourself if all the messengers have gone.'

Half an hour later Selkirk was crossing Westminster Bridge. A crowded police launch passed beneath him, then another and a third; more trouble expected tonight. He noticed half a dozen ambulances drawn up in the courtyard of St. Thomas's Hospital. Under one arm he carried a roll of tweed, Thorganby's farewell present, in the other hand the letter to Ralston. Thorganby had followed the old rule that if you give a gentleman a letter to deliver you leave it unsealed.

Selkirk had always liked his employer, and enjoyed their formal, good-tempered, unexacting relationship. He was angry with the dramatic suspicions crowding into his brain. Thorganby and Coper, working together to thwart the Government, using violence, perhaps even mutiny, for their ends? He had no proof, no evidence even, and he swore at himself for letting the crisis upset his judgment. He longed to turn back and have it out with Thorganby. ('What were you saying to Coper on the sofa at 11.07 last night out of earshot of your other guests?')

Selkirk glanced at the envelope in his hand. That might show a clue. He had never before opened a letter not meant for his eyes, and his fingers shook slightly as he slipped it out of the envelope. He decided that if there was nothing unusual in the letter he would forget the whole thing.

Dear Dennis,

Many thanks for your letter. What you write confirms my own feeling, and for the present I shall stay in London.

Yours ever,

David T.

Selkirk put the letter back. Nothing of course. How could he have expected anything else? He did not know whether to feel disappointed or relieved. He walked on towards Herakles House, the roll of tweed heavy under his arm.

7 pm

'I don't see what you can do at the moment, Mrs. Steele. There's nothing you can tell the police, so you're let out of that one. Obviously Harry has more to say and he wants to say it to you first. So stay where you are and wait for him to ring again, as he said he would. All right now? Try not to worry; I'll ring back at nine.'

Kemble replaced the receiver in the call-box and returned to the bedsitter in Pimlico where his mother had laid out two farewell glasses of sherry. The television was on, and the news began with a picture of chanting crowds marching down a street in Oxford. '. . . film taken earlier this afternoon during preparations for the meeting organised by the "Hands Off Rhodesia" movement. Police estimated that by six o'clock this evening a crowd of five thousand people had collected in Saint Giles for the meeting, which is being addressed by Mr. Barnett Coper, M.P. Police reinforcements were called for, but before they could arrive, counter-demonstrations broke through police cordons in Banbury Road and Broad Street, and fighting began. The first serious casualty came when a Lincolnshire schoolteacher fell to her death from a second-floor window in Balliol College. The teacher—Miss Molly Fane, from Skegness—was attending a conference of modern teaching methods at the College. She was 28. We have just heard that seven more deaths have been confirmed, two by shooting, and approximately 50 people have been injured, including Mr. Coper, who was struck on the head by a flying brick. It appears that some demonstrators on both sides had come to Oxford armed and prepared for a fight. Troops have been called in, and it is hoped to clear the rioters with tear gas. It was announced tonight that in view of the Rhodesian situation the King has decided to cut short his holiday in Italy and fly home tomorrow. Immediately after his return, the King will address the nation at 5 p.m. from Buckingham Palace. The address will be broadcast live on sound radio and all television channels. . . . The Russians today finally abandoned attempts to restore radio contact with the four cosmonauts who landed on the moon's surface three weeks ago. There is now no hope that . . .'

Mrs. Kemble switched off the set and they raised their glasses in a silent farewell toast. The room was cluttered with photographs and relics, a lonely widow's consolation.

'What a mess we're in,' she said. 'I'm glad the King's coming back, he'll sort things out.'

One safely fashionable opinion which Kemble had retained

89

from his left-wing days was a contempt for the Monarchy. 'I don't see what difference he can make,' he said.

'Oh, you'd be surprised, Jack. You don't see what I do in my job. When things go wrong people expect a lead from the King—it's what holds the nation together. A word from him and they'll all come into line, you see.'

'Well he should start on the Grenadiers, he's their Colonel-in-Chief. They'd give him a rough ride.'

'Don't be soft, 'course they wouldn't. Soon as they heard he was coming they'd be polishing their boots, trying to look their best.'

'You think so?'

'I do. Anyway, what did Mrs. Steele want? When they said she'd phoned the pub looking for you, I thought it must be urgent.'

'She had a call from Harry, but he rung off before she could find out where he was. Said he would ring back.'

'What did he say?'

'That he didn't kill him—the Sergeant of the Guard, that is, not Reith. The Lance-Corporal, Evans, is dead, and the whole job was done by a man calling himself the Major and a man with a scar on his face and an eye-patch. He thinks the second man is French. He's being held in a house in the country with about ten others, but he didn't get round to saying where. His main worry seems to have been to convince his mum he didn't shoot the Sergeant. Understandable, if he's innocent.'

'Jack, he's telling the truth.'

'Sure, Mother?'

Her reply wiped the patronising smile from his face.

'Yes, because I've seen that Frenchman, and the other one. They came to the pub twice last week. You couldn't miss that scar, horrible it is, looks like a burn. And you know who they came to meet? That other boy who escaped with Harry—his picture was in the papers.'

'Meredith, eh? That's interesting. Mrs. Steele says she saw two men in a Ford drive off after the business at the barracks, and one had a black eye-patch. She might lie to support Harry's story, but you wouldn't.'

'What are you going to do?'

'Ring Hollis. He might be able to get a line on those two characters.'

'Hollis? But I thought he just sacked you?'

'Not his fault. I think it broke his heart to see all that training go to waste. Kemble the man he never fancied, but Kemble the journalist—that was his own work. This can be a farewell present for him, a last tribute to the old master from the young pupil. The soldier who went on fighting when they told him the battle was lost, that's me. Another sherry, Mother, before I break up.'

7.30 pm

'Remember that ball in Inverness?' Selkirk said.

'The one where that dreadful woman was sick in the middle of our sixteensome?'

'That's it. And that crazy Frenchman, de Picardat, started shooting rabbits from the drawing-room window at six in the morning—terrible chap.'

Anne laughed. 'Picardat's a Tory M.P. now you know, British as they come.'

'You still go to that sort of thing?'

'No, I lost touch.'

'Me too. Have another of those. Sorry there's no Campari.'

'Thanks.'

'Two halves of Red Barrel, please.'

They chattered on, pumping the past for common memories, filling in the missing years, searching the present for points of contact. The Sherlock Holmes was warm and crowded with late-working civil servants breaking the walk to Charing Cross. It was a good pub for a girl to wait in; you could browse among the relics of the great detective instead of staring foolishly at your glass. But Alan Selkirk had been as punctual as she thought he would be.

'You know this place?' he said.

'Yes, it's a favourite haunt of the defence correspondents. Do you know Jack Kemble? He's on the *Globe*. Was, rather.'

'No, I don't think I've heard of him.'

'He and I have been going out for about a year; I
91

think he wants to marry me. We're going to Rome together tonight. God knows what Daddy will say, he's not really his type.'

'And will you marry him?'

'I might. He's great fun, and I'm very fond of him.'

'Oh.'

Selkirk lifted his glass to hide the disappointment. She thought: poor Alan, so artless. Never had time for girls and now regretting it. A man who was 'great fun' would be the hardest competition.

'You must have a fascinating job,' she said.

'Job? At this moment I am unemployed. Lord Thorganby resigned after the Cabinet.'

'So he did. Did you expect it?'

He thought before replying. All his words are weighed she thought, and that could get on your nerves. 'Yes,' he said finally, 'I expected it.'

'And what do you think of it all?'

His finger stopped tracing patterns in the beer rings and he looked at her directly. 'You want to know what I think? All right, I'll tell you.' He was definite now, sure of himself. She had him on his home ground. 'Morally, I'm on the other side. The whites who have taken over in Rhodesia are a thoroughly bad lot. Smith, and the people who followed him—one could sympathise with them. Basically they were decent men, feudalists really. Lots of them came round in the end to the multiracial idea. But behind them, getting stronger all the time, there's always been this other lot—and they are different. The pure fire of racism burns in them. Grind the blacks, make money and to hell with the world is their philosophy. I think Lord Thorganby has missed the distinction.'

'It's nice to hear someone with opinions. I thought you civil servants always sat on the fence. But Alan, you talk about it all in terms of the whites. What about the Africans? Surely they're the wronged party, they are the ones we should worry about more.'

'Not more. Equally.'

'All right, equally.'

'The trouble is, now the Brotherhood are in, the Africans

92

have been taken over by their own extremists. Usual story. They must be stopped too. We must get in there as soon as we can, and save the day for moderate men, black and white.'

'One man, one vote.'

'Well, yes—as soon as possible, anyway. That principle's all right unless it gets the voters killed. We shall have to see that it doesn't.'

'And what about the South Africans?'

Suddenly he looked cautious. 'Well, their position is quite simple. They were happy with the *status quo*, but now it's gone they don't think the black extremists can be stopped except by force, so they support the white extremists. Let's hope they don't do something silly.'

The Official Secrets Act slid between them like the shadow of a stranger. Selkirk's words had become self-conscious.

She said: 'The South Africans have a lot of enemies, don't they? Since they sabotaged that régime in Botswana and shot those British teachers, people feel more strongly.'

Selkirk ordered two more beers. When they had come, he said in a quiet voice, wanting it to sound like an after-thought: 'They have friends, too.'

'Who do you mean?'

He laughed; she was too quick. 'Critten, Coper, plenty of M.P.s, the mutinous guardsmen, the man who blew up that statue perhaps.'

'But that hurt their own people.'

'And whipped up sympathy for their cause.'

'What a preposterous thought!'

'It's not the only preposterous thought I've been having.' His voice was now very quiet. 'My ex-boss has been keeping strange company. These people could make bad trouble for Harvey.'

'But Alan, Harvey's the Prime Minister, he's still got a majority—he can do what he likes.'

'The British constitution, Anne, is a funny thing. Everyone takes it for granted, thinks it's what protects us. But at times like this . . . Let's say that, in the wrong hands, it could be a very flexible instrument.'

'What on earth do you mean? You're talking riddles.'

'*Honi soit . . .*'

From the television in a corner of the bar a quartet with guitars were fighting to drown the conversation. They were interrupted in mid-song by a grave-faced announcer. In the sudden hush all heads in the pub turned towards the screen. 'In five minutes we shall be interrupting this programme for a broadcast by the Prime Minister, the Right Honourable Patrick Harvey, on a subject of national importance. Please do not adjust your sets. The Prime Minister's address will be broadcast simultaneously on all channels.' Unaware of the interruption, the singers returned to the screen.

'We must watch that,' Anne said.

'Yes, I should like to.'

'I'll phone Jack and tell him I'll be late. Won't you join us for supper? I know he'd like to meet you.'

'Well, if you're sure he won't mind . . .'

'I'm sure.'

Kemble was not so sure.

7.50 pm

The Prime Minister fretfully declined a ready-made whisky and soda. The B.B.C. always mixed them too weak.

He resented having to go to Shepherd's Bush at all. Surely even at such short notice they could have rigged up the TV apparatus at No. 10? That's where the Prime Minister ought to be at times like this. He had enjoyed his victory at the Cabinet that morning. He had enjoyed lunching alone with his wife in the garden; she was worried because the wistaria seemed to be dying back, and they had decided where to put the new daffodil bulbs for next spring. He had enjoyed manoeuvring Critten out of office in the early afternoon. He had felt like a man at the tiller when a breeze fills the sails. They were no longer becalmed, there was a course set.

Then the Chief Whip and the Foreign Secretary had both telephoned to say he must broadcast that night, that people wouldn't understand if he did not appear on their screens at such a time. Normally Harvey liked appearing on TV; indeed he had made his name fifteen years before when, as a backbencher, he had scored heavily on *Panorama* over an exhausted Labour Chancellor. 'You see, Callaghan has confused two quite different things. It's quite simple really. The rise in the cost of living . . .' and he had bent confidentially towards the cameras, the thick grey streak in his black hair coming attractively into view. Those were the days. Now it was all grey, with no black, and it was he who was exhausted and having to deliver a speech written for him by others to an enormous audience. Indeed he had only had time to read the script through in the car, passing down the Cromwell Road in a thicket of police motorcycles. It was stodgy, adequate stuff; an account of all that had happened in Rhodesia in the last six months, of the discussions at the U.N., of the issue before the Cabinet, then a peroration about unity. The King could do that sort of thing much better; why not leave it to him the following night? But his two colleagues had been adamant.

The make-up man brushed some powder into his eyes. There were so many real things to be done: the Home Secretary and Lord Chancellor to be talked to about a state of emergency, the Chief of Staff to be told that the Foreign Secretary would be in charge of Operation Constable while the Ministry of Defence was vacant, Thorganby to be persuaded if possible to stay silent—all to be done today and tomorrow morning before he went to the airport to meet the King. There was no time to be lost. He got up abruptly.

'That will have to do, thank you. I must look at my script again.' The telephone rang and the make-up man held it towards him. It was Ryder Bennett. His voice was high. 'There's very bad news from Oxford. I wasn't sure whether to tell you before the broadcast. The Chief Constable now reports eighteen people killed at least and several hundred knocked about. The police have got control at last. The point is that someone deliberately stirred it up. Perhaps Coper—he was hit by a brick, pity it wasn't a bullet. I've talked to the Chief Constable—the man's a fool —keeps muttering about black undergraduates, as if they

95

kept rifles under their beds. It's pretty serious, Patrick. The Home Secretary's in a state; full of brandy since tea-time, but it makes him tearful and with another glass or two he'll resign. Perhaps that would be best. . . . Anyway, you'd better mention it, I suppose. Good luck.'

Patrick Harvey realised that his Foreign Secretary was still enjoying the excitement. A buccaneer could not help enjoying himself when debates, votes, speeches suddenly gave way to action. Harvey was not a buccaneer. He imagined a black and white picture, as on a television screen, of small untidy heaps lying around the Martyrs' Memorial in Saint Giles, then being carried carefully, uselessly into ambulances.

On his way into the television studio he swallowed half a glass of whisky and dropped the script into the producer's waste-paper basket.

'Good evening.

'I came to the studio this evening to talk to you about Africa. I came to explain why, after much thought and argument, my colleagues in the Cabinet and I have decided that British troops should be used as a United Nations force to restore order and the rule of law in Rhodesia. This operation will mean violence and loss of life. We thought you should know at once why we believe it to be necessary.

'But today there has been violence and loss of life much nearer home. I have just heard that eighteen people were killed in a riot at Oxford a short while ago. I do not yet know the details. But I know enough to say this. We have had three weeks of growing political violence in our streets and squares. On these fine summer evenings, when everything in our cities and countryside has been looking its best, we have betrayed ourselves. Is that too strong a word? People have been killed, innocent people, eighteen of them today, because a handful of extremists are trying to force the will of your Government and your Parliament. Forget how you voted last time. Forget what you think about Rhodesia. Help us to keep Britain a place where . . .'

A tall young figure in a dark suit moved quickly between

the camera and the Prime Minister. Harvey began to rise from his chair; the young man swivelled to face the camera. The dark, tough good looks, the aquiline nose, the eccentric cloak were known in every lounge, parlour and drawing-room which the B.B.C. could reach. He played the defence lawyer in *The Revengers*, every Tuesday, 10 p.m. He was already made up for the part, but tonight he was cast for farce. 'We, the people of England,' he intoned, 'hereby accuse Patrick Harvey of imbecility and cowardice.' He turned, drew something from his right coat pocket and threw it at Harvey. The screens of Britain went blank a split second after the tomato squashed on the Prime Minister's face.

'The B.B.C. wish to apologise to viewers for the interruption to the Prime Minister's broadcast. An apology has also been offered to and accepted by Mr. Harvey, who has now left the studio.'

8.30 pm

The avocados came and went. The theatre-goers had left and the box pews of Jasper's Eating House were filling with a second wave of diners. The boatered waiters jostled at the kitchen hatch, and the buzz of conversation grew till each speaker was forced to speak a little louder, edging the noise-level up again. The phrase 'poor Harvey' recurred again and again, followed by peals of laughter. At Anne's insistence, Selkirk told what he knew of Thorganby's attitude and his connection with Coper, and Kemble told of his conversation with Mrs. Steele and his mother's comments. The steak and kidney puddings arrived with a bottle of Beaune.

'Of course,' Kemble said, 'there might be a connection.'

'What do you mean?' Anne said.

'If Steele and Meredith were sprung from the barracks, what else have the gang been up to? If you want to bring a government down or create a pretext for unconstitutional behaviour the best way is to make trouble in the Army.'

'And what about Oxford?' Selkirk said. 'Someone there

was out to cause bloodshed. Could have been the same people.'

Kemble said: 'I should think the lunatic fringe of Coper's outfit are capable of anything.'

Anne said: 'They found revolvers on two Negroes, you know, and the grenade that killed that old woman came from a bunch of students. Makes you wonder whose side you're on.'

Selkirk said: 'What makes you think Coper's so innocent, Jack?'

'He's too much to lose,' Kemble said.

'I don't think he makes that sort of calculation. At Thorganby's dinner the other night he showed all the symptoms of fanaticism.'

'That man's just too stupid to be dangerous,' Anne said, for the second time.

Kemble left the table to telephone Mrs. Steele. While he was gone, Anne and Selkirk lit cigarettes and sat in silence. It seemed a natural thing for Selkirk to rest his hand on hers, as if they shared responsibility for the state of the nation. When Kemble returned it was obvious from his face that the news was bad.

'They've found Harry,' he said.

'Where?' Anne said.

'In a telephone box by Nuffield College. Someone's bashed his head in.'

'Is he dead?'

'No, in a coma, at the Radcliffe Infirmary. It's touch and go. Mrs. Steele wants me to go down there with her. Poor old thing, she needs help, someone who knows the ropes. The Press, the Police, the Army, they'll all be there—it's too much for the old girl to handle alone.'

'But, Jack, you can't—' Anne said.

'I'll go,' Selkirk said.

11 pm

The undercarriage lifted with a crash and the engines slowed to spare the ear-drums of Staines. Knuckles whitened

98

on arm-rests, eyes stared ahead, jaws chewed on barley sweets. The plane continued its steady climb into the night, and faith returned. Smiles were exchanged to left and right, a mutual reassurance that the moment of weakness would be forgotten. But Lady Molly Downes believed in speaking her mind.

'Scare the bloody pants off me, these things do,' she said.

'I quite agree,' Anne said. 'Let's have a drink.'

Kemble lifted his hand from the air jet which was adding frostbite to the injuries sustained by his left ear in the Strand, but before it could reach the steward's bell it was intercepted by another hand, brown and hairy, rising swiftly from the seat in front. The hand was followed by a handsome, dark-jowled face.

'Allow me, Lady Downes.'

'Why, it's Signor Silvestri!' (Lady Downes refused to be seduced by the Italian custom of addressing people as Engineer, Advocate, or Doctor: her universal 'Mister' offended all, and therefore none.) 'What a nice surprise!' Kemble deduced from the fixity of Lady Molly's smile that the surprise was anything but nice. 'This is my daughter Anne.' To Kemble's relief the alien lips stopped short of Anne's upraised hand. 'And this is Mr. Jack Kemble, he's coming to stay with us in Rome.'

'Enchanted, Mr. Kemble.'

The enchantment was so thin that Silvestri continued to look at Anne as he offered Kemble his hand. The handshake was just firm enough to establish superiority. Kemble resented feeling inferior, but could not deny or explain it. The man was running to fat, his hair was thinning, his teeth were peppered with gold fillings, yet he had a certain natural sexy grace—that air of physical ease with which Negroes and Latins score over Anglo-Saxons. Kemble decided that if he was not to be allowed to read last week's *New Statesman* in peace, he would at least find the heel of this Achilles. 'And what do you do for a living, Mr. Silvestri?' he said.

That's a bit blunt, thought Lady Molly, and wondered once again what her daughter saw in this rather uncouth young man.

'I think you should allow me to buy the ladies a drink, Mr. Kemble, before giving you the story of my life.'

Anne tittered. Jack the Giant-Killer.

But Silvestri's vanity would not allow the question to go unanswered, and when the drinks had arrived he turned to Kemble again. 'I make planes, Mr. Kemble. Apart from the Finsider Steelworks at Taranto, the Silvestri aircraft factory at Naples is the biggest plant in southern Italy. I should be happy to show you round.'

'What sort of planes?' Kemble said.

'Our most successful product is the Cavaliere, a twin-jet executive four-seater. Many of the components are British, of course.'

'Oh? And who makes them?'

'Wolverhampton Precision Instruments, or WOPI, as my men prefer to call it. "Wolverhampton," you realise, is a difficult word for us Italians. I have just been negotiating new deliveries with them; a fine company.'

'You saw the Chairman, I suppose.'

'Of course. These things are always discussed at the highest level.'

'I'm surprised he had the time.'

Silvestri glanced into Kemble's eyes. The trouble with the English was you could never tell when they were being funny. 'And why should you be surprised, Mr. Kemble?' he said.

'Well, it's Mr. Barnett Coper, isn't it? And he's been pretty busy with other things.'

Silvestri now looked put out; he had underestimated the intelligence of his audience. Kemble took a triumphant swig of his gin and tonic. 'Yes,' Silvestri said, 'but Mr. Coper is very successful at mixing business with politics.'

'He got a brick on the head tonight,' Kemble said. 'That must have been good for business.'

Lady Molly began to look unhappy. Anne laughed and said: 'Tell me, Signor Silvestri, what do *you* think about Rhodesia?'

'I prefer to leave politics to the politicians, Miss Downes. And now if you will excuse me, Lady Downes, I will return to work.'

100

Kemble reached for his *New Statesman*. Game, set and match.

11.30 pm

Syrian Arab Airlines Flight 362 from Damascus, Athens and Naples was half an hour late at Heathrow and because she was late, the elderly Comet had to circle for another twenty minutes in the stack before she was called down. The first passenger off was a thin, grey-haired Englishman, carrying a dispatch case with a crown on it. After a word with the immigration desk he was shown straight to a small V.I.P. room, and one of the duty officers detached to look after him.

John Lavering was only twenty-one, and the world of kings, ministers and rapid telephone calls into which he was suddenly thrust remained vivid in his memory for years to come. In the V.I.P. room Sir James Courthope ignored the tray of drinks and went straight to the phone. 'Please place an official call to Italy, Ravello 3619, Province of Sorrento. It's a hotel. I want to speak to Mr. Perkins. Meanwhile get me a London number—126-7145. If the Italian call comes through while I'm talking to London keep it open. Is that clear? Good.' He put down the receiver, turned to Lavering and said: 'Would you be kind enough to fetch my suitcase? It should be off the plane by now. Here's the tag. And both the evening papers, please, last editions.'

The suitcase was ready, but the nearest news-stand was shut, and Lavering had to take the two newspapers from the Press Officer's desk at the far end of the building. The long corridors were almost empty, and his footsteps echoed importantly. As he came back into the V.I.P. room, he heard Courthope saying: 'There's some risk either way, but on balance I think you're right. I'll change the plan as you suggest. Goodbye then.'

As he put the receiver down the telephone rang again. 'Ravello? Good. Is that you, John? I must speak to Mr. Brunswick . . . Yes, I expect he has, but he won't be asleep. I'll wait. . . . Hallo, sir, I'm sorry to disturb you,

101

but I've just been talking to Number One. Things are fairly desperate . . . Oh, you've heard about Oxford. He's worried about the resignations too, and the effect they may have on morale. He's thinking particularly of the thing on Thursday morning. . . . Yes, sir, he made the same point—T. more important than C. He wondered if you could possibly fly back at once and see T. in the morning. A word from you might stop him coming into open opposition. . . . Yes, certainly unusual, but frankly, sir, Number One sounded fairly desperate, and if you want to keep him in one piece it might be a good idea. . . . Yes, the Swanstar will be at Naples by now. . . . Fine. I'll tell Number One at once, he'll be delighted. Shall I speak to Perkins? . . . John, you're off tonight—yes, he's just agreed. You know the form. Get on to Naples Airport and tell the Wing Commander the new ETD. It'll be Stocks, I expect—the young one with fair hair. You could be in the air just after four, I suppose, by the time you've packed and driven down to Naples. Stocks will fix it with Naples Traffic Control. Be sure to ring the Ambassador before you leave Ravello. I'll tell them here to expect you about 7.30 a.m., your time. That'll be 6.30 here. Anything else? . . . Yes, they always send the bill to the Embassy, but you do the tips. All right, then? Make him sleep in the plane if you can, he'll have a full day tomorrow. Goodbye, and thank you.'

Courthope turned to where Lavering was standing. For the first time Lavering noticed that he looked crumpled and exhausted; a vein was throbbing visibly in his neck. The flight must have been quite an experience.

'You heard that then?' Courthope said: 'A change of plan and I must talk to the Chief Traffic Controller to tell him the King's arriving first thing in the morning. Could you take me to his office? And then could you ring up Windsor and say I shall be sleeping there tonight, and not at Buckingham Palace? Perhaps you could do that now from another telephone, while I make one more call on this one.' As he left the room, Lavering heard Courthope say softly: 'I want to speak to the Prime Minister.'

It was 3 a.m. before Lavering finally went off duty—an

hour later than usual—and 3.30 before he let himself into his bungalow in Twickenham. His wife lay asleep with the light on, a lurid paperback sprawled open on the eiderdown. He thought of waking her up, but his thriller could wait till the morning.

Midnight

Extract from the diary of Alan Selkirk
Eastgate Hotel, Oxford   AUGUST 5

What a day!

T. resigns after Cabinet, as I feared he might. Gave me a roll of tweed. Typical. Am v. fond of him I discover—a real patriot, out of his time. Thinks Rhodesia the last bastion of the great and good British Empire; not a racist, but will be pulled in with them unless he's careful. Can't believe he will break the rules to get Harvey out, though.

Drink and supper with Anne. What a lovely girl—pretty, vivacious, bright, stylish—my type! Was not so keen on journalist friend, but warmed to him later. Seems I've missed the boat again.

Drove down here with Mrs. Steele, a really fine old lady. Father, brother, husband all soldiers, all dead—and now Harry. Seemed to expect it: no sense of injustice. Harry in private room at Radcliffe Infirmary, Military Police and C.I.D. at bedside. Head covered in bandages, only lips visible. Doctor said whoever hit him knew how to do it. Recovery still doubtful, permanent brain injury probable. Mrs. S. tried to communicate but couldn't get through. Delirious mumbling. Dreadful. Only time I saw her weaken. Thought I heard Harry say 'Coper' twice—and another word, beginning with 'B,' but couldn't make it out. Coper also in Radcliffe: will call on him tomorrow.

Wednesday, August 6th

DEFENCE AND OVERSEAS POLICY COMMITTEE

OPERATION CONSTABLE

DOPC (P) 43/75

1. *Background*.

(a) In order to implement U.N. Security Council Resolution No. S/4568 of August 5th, it has been decided (Cabinet (M) 31/75, Item 1) to mount military operations against RHODESIA with all possible speed.

(b) Contingency Plan No. 4 (COS (P) 271/73) will provide the basis for operations, which have been given the code name "CONSTABLE".

(c) The Joint Intelligence Committee assessment of the situation in RHODESIA will be issued separately; this will include strengths and locations of all forces available to the Rhodesian Republic. A special appreciation will be provided concerning the African Nationalist guerrilla forces.

2. *Objective*.

The object of CONSTABLE will be speedily to impose, with the minimum of casualties and damage, conditions under which a government might be set up that will satisfy the requirements of the Multiracial Settlement of 1968. It will be necessary as an interim measure to create a Military Government; to this end a Civil Affairs Unit will be placed under command. On the termination of military operations the G.O.C.-in-C. CONSTABLE will assume the additional title of Military Governor.

3. *Command.*

The combined force will be under command General Sir Robert Bentlay. He will be directly responsible to H.M. Government, but will give full co-operation to the U.N. Observer and his staff, who are responsible directly to the Secretary-General U.N.O.

4. *International Support.*

The Zambian and Tanzanian Governments have placed their full resources at the disposal of H.M. Government. At the special request of the President of Zambia, one infantry battalion group of the Zambian Army will be included in the occupation force. The U.S. Government have agreed to deploy logistic units and aircraft, including helicopters, in support of operations. In no circumstances will U.S. forces be used in a combat role.

5. *Forces Available (Under Command).*

COMD: One H.Q.

R.N.: Two opposed Landing Task Forces, three Squadrons Helicopters, two Underwater Demolition Teams.

ARMY: One Regiment R.T.R. (Amphibious Tanks), three Squadrons Household Cavalry (Armoured Cars), three Field Regiments R.A., one Anti-Aircraft (SAM) Regiment R.A., four Field Squadrons R.E., two Bridging Squadrons R.E., five Hobart Bricks R.Sigs., five Infantry Brigade Groups, 16 Parachute Brigade (less one battalion, plus two Squadrons S.A.S.), 2nd Royal Marine Commando Brigade plus two batteries light artillery, miscellaneous support and logistic units.

R.A.F.: Det. Strike Command, 38 Group (reinforced), Det. Strategic Transport Command (including tanker aircraft), two Squadrons Hovercraft, two Squadrons Surface-to-Air Missiles (Mobile), two Squadrons R.A.F. Regiment.

MISC.: Civil Affairs Unit, Psy-war Unit, Forces Broadcasting Unit, two P.W. (Special Interrogation) Units.

ZAMBIAN: One Infantry Battalion Group.

6. *Method and Phasing.*

D-day will be Thursday, August 7th. H-hour will be 0300 hrs. G.M.T. To ensure surprise, the entire operation will be mounted from the U.K. Refuelling will be by R.A.F. tanker aircraft based at Malta, Cyprus and Aldabra, B.I.O.T.

Phase I

(a) H—4 hours. Advance elements 38 Group will occupy airfields at LIVINGSTONE and LUSAKA (reception parties already in place under civilian cover).

(b) H—3 hours. Troops for Phase III onwards land at forming-up areas vicinity LIVINGSTONE-LUSAKA.

Phase II

(a) H—15 minutes. Elements of 38 Group will attack and destroy airfields at GWELO, BULAWAYO and SALISBURY.

(b) H-hour. Three company groups R.M. Commandos will seize and hold bridges across the Zambesi at CHIRUNDU, KARIBA and VICTORIA FALLS.

(c) H+30 minutes. Elements of Strike Command will attack communications on Rhodesian side of borders with SOUTH AFRICA and MOZAMBIQUE. Centres of population will be avoided.

Phase III

As soon as bridgeheads established, two Battalion Groups supported by Armoured cars will pass through to gain control roads CHIRUNDU-SALISBURY and VICTORIA FALLS-BULAWAYO. If the Zambesi crossings are destroyed, units taking part in this phase will be lifted by U.S. Navy helicopters.

Phase IV

H+2 hours. 16 Parachute Brigade will seize airfields at SALISBURY, GWELO and BULAWAYO.

Phase V

H+4 hours. Four battalion groups will be helicopter lifted to SALISBURY (two bn gps), GWELO (one bn gp) and BULAWAYO (one bn gp) in that priority.

Phase VI
D+1. Reserve formations and support units will be helicopter lifted on call from Tactical H.Q. to be established at SALISBURY.

Phase VII
D+2. Pacification operations begin.

Phase VIII
D+3. Logistic airlift begins to forward areas.

7. *Civil Affairs.*
(a) The Chief Civil Affairs Officer will be authorised to take over the police and judiciary; in so far as is possible the maintenance of law and order after pacification will be the responsibility of Civil Affairs supported by military forces in an emergency only.

(b) All public utilities, services and urban and rural administration will be placed under the control of Civil Affairs.

8. *Logistics.*
(a) Logistic support will be maintained from U.K. sources. Logistic reserves afloat will not be used except at order from MOD.

(b) Ten days' maintenance stocks will be built up from D-day onwards in the vicinity LIVINGSTONE-LUSAKA and kept at that level until the operations stage is complete.

(c) Fifteen days' maintenance stocks will be built up from D+3 onwards dispersed between BULAWAYO-GWELO-SALISBURY at G.O.C.-in-C's discretion. This level will be maintained until orders for the force to be evacuated are given.

5th August, 1975.
Cabinet Offices,
LONDON, S.W.1.

3.30 am (4.30 am, Italy)

Sir Peter Downes hated flying into Naples Airport even by day. At night the hulk of Vesuvius felt the more threatening for being invisible, and the Herakles Witch, though well piloted, seemed dangerously small and insubstantial. Besides he was in a bad temper. He believed in routine, and solid plans solidly adhered to. 'Order, counterorder, disorder' was one of his favourite maxims. Yet here was the King, rushing off in the middle of the night, to the great inconvenience of all concerned. That young Perkins had said that he need not come down to see the King off. But of course that was wrong; he was the Ambassador and this was the King, private holiday or no private holiday. The Rolls would not have made it in time, but luckily Ralston had offered the use of his plane sitting at Ciampino Airport for the Air Show, and in the end had come himself. Interesting chap, talked well, and kept good whisky in his flask. Even so it was a dismal way of spending the night, and no doubt there would be the usual wait before the King took off.

The Witch taxied in and parked beside the Swanstar of the King's Flight. The sleek white shape, shining under the arc lights, looked not unlike a swan. The Ambassador deduced from the lack of activity round her that she must have finished refuelling. At the foot of the ladder a young Carabiniere captain saluted as they came down.

'Excellency, it will please the Commandant if you will come suddenly to his office. The English Wing-Commander is there now.'

'Has the King arrived?'

'Not yet, Excellency. His Majesty left Ravello at 0345 hours. We expect him within twenty minutes.'

Like Lavering at Heathrow, the Captain of the Carabinieri was enjoying the new world of Excellencies and Majesties into which he had been momentarily thrust. Exploiting every moment to practise his little-used English, he led the way to the Commandant's office.

It was clear at once that inside the room a storm was brewing. The Commandant of Naples Airport, a handsome man with silver hair, sat at his desk under the portrait of President Fanfani. His face was reddening with suppressed anger, and his A.D.C. fluttered round the room like a wounded hen. Opposite him stood young Wing-Commander Stocks, fair hair cut very short, a stubborn twist to his mouth.

'*Sua Eccellenza l'Ambasciatore di Gran Bretagna e Sir Railston,*' intoned the Captain.

'Thank God you've come, sir,' said Stocks. 'We're in bad trouble. There's a serious hydraulic leak on the Swanstar. We found it twenty minutes ago—fluid pouring out of the undercarriage. We don't know how it happened, but it means we're stuck.'

'Stuck, why stuck? They must surely be able to replace the fluid here.'

'Yes they can, but the pipe has a ten-inch hole in it, and that they can't replace. Now the Commandant here—'

'Allow me to state my own position.' The Airport Commandant spoke slowly to control his temper; his English was perfect. 'The Wing-Commander has explained to me that the accident which his plane has suffered, for which incidentally no Italian can be held responsible, necessitates a delay of several hours, perhaps eight, perhaps ten, before a replacement can be flown out from England. I also understand that His Majesty your King is anxious to leave at the earliest possible moment. It happens that we have here at the airport the personal Cavaliere aeroplane of Signor Silvestri, who is known to you, Excellency. He returned from Rome in this aeroplane only half an hour ago. It is of course a smaller plane, but in comfort, safety and performance, it is in every way the equal of the Swanstar, if the Wing Commander will permit me to say so. I should add that Silvestri is the cousin of my brother's wife. As soon as the Wing-Commander told me of his misfortune I took it on myself to telephone to Silvestri at his house in Salerno where he was on the point of retiring to rest. He at once said that it would be an honour and privilege if His Majesty would accept the offer of his plane for the journey to London. The plane is now being refuelled and will be ready to take off in half an hour. Silvestri himself is on his way here to salute His Majesty and wish him *bon voyage*. It seems to me, Excellency, that we have solved your problem for you.'

'I've been trying to explain for the last ten minutes,' broke in Stocks, 'that by our rules the King has to fly in one of the Flight planes. He can't fly in anything else. It's not an insult to anyone, it's just a rule. But he won't understand it.'

'What I understand, Excellency, is that the Wing-Commander's "Flight Planes" are at Benson in Oxfordshire, except for the broken one here, and that the King is in a hurry. When Kings are in a hurry, rules can be stretched, is it not so?'

The Ambassador interrupted: 'Wait a minute, Stocks. Have you reported this to Benson?'

'Yes, sir, immediately after the accident was discovered. They got Air Vice-Marshal Sharp out of bed and I spoke to him personally. I am afraid the other Swanstars are in Thailand with the Princess, but he's checking on the spares position and will ring me back here. Whatever happens, there'll be a delay of several hours. As I see it, we shall have to explain to the King . . .'

The Ambassador took Ralston aside. 'You know these planes, Ralston. What would you advise?'

'Well, Silvestri's after the publicity, naturally; he's my competitor and I'm an interested party to that extent. I would think the Cavaliere is a safe enough plane, but of course if anything were to happen. . . . I wonder if perhaps—'

The telephone rang on the Commandant's desk. The Commandant picked it up, listened, passed it to Stocks with a smile. 'Here is your poor Air Vice-Marshal.' Stocks listened intently, and when it was over turned to the Ambassador.

'There's a spare pipe at Benson, sir, and they could get it in the air within an hour. Once it was here, there'd be the welding to be done, and the Air Vice-Marshal is not too happy—' he glanced meaningfully at the Commandant —'anyway, he would prefer to get Transport Command to send out a Comet.'

'That would mean the King could leave at what time?'

'The Comet should reach here by 8.30 Italian time, then she'll have to be refuelled and tested. Take-off would be, say, 9.30.'

At this point the crowd in the overheated little room was joined by Perkins, Assistant Private Secretary, with the news that the King had arrived and was waiting in the V.I.P. Reception Room. His Majesty was anxious to leave immediately. The Ambassador volunteered to explain the situation. As he left the room, Ralston slipped a piece of paper into his hand and said: 'This is awkward in front of the Italians. Before the telephone rang I was about to suggest that the King take my Witch. It is perfectly safe and will get him to London in four hours from now. There's room for all his party. Here is a note for him.'

The Ambassador's departure was followed by a constrained silence. The Commandant's A.D.C. switched on the ceiling fan and the Commandant told him to switch it off. A white-coated waiter offered little glasses of brandy from a battered metal tray. Shaking hands reached gratefully for the medicinal fluid. But Wing-Commander Stocks, remembering the Borgias, refused abruptly. Only Ralston was at ease; he sipped the brandy, pulled *The Economist* out of his dispatch case and began to read. The rattle of a twin exhaust distracted him. Looking out of the window, he saw a scarlet Alfa Romeo halt below them. A man in a white raincoat jumped out. 'I think Silvestri has arrived,' he said to the Commandant. The Commandant snapped at the A.D.C., who left to escort Silvestri upstairs. Before he reappeared, Sir Peter Downes returned and the Commandant rose to attention.

'Commandant,' the Ambassador said, 'the King has decided to take Mr. Ralston's plane. Nothing would give His Majesty greater pleasure than to fly in Signor Silvestri's Cavaliere, which I am sure is excellently equipped and thoroughly trustworthy. But he is already breaking one rule by flying in a private plane; he cannot break another and fly in a foreign private plane, however admirable. With your long experience, Commandant, you will understand how this is, and I ask you to explain to Signor Silvestri why the King cannot accept his courteous offer.' Then to Stocks:

'Tell Air Vice-Marshal Sharp the King is adamant. The Comet would be too slow. With the home situation as it is, he is determined to be in London first thing.'

As the Wing-Commander began to speak into the phone, Silvestri appeared at the door and bowed low over his paunch before noticing the absence of royalty. The Commandant explained fast and apologetically in Italian. Silvestri looked dumbfounded, then caught sight of Ralston and laughed in a flash of gold.

'Sir Peter, I do not know by what miracle Mr. Ralston is here, and with one of his famous Witches, too. I thought him safely asleep in Rome. He is an old enemy of mine, but I must admit he is a faithful subject of His Majesty, and I yield the prize to him. I know how these things are. It would be a strange day indeed if President Fanfani ever took flight in a Herakles Witch.'

The Commandant looked enormously relieved, laughed very loud and urged the brandy round. Ralston slipped out with Perkins and Stocks to give instructions to his crew. The Ambassador ushered Silvestri and the Commandant into the royal presence and conversation turned to the Rome Air Show. The King knew Italian and was a qualified pilot; awkward silences were avoided.

The wait lasted thirty-five minutes, the King occasionally looking at his watch. Ralston reappeared to say the Witch was ready and the rest of the King's party already aboard; Ralston's pilot and navigator were presented on the tarmac; the King shook hands with the Italians and the Ambassador, spoke a special word of thanks to Ralston, then climbed the ladder into the plane, preceded by Perkins. At the top of the steps he turned and waved. He was outside the pool of brightness cast by the lights of the terminal building, but his silhouette was clear against the open cabin door.

The ladder was folded inwards and the door slammed shut. Clutching their hats in the wake of the whistling engines, the little group of dignitaries watched the plane taxi away into the darkness. There was a short pause at the end of the runway, then they heard the twin jets roar along the avenue of lights and smoothly into the air.

The Ambassador looked at the airport clock: 5.15. A

faint ragged light showed in the east behind Vesuvius and he shivered in the breeze. Well, that was over. Now, how were he and Ralston to return to Rome? The Consul-General would have to disgorge his Humber.

They said goodbye to the Italians. Silvestri watched the Witch's lights disappear over the sea and said: 'Short take-off, but the Cavaliere's is shorter.' Distributing short little hand-clasps all round, he jumped into his car and roared away, leaving two strips of Michelin X on the tarmac. Now that the King had gone, he was barely bothering to hide his pique.

Stocks looked worried, and the Ambassador put a friendly arm round his shoulder. 'Cheer up, Wing-Commander! Not your fault; you were overruled. You'll have to stay here and wait for a new pipe, I suppose. The Consul-General will help you with anything you need.'

When they had gone, Stocks walked gloomily over to the Swanstar. The sticky fluid had formed a pool around the wheels. In the half-darkness it looked like bile seeping from a wounded body.

5 am

The automatic control on the bedside radio switched on B.B.C. Radio Two and woke the Prime Minister up. Through the fog of sleep he heard of an anticyclone persisting over the British Isles. Somehow fine weather was important, and Harvey half-consciously looked at the chink in the thick blue curtains to see if the sun was up. No, of course, too early. They needed good weather for Constable (the airlift would be under way by this afternoon) and good weather for the King, who would be in the air by now.

Slowly the events of the night before began to marshal themselves in his memory. James Courthope had telephoned from Heathrow to say the King would be back about 6.30 in the morning instead of in the afternoon. All the better; there would be time for a good talk with him before his broadcast. He must remember to take the plan for Constable to the airport.

113

As the pips went for the news, Harvey remembered last night's tomato, and waited bitterly for the prim B.B.C. voice to narrate his humiliation. But the tomato did not come first.

'In the last few hours there have been persistent reports of unrest and undiscipline among units of the Army. The Commanding Officer of the 15th/21st Hussars has just telephoned our northern studio from Catterick to say that he has resigned his commission. This follows a serious incident at Catterick last night when a number of officers and N.C.O.s are reported to have told Colonel Patrick that they would not obey a movement order given to them earlier in the day. Incidents are also reported from Tidworth and near Hanover, where three officers of the British Army of the Rhine are said to have asked the Federal German Authorities for political asylum.

'There have been no further reports of unrest in the First Battalion of the Grenadier Guards. The battalion is now in a state of operational readiness at the Transport Command Air Base at Brize Norton in Oxfordshire. Two of the battalion's vehicles were found abandoned yesterday morning in a wood near Eynsham, two miles from the A.40, on which they were travelling to Brize Norton. Twenty-three men and a quantity of ammunition are still missing, and police throughout the West Country have been alerted. Guardsman Steele, one of the three men who escaped early yesterday morning from the guardroom at Chelsea Barracks during investigations into the death of the battalion's Sergeant-Major, was found last night in Oxford with severe head injuries. His condition is still critical. In an official statement the Ministry of Defence said that there were strong grounds for believing that the battalion had been the object of outside interference. The Ministry's spokesman went on to stress that with minor exceptions—which were inevitable in the present circumstances—the loyalty of the Army to the Government's policy was beyond question.

'The King has cut short his holiday in Italy because of the Rhodesian crisis. He left Naples airport an hour ago in a Herakles Witch lent to him by Mr. Dennis Ralston, Chairman of Herakles Aviation.

'Adam Rawthorne, the actor who has become well known for his part in the B.B.C. Television series *The Revengers*, will be charged with assault today at a London Magistrates' Court following an incident during last night's televised broadcast by the Prime Minister.

'Following yesterday's riot at Oxford, in which eighteen people were killed and over a hundred injured, the police . . .'

Harvey switched off irritably. If that glamorous young thug had hit him with a microphone and drawn some blood, it might have been useful politically. A tomato was farce, serious people did not get hit with tomatoes, Prime Ministers who got hit with tomatoes did not last long. But it had happened, and the only thing was to ignore it.

The trouble in the Army was much more serious. Damn Joynson! A shallow, ephemeral man. Too clever by half. That line for the Press yesterday about an outside organisation was no use; he should never have agreed to it. No evidence —and without evidence, wholly incredible. Better to admit a certain amount of genuine unrest, and use the King's broadcast to kill it.

His wife came in with the tray. (Juice, egg, coffee, napkin in a silver ring from the Sutton Conservative Association.) She must have seen the tomato, but had gone to bed by the time he returned. She made it a rule never to talk politics. He knew it was a favourite joke of the lobby correspondents that she had only agreed to move to Number Ten because she liked the garden better than the poky plot they had left in Blackheath. Normally he was refreshed by her detachment. This morning, as he watched the neat perm bob about her face when she put down the tray, he desperately wanted to talk to her about the troubles crowding in. But he knew it was no use; the busy way she was fussing with the tray was a plea to him not to bring her into it. She wanted always to pretend that they were ordinary people.

'I thought I'd better sleep in the dressing-room as you'd gone to bed,' he said.

'That was thoughtful, Patrick, and in return I got up and brought your tray. I'm glad we don't wake so early every

115

morning. No papers yet, I'm afraid. I gather you're off to the airport. Will you be back for lunch?'

'Yes, I think so, but it had better be sandwiches again. I don't know when I'll have time to eat.'

'Very well. If you're quite happy, then I think I will go back to bed. A busy day for me too—the Sutton Flower Show, and I have to make a speech.'

As she closed the door Harvey thought of something odd about the news bulletin. He lifted the bedside phone. 'Duty Officer, please . . . What's all this about the King travelling in a Herakles plane?'

'Oh, you've heard it on the news, sir? I was just going to ring you. R.A.F. Benson are in a flap and wanted you to know as soon as you woke up. They flew out their only available Swanstar to Naples yesterday but heard early this morning that it was damaged in some way. No details yet. Transport Command offered a Comet but the King wouldn't wait and took Ralston's plane, which happened to be at Naples already.'

'I see. No wonder they're in a flap. There will have to be a full investigation. When is the King due at Heathrow?'

'ETA is now 7.30, sir—an hour later than before, because of the delay at Naples. Your car's ordered for half past six.'

That meant a little more time to think. Harvey drew back the curtains; it was just light. He climbed back between the luxuriously warm sheets and decapitated the egg. It was underdone. There was nothing Harvey hated more in the world than an underdone egg. (Days which started thus never ended well.) Fidgety with irritation he spooned out the slippery translucent mucus to get at the yolk, then, sipping his coffee, jotted on a postcard the thing he must mention to the King.

1. Constable—explain plans.
2. H.M.'s broadcast—go over text. Special passage for armed forces?
3. Recall Parliament—? 13 August.
4. Emergency legislation—special powers for police? Expel Coper from House so that he loses immunity.
5. Sack H.P.

Harvey's pen lingered over the last item. Risky, but

116

necessary. Humphrey Pallman, the Home Secretary, had a massive chin and weighty legal manner, and was highly regarded in the Party as a man of substance because he spoke slowly and in many syllables. Adequate in ordinary times, but now a lump of jelly. Harvey would take over the Home Office himself for the time being, and steer through the emergency legislation. He looked at the list again. The King might need some persuading on 4 and 5, but it would be good to have him back. Better than anyone else he could share the Prime Minister's loneliness.

5.20 am (6.20 am, Italy)

The Consul-General's Humber wove through the concrete rubbish heap of suburban Naples and turned on to the *Autostrada del Sole*. Up the clover leaf, through the toll-gate, under the hundred-metre span of a Pavesi restaurant, past the six-legged dogs, black on yellow, of an AGIP Service Station—and they were in space, cruising at 140 k.p.h. along a double swath of black macadam through the hills to Rome. The sky was turning from grey to pink behind the mountains to their right. The windsocks, placed to warn the motorist of the fearsome gusts which sweep this road in winter, were hanging limp.

'The Motorway of the Sun,' said Sir Peter Downes. 'Sounds better than the M.6, doesn't it?'

'Better cambered, and I like the markings, but I'm not sure about the surface,' Ralston replied, prosaic as always.

Sir Peter rested his head against the back of the seat and closed his eyes, then opened one to examine the speedometer in the heavy walnut fascia. '*Basta*,' he said, '*cento quaranta, non più*.' The driver let the needle fall back and silence returned.

After ten minutes Ralston said: 'Tell me, Sir Peter, did anything strike you as odd about that scene in the Commandant's Office?' The Ambassador was thinking of his breakfast and did not hear the question, so Ralston repeated it.

'No,' Sir Peter said, 'can't say I did. A very typical scene all round. What are you thinking of?'

'Well, it's only just occurred to me. Stocks said they found the leak twenty minutes before—in other words about ten minutes after Silvestri had landed from Rome; and the Commandant said he had then phoned Silvestri at his home in Salerno. Ten minutes after our arrival Silvestri arrives back at the Airport. That's fast travelling in both directions, even for an Alfa G.T. In fact, I would say, impossible.'

'Yes, I see what you mean. It is odd.'

'Another thing. The damage to that hydraulic pipe—I had a look at it while we were fuelling the Witch, and I didn't like what I saw.'

'Yes, it was obviously a great blow to Stocks.'

'I don't think you quite follow me, Sir Peter. Several things could have caused that leak, but if you asked me to bet on it, I would put my money on a blow from a heavy instrument.'

The Ambassador's eyes opened wide. 'Good heavens! What —a deliberate blow?'

'I would say so, yes. It seemed to have been hit twice.'

'Are you sure? That plane was guarded, you know.'

'No, not sure. But anyone working on the plane could have done it easily.'

'Sabotage! But why didn't you speak out? What about Stocks? Didn't he notice anything?'

'He had noticed all right. That was why he was so keen for a fresh plane.' Ralston smiled with the sympathy of one airman for another, and added: 'Poor fellow.'

Sir Peter sank back on the leather seat, feeling at a loss. Mechanics, engineers, technicians of any kind provoked his envy and recalled the vices of his own profession. He looked at Ralston; the pale blue eyes were fixed on the road ahead, devoid of alarm or doubt. You could *feel* the man's authority, tempered by years of decision, risks, responsibility—all the things denied to an Ambassador; but he was not a subtle thinker, that was for sure. These alarming remarks of his were altogether too hasty. Already in Sir Peter's mind a mass of qualifications had settled on the simple conclusion, like flies on an apple, blurring its outline. 'You are suggesting,' he said, 'that Silvestri, in collusion with the Airport Commandant, had the plane fixed so that the King could ride in a Cavaliere. That's quite an allegation, Ralston.'

'Your allegation, not mine, Sir Peter.'

'Well, that's what you're saying.'

'It is *not* what I'm saying.' The correction was brusque, irritated. 'I have merely pointed out two aspects of the situation which may need further explanation.'

Although it was not yet hot, the Ambassador mopped his brow and ran the handkerchief round the inside of his collar. 'Well,' he said, 'thank God you had the presence of mind to offer the Witch.'

Silence settled between them; Ralston resumed the *Economist* and Sir Peter lit a cheroot, wondering how his companion would receive the suggestion that they should pause at Frosinone. Frosinone had a coffee bar. His thoughts of breakfast were interrupted by the swooping howl of an Italian police siren. The Humber was overtaken as if it were standing still by a khaki Alfa Romeo Giulietta, blue beacon flashing on the roof, hands waving stop signals from every window. They pulled into the emergency lane behind the other car. A Carabiniere captain—the same man who had met them at the airport—ran back and leaned in the window.

'*Eccellenza, l'aereo del Re non risponde alla radio!*' Seeing Ralston's bafflement, the Captain searched for the English words. 'The plane, sir, it is not speaking to control.'

One minute later the two cars bounced through the azaleas on to the southbound lane and headed back to Naples.

7 am

The Prime Minister's battery-powered Austin Electra drew up at a side-door of the Europa Building at Heathrow. As he closed the door after Harvey, the chauffeur took off his cap and wiped his forehead; he had never been asked to drive so fast or break so many rules.

Without a handshake or a greeting, Harvey swept through the knot of harassed-looking officials who had gathered to meet him. Half-hanging from his coat pocket was the message he had been given as he stepped into the car at Downing Street.

'Well, have they regained contact?' Harvey threw the question at the tall grey-faced man in R.A.F. uniform who saluted him at the entrance.

Air Vice-Marshal Sharp, Captain of the King's Flight, shook his head. 'No sir, last radio contact was at 5.45 Italian time—half an hour after take-off—and Italian radar lost the plane shortly after that.' The two men stood together in the open doorway. 'But there's worse than that, sir. The Foreign Secretary rang two minutes ago hoping you'd arrived. He's just heard from Rome that an Italian tanker has reported an explosion in the air between Sardinia and the Italian mainland about 6 a.m. their time. No further details. The tanker said she would go to the spot and signal again. The Italian Air Force are mounting a search. H.M.S. *Dalkeith* has been ordered to investigate, and should be there about now. That's all there is, sir. I've just telephoned Sir James Courthope to let him know.'

'Thank you, Air Vice-Marshal.'

The group of airport officials, who had been ordered to keep their distance, saw the Prime Minister gaze abstractedly at the rubber floor; the Air Vice-Marshal spoke again, too softly for them to hear. 'Of course, sir, as I told Sir James, there's no proof yet that the two events are connected, and we should not assume the worst until we hear more. I've known false alarms like this before.'

But Harvey knew that the King was dead, and his mind began to grow numb. There would be hours of waiting, confusion and false hopes; but in the end he would be dead. Still, one had to go through the motions.

'Come and sit in the car for a minute,' he said, and when they were in the back of the Austin: 'How does the time and place of the explosion fit with the course you'd expect the Witch to take?'

'Slightly west, and a bit slow, sir. She should have been

120

past Sardinia by then. But there was a head wind, and there's no sign of her on the French radar.'

Harvey saw that the Air Vice-Marshal too knew that the King was dead. But there was a difference; Sharp had had time to think of the consequences. He sat hunched in the car, his left hand fiddling with the ashtray. No use to say he had been miles away when the wrong decision was taken, and that the King had overruled his subordinate. He, Sharp, was the Captain of the King's Flight, and the worst thing that could happen to that officer had happened to him. His voice was monotonous with misery. 'Would you like some breakfast, sir, while we wait? I told them to fry some eggs for you. There's a private room.'

'No, thank you,' Harvey said. 'Nice of you to think of it, but I must go back to London at once. Please telephone the Foreign Secretary and tell him to come to Number Ten, and get the Lord Chancellor, the Home Secretary, the Secretary to the Cabinet and the Chief Whip to do the same—yes, and Sir James Courthope. No, on second thoughts, we'll meet in the Foreign Office. And tell Ryder Bennett that nothing whatever must be announced until we've talked. Joynson must get on to the B.B.C., I.T.V. and the editors of the evening papers and tell them there'll be a statement later but meanwhile they should hold everything. Reports from the Cabinet will be coming in any time now. And I rely on you to see that nothing comes out from Heathrow.' For the first time Harvey noticed and understood the grimness of Sharp's face. 'Don't ask yourself too many questions, Air Vice-Marshal. And eat those fried eggs yourself. We shall need all your experience today.'

The traffic was beginning to thicken on the Chiswick flyover and a man in a Jaguar hooted insolently when he recognised the Prime Minister in the Electra. Harvey did not notice. He sat rigid, trying to push the numbness out of his mind, forcing himself to think of what had to be done in the hours ahead. The white card of headings in his neat handwriting under the title 'Points to be raised with the King' dropped through his knees to the floor.

7.45 am

'You may go in now, Mr. Selkirk.' The Sister disappeared down the corridor with a rustle of starch and a squeaking of rubber-soled shoes, and Selkirk knocked lightly on the open door.

'Come in, come in!' The voice had lost none of its volume and bounce. The familiar, fat, drink-reddened face, now wearing a large dressing over one eye, rose triumphant from a mountain of pillows and morning papers. 'Young Salcock, isn't it, Thorganby's P.S.? Good of you to come, my boy. Sit down.

Selkirk pulled up a chrome and green plastic chair. 'How are you feeling, sir?' he said.

'The quack says I'll be laid up for another couple of days, but it's not mortal. Three stitches, y'know—here. Scars of battle, what?' Coper was delighted to be martyred so easily. 'Now tell me, Salcock, what brings you to Oxford?'

'Selkirk, sir. Someone I knew was hurt. I brought his mother down.'

'No message from your master?'

'No.'

'Mm, pity—I thought he'd sent you. Friend of yours got hurt, eh? Nothing serious, I take it.'

'He may die.'

Coper began to busy himself with an old brier pipe, kneading, stuffing, tamping the bright yellow tobacco. 'I'm sorry to hear that,' he said. 'Whole thing got out of hand. Never expected to see casualties like this at a British political meeting. Damn it, we're supposed to be a democracy —the Movement's got every right to put its point of view. But free speech never meant a thing to the Bolshies. Do you know, some of those long-haired little devils were *armed*? Pistols, bombs, knives, you name it. Damn shame we don't have capital punishment, prison's too good for 'em.'

Selkirk's anger reached a pitch. He rose to his feet and said: 'What did you expect? Violence breeds violence.'

Coper stopped playing with his pipe. 'Just a minute, young

man. Are you seriously suggesting that the Movement would stoop to violence?'

'And are you suggesting that all yesterday's damage was done by left-wingers?'

'They started it, with a planned and organised attack. Our people had to defend themselves.'

'With respect, sir, that is nonsense and you know it. Plenty of your people came prepared for violence too—looking for it. There have been fights and arrests at every meeting the Movement has held since it began; you have never explicitly condemned such behaviour, and so you must take responsibility for it. More than that, by supporting the White Rhodesian Brotherhood you are actually promoting a violent solution.'

In the silence which followed Selkirk was aware that he had done a very uncharacteristic thing. For the moment he was appalled by his own recklessness, but knew already that he would not regret it. Coper's reaction, though unexpected, was more characteristic: his wrath boiled over and subsided wordlessly. He looked at Selkirk with something approaching kindness. 'You're wrong, boy. But you're entitled to your opinions and I admire your courage in stating them. And Selkirk—'

'Yes?'

'I'm sorry about your friend.'

'Thank you, sir. I apologise for speaking the way I did. It's just that—'

'Forget it.'

The door opened to admit an immaculately groomed woman, dressed in yellow silk and carrying a Norfolk terrier. The faint reek of ether was subdued by a blast of *Arpège* by Lanvin. Selkirk stepped back in admiration; at Thorganby's dinner the attractions of Mrs. Coper had been less obvious.

'My poor darling, 'ow are you feeling?' Except for the missing 'h' the accent was perfect. But the musical intonation and the slightly sensual pursing of the lips gave her away: Mrs. Coper was French—a long time in England, but still French.

Coper closed his eyes for a kiss, beaming proudly, then

waved a hand in Selkirk's direction. 'Louise, this is Mr. Selkirk. You remember, he was at Thorganby's on Monday.'

'But of course.' The hand that shook Selkirk's was cool and smooth-skinned.

'Hallo, Mrs. Coper,' Selkirk said. 'We hardly spoke, did we? I'm just leaving.'

'Please don't go, Mr. Selkirk. I'm not staying long and you may be able to help me. When I leave here I want to hire a car, but I don't know Oxford well.'

'I know a place; I'll drive you there.'

'What's all this?' Coper said. 'Where are you going, sweetheart?' Selkirk guessed that he was a jealous husband; she must be at least fifteen years younger. She laughed —a liquid mischievous chuckle—and said: 'Well it was to be a surprise, Barnett, but since you're so smart I'll tell you. I'm going up to Burford to get the house ready. We haven't been near the place for six months, and there'll be a lot to do. Dr. Swanwick says that when you come out you'll need a few days' rest, so we're going to have a long weekend in the country, just the way we used to. I've told June to cancel all your appointments till Monday.'

Coper was incredulous. 'Now look here, Louise,' he said, 'you know perfectly well . . .'

Selkirk was deaf to the domestic squabble. A single word was reverberating in his head and he was listening again to the low groans and faltering exhalations, waiting for the cracked lips between the bandages to form a second syllable.

'Mrs. Coper,' he said, 'did I hear you say you had a house in Burford?'

They both looked at him in surprise, as if they had forgotten he was there. Coper recovered first. 'Yes,' he said, 'bought it from a clapped-out farmer two years ago. Never go there much, but Louise likes it. Why? You know that part of the world?'

'Yes, fairly well.' A British M.P.? It was impossible. 'But I was just thinking—well, I'm lunching at Eton, but I have nothing to do this morning, and I'd be happy to drive Mrs. Coper out there.'

Selkirk saw the mascara-coated eyes dilate, and a red

patch appeared above the pearl necklace. Her poise was gone. 'That's very kind of you, Mr. . . . but I think I would prefer to go alone.'

'Nonsense,' Coper said. 'A very kind offer. Let your young friend take you to Burford, and see that he's looked after when you get there.' He squeezed his wife's hand. 'Now off you go, the two of you, I have some telephoning to do.'

She tried to refuse twice more before they reached the car, but he insisted.

8 am

From Lupton's Tower the clock struck eight. Even the notes of the bell sounded leisurely now that the summer holidays had begun. Leslie Trumper turned over in bed. At this hour a week ago he had been trying to ram a little history into an unruly mob of fourteen-year-olds (after twenty years at Eton discipline was still a problem), but now he could relax. A pile of school reports waited for him downstairs, but he had never found those a penance. In the deck-chair by the summerhouse he could deal with them quite comfortably, surrounded by the deep red roses for which his garden was famous.

Then he would have to work out the next stage of the Prince's teaching. Educating the heir to the throne could not be taken lightly. Macaulay, perhaps, and of course Bagehot to end up with. If the wireless was right Courthope would be returning with the King that day. Perhaps he should ring Buckingham Palace that evening to find out when they expected the Prince at Balmoral. Mid-August, Courthope had said. No hurry; he liked having the Prince in his house, and the guineas were useful. The housemaster sipped his morning tea: no milk, pink and grey Worcester—not, of course, for use by the boys.

Yes, definitely Macaulay, good old-fashioned medicine for English royalty. Perhaps not so old-fashioned; Trumper had heard the night before that a favourite pupil was in hospital in Oxford with a bullet in his thigh. He looked out of the window round which the Gloire de Dijon roses clustered. Perhaps riot and revolution were coming back, and his England of order and quiet gardens had just been a misleading interlude. It would be interesting to hear what young Selkirk had to say at lunch; he worked at the centre of things.

Trumper had just decided to drift back to sleep when he heard the telephone ring in the drawing-room below. Under the sheets he went rigid with annoyance. There was only one man who would telephone at such an hour. Edward Risington, the new Headmaster, had been chosen because his experience in running Thamesmead Comprehensive School, the largest in London, would be useful in dealing with the inflow of 500 state schoolboys which Eton had accepted. (His enemies said that Risington also favoured schoolgirl Etonians, but Trumper, a fair-minded man, could hardly credit that.) Risington left his bed at 6.30 and assumed that his staff did the same. During the half this was unpopular, during the holidays surely an outrage. The man would be fretting already about next half's timetable. In impotent rage Trumper heard his maid answer the phone and start the journey upstairs. He found his ancient silk dressing-gown and met her half-way.

'It's Sir James Courthope, sir, from Windsor Castle.' Betsy's excitement sounded in her voice. Trumper shambled crossly to the receiver.

'Is that Leslie Trumper? Courthope here. Sorry to disturb you so early. Something has happened which means I must come and collect the Prince at once. I can't say more on the telephone. Can his things be packed in half an hour? . . . Right, I'll be with you before nine. Don't say anything to him, or to anyone. I'll do the explaining.'

Trumper replaced the receiver and said to the maid, standing wide-eyed in the doorway: 'Where's the Prince then, Betsy—still in bed?'

'Oh no, sir, he's gone to the pool for a swim, like he does every morning, rain or fine. "You'll turn into a fish," I said, but he just laughed.'

'Well, he's leaving straight away, so will you go upstairs and pack his suitcases as best you can?'

'Good heavens, sir! Whateve 's happened?'

'Nothing, Betsy, nothing at all. Just a change of plan.' But her black eyes were full of drama as she marched off to tell Cook.

When Courthope appeared, the Prince was eating breakfast. Trumper met the Private Secretary in the hall, where three smart black suitcases were ready.

'I simply said you were coming to see him,' Trumper said. 'He's in there. No one will disturb you.'

'Many thanks. You'd better know what has happened. The King's plane crashed in the sea a few hours ago off Italy. There are no survivors. It is as simple as that, so now I must tell that boy in there that he is the King of England and take him away to begin his reign.'

'But what happened to the plane?'

'I don't know, no one knows. An explosion, they say —that might mean anything.'

'I'm sorry, Courthope. It must be particularly hard for you.'

'Yes, he was a good master. But there will be so much to do now that we shall not have time to think about that. Excuse me then, I will go in.'

After the Prince had left with Courthope, the big black car cautiously negotiating the narrow lane away from the house, Trumper tried to think of the late King, whom he had never met. But instead his mind kept turning to Courthope. Not as he was now with his strained expression and the vein throbbing in his neck; but as a tall seventeen-year-old with a sharp, strikingly handsome face, pale above the black gown, declaiming in that same tense voice against Catiline in Upper School. Something else, had there been? Trumper's memory, never strong outside academic subjects, gave up the struggle.

Betsy reappeared, nursing in astonishment the five pound note which Courthope had given her. 'Ah, Betsy,' Trumper said, 'we'll be two for lunch now, just Mr. Selkirk and myself. Perhaps Cook could find us some lamb?'

8.45 am

Waiting at the park door of the Foreign Office Jane
Richardson yawned in the morning sunshine. She had
had perhaps three hours' sleep that night, and wondered
not for the first time why she had volunteered for a period
as Resident Clerk. Partly to be the first female member of
the Diplomatic Service to do it, as the gossip columns had of
course noted. Partly for the cash, a good allowance, and
a rent-free flat on the top floor of the Foreign Office, done
up in the sort of dingy discomfort which men pretended to
like. The view over park and Palace continued to delight
her, but when there was a crisis the view was well paid for.
Could it be that after all women needed more sleep than
men? Jane brushed aside the heresy.

Pretty girls in ones or twos tripped along the path which
led across the park from the direction of the tube station.
Jane looked at her watch—8.45, too early yet for the
bowler hats. The Prime Minister should arrive soon. A
man in a raincoat and a grey trilby was talking to a pelican
under the fig tree where the path came nearest the lake.
Across the road on the Horse Guards' Parade another man
was polishing an official-looking car. Funny, same hats.
. . . Then she remembered the special security arrangements
brought into operation that morning.

She wondered if the Prime Minister would recognise
her; she had been at school with his daughter, and long
ago there had been a half-term picnic with embarrassingly
mushy strawberries. She decided her green suit was definitely
too bright. Too late to do anything about it now. Would
she have time that day to fetch her black from the cleaners?
Court mourning for at least a fortnight, she supposed.
Nervously she crumpled the piece of paper in her pocket, then
took it out and tried to get rid of the creases by flattening it
against the wall. She was sure the lift would stick as
it carried Harvey and herself up to the Secretary of State's
room. By the time the Prime Minister's car turned the
corner and drew up beside her, Miss Jane Richardson,

First Secretary, was in a state of panic. She began to speak very fast.

'Good morning, sir. The Secretary of State asked me to meet you and take you up . . .'

'Good morning.' For an alarming moment the Prime Minister's eye rested on the green suit, but he did not see it. 'Anything from the *Dalkeith*?'

'Yes sir, here it is.' Jane offered the piece of crumpled white paper. Harvey stopped to read it in front of the chiselled portrait of Edward Grey by the entrance, and Jane noticed the two men had the same nose. Then, still quaking, she led the way into the lift. It creaked alarmingly, but decanted them without mishap on the first floor. Harvey was re-reading the message from H.M.S. *Dalkeith*.

'0815 OIL AND FLOATING WRECKAGE SIGHTED LONGITUDE 9° 15' LATITUDE 44° 7' PORTION OF TAIL RECOVERED IDENTIFIED AS FROM HERAKLES WITCH NO TRACE SURVIVORS ITALIAN TANKER CORONA DI BOLSANO HAS RESUMED VOYAGE LA SPEZIA GRATEFUL FRESH INSTRUCTIONS.'

In the corridor between the lift and the door to the Foreign Secretary's room Harvey paused for a moment and for the first time was conscious of his companion. 'You're Jane Richardson, aren't you? At school with Lucy, weren't you? Didn't know you had this job. Tell me, who's in there?'

'The Secretary of State, the Lord Chancellor, Joynson from Number Ten and Sir Norman Birchett. I spoke to Sir James Courthope at Windsor, and he said he would certainly come if you wanted him but it would take him nearly an hour to get in.'

'At Windsor? What's he doing there? I thought he was at Buckingham Palace.'

'Would you like me to call him again? He said—'

'No, no, perhaps it's as well he's down there. I'll talk to him myself when we've finished.' He was half inside the door, then turned back. 'You'd better come in too. Got a pencil? Make a note of what we decide. Not minutes, just the decisions. We may be too busy afterwards to remember.'

Three men stood talking in low tones by the far window

of the Foreign Secretary's room. Jane knew Bill Joynson, the Press Secretary from Number Ten, short and bald with a scruffy moustache. As usual he looked as if he had slept in his suit; this time he probably had. The Lord Chancellor and the Secretary to the Cabinet looked remarkably alike: grey-white hair carefully brushed so that its thinness did not show, stiff collars, dark heavy suits with waistcoats in mid-August, watch-chains, glowing shoes. Handsome and sixty, thought Jane; first-class brains, first-class incomes, and all their emotions behind them. She turned to Ryder Bennett who sat at his wide mahogany desk, flipping through a red boxful of telegrams. But Harvey explained her presence for her.

'Here I am, Ryder. Perhaps Miss Richardson should stay and record for us.'

They all sat round the big oval table which ran along one side of the room. The Prime Minister poured himself a glass of water. Everyone there had been trained to believe that crises and tragedies were best dealt with in an orderly, businesslike manner, sitting round a table, with a white pad and sharpened pencil by each place and some-one taking the record.

'Let's deal first with the message from the *Dalkeith*,' Harvey said. 'You've all read it?'

'Excuse me, Prime Minister.' It was the Lord Chancellor. 'Before we begin, I wonder if the Home Secretary and James Courthope ought not to be with us? It might save time in the long run.'

'Courthope is at Windsor, and the Home Secretary will have resigned before the day is out. So we must make do as best we can. I would first like to ask each of you in turn: how conclusive is the message from the *Dalkeith*?'

Ryder Bennett cut in first. 'It's perfectly clear to me. The Italian tanker has been on the spot for two hours, the *Dalkeith* for one, and they've found no survivors. No other ship is within miles; it's beyond the fishing-ground. The Italian fighters have nothing to report. The *Dalkeith* has proved it was a Witch that crashed. We've checked with Herakles; there's no other Witch in the Mediterranean. Therefore the King is dead. I'm against delay or messing about. With the country in its present state, and Constable starting tomorrow, the only safe thing is to make an announcement at once and proclaim the Prince.'

There was a silence. Ryder Bennett, the youngest man present, had spoken too abruptly. He pushed his hand savagely through his stiff brown hair as he realised it. Even Jane Richardson was thinking of the King. It could not be decent simply to sweep him and his reign aside and go on as before. There should be bells, black coats and ties, a gun carriage, the 'Dead March from Saul,' before life could properly start again.

The Lord Chancellor's anger showed in his voice. 'With respect, I think that's going far too fast. No court of law would accept the information we have so far as evidence of death. If after two or three days there is no further relevant information that is a different matter, and we could reasonably presume a demise of the Crown. To take one point only, how can the captain of the *Dalkeith* be so sure that the piece of metal which he has recovered is from a Witch? He is not presumably an expert on aeroplanes. The tanker which saw the explosion said nothing about a Witch. Ryder Bennett mentioned Constable. I have supported that operation as you know, Prime Minister, with some reservations, but it surely must in present circumstances be postponed. I am in favour of saying as little as possible to the Press, continuing a stringent inquiry locally and avoiding, for two days at least, any definite assumption about the King.'

The Lord Chancellor looked across the table at Birchett for support but failed to catch his eye. As was his habit when senior Ministers disagreed, the Secretary to the Cabinet was gazing at the chandelier. Ryder Bennett and Joynson both started to speak at once, but Harvey stopped them. 'I should like to take one point out of our present discussion. There can be no question of postponing Operation Constable. If it does not begin tomorrow it will never take place. The reasons which led the Cabinet yesterday to approve the operation remain valid. Now, Ryder, you had something to add.'

The Lord Chancellor crossed his legs in a quick, almost

nervous gesture. Jane Richardson could see that he disliked
the edge in the Prime Minister's voice. He was being hustled.
A mounted police patrol clattered in the street outside on
their way to man the approaches to Trafalgar Square.

'I just wanted to say,' said Ryder Bennett, 'that the
Dalkeith, like all naval vessels in active service, carries an
aircraft recognition chart. I have checked that the latest
supplement which she received includes details and drawings
of the Witch.'

'Thank you, Ryder. Now you, Joynson.'

Joynson got up, marched to the window and gazed out
at the policemen. His trousers looked even baggier from
the back. He turned round suddenly to face his audience.
Joynson had never learnt the urbane ways of the upper
bureaucracy; at first this had been a handicap, but now
he exploited it as an asset. Marking each point with a
downward wag of his index finger, he said: 'It's bloody crazy
to try and hold this up. We all know the King's dead. Every
newspaper office in Britain will have the story by lunch-
time. That tanker will be in La Spezia, the crew blabbing
away, then there are the owners, the pilots of the Italian
fighters, the Embassy in Rome—there must be a hundred
people already who know the guts of it. I've nobbled the
evenings and the broadcasting organisations—they'll say
nothing in the early editions or news bulletins—but I've
promised them something this afternoon at the latest. However, that's not the main point—'

The Lord Chancellor cut in. 'You don't seem to understand, Joynson. This is a national emergency, without
precedent I should say. I don't know what authority you
had for what you've done. We really can't let ourselves
be stampeded into ill-considered action by the Press.'

Joynson looked quickly at the Prime Minister and, seeing
nothing to discourage him, went on. 'That's just what I
was going to say. This is an emergency, a crazy situation,
crazier than most people realise. It's not just the Press.
Look at it this way: tomorrow we're starting our biggest
military operation since Suez. We need calm nerves, national
unity, pulling together as a team, all that stuff. And what
have we got? Riots and shooting, Ministers resigning, the

Guards off their heads, army officers deserting in droves, Fleet Street humming with preposterous rumours—and now the King's gone up in a bang on a summer morning, no one knows how or why.' He came back to the table, and stood over the Prime Minister. 'There's only one thing to do, sir. Play it straight and simple. Tell everything we know, get the Prince on the throne and the troops into Rhodesia. If we try to cover up and put out a lot of platitudes and ambiguities, we'll have half Fleet Street believing tonight that the Foreign Secretary made the bomb and you put it in the Witch yourself. That's the kind of jitters the country's in.'

Joynson found a large red handkerchief, mopped his brow, and shambled defiantly back to the window. There was a pause.

'I really can't believe'—began the Lord Chancellor, but Harvey interrupted.

'That carries us some way from the immediate problem. What do you say, Sir Norman?'

Birchett reluctantly detached his gaze from the chandelier. His mind had not been idle. 'Perhaps I could make a proposal which would be generally acceptable. I suggest that we say nothing at all until 4 p.m. this afternoon, and meanwhile instruct the *Dalkeith* to continue the search for survivors. If by then neither she nor the searching aircraft have anything further to report, then we should announce the King's death.' He drew the gold watch from his waistcoat. 'That gives them six hours more. At the same time I suggest that you appoint a senior Minister to fly to Italy at once and make an immediate investigation into the crash. If the Lord Chancellor were able to do this himself I believe that the public would be greatly reassured. Then there are other problems. For example, the Prince . . .'

'One thing at a time,' Harvey said. 'Sir Norman's proposal for an announcement strikes me as about right.' His tone was even, but as he poured himself a glass of water, Jane Richardson noticed that the decanter shook slightly in his hand. 'But I'm not going to take a vote. This is something we've all got to agree. If you, Robert,' turning to the Lord Chancellor and calling him for the first time by his

133

Christian name, 'give us your considered advice that we are acting too hastily, then we must take that advice and think of another way.'

There was another silence. Even the noise of traffic outside seemed to die down, and Jane was conscious of the heavy tick of the clock on the marble mantelpiece. Ryder Bennett started to scribble angrily. The Lord Chancellor put his head in his hands, but said nothing. Harvey spoke to him again. 'Remember the sad old saying "*inter arma silent leges*"?'

'What's that mean?' Ryder Bennett was impatient. His pencil snapped on the pad.

'It means,' the Lord Chancellor said, speaking slowly but smiling for the first time, 'that when there's a real crisis, the Lord Chancellor should keep his mouth shut. Which I accept. In fact, I agree to what Birchett's suggested. If wanted, I am ready to fly to Italy at once.'

Harvey leant back in his chair and took from his pocket a white House of Commons card covered with neat black jottings. 'That's fine. I am very grateful. Now we have an immense amount to do in a short time and we must divide our energies. Ryder, you must concentrate on Constable, and I suggest you move over to the Ministry of Defence and let one of the Ministers of State look after the Foreign Office. The Lord Chancellor will be in charge of the investigation into the crash. I leave that entirely to you, Robert. You will probably find it useful to take Air Vice-Marshal Sharp with you. Sir Norman, I want you to look after all constitutional formalities, proclamation of accession at St. James's Palace, that sort of thing. And send me a list of what I personally must do. Either the Prince or I should obviously broadcast this evening; let me know by lunchtime what you recommend. Joynson's first job is to draft the statement for four o'clock. Clear it with Sir Norman before you show it to me. I will look after the recall of Parliament and emergency powers to deal with the Movement.

'One important point which you may not all know: the King's will provides that there should be no public mourning at his death and no disruption of ordinary life.

134

Make sure that goes into the statement, Bill. I shall telephone Courthope now and tell him what we've decided. He should get down to Eton straight away and bring the Prince to London, then he can help you with your side of it, Norman . . .'

The meeting continued briskly and Jane Richardson was hard pressed to record the main decisions. Footsteps could now be heard more often in the corridor and in the anteroom beyond the connecting door. A uniformed messenger carrying the daily papers poked his nose round the door, gaped, and disappeared. Somewhere a kettle boiled fussily. The Foreign Office was setting about its daily life. Jane, who was breakfastless, began to think about a cup of coffee.

'. . . I think that is all then, gentlemen. Miss Richardson will let us each have a copy of our conclusions.' Harvey had brought the meeting down to the humdrum and matter-of-fact. As he left the room he looked almost cheerful, and Jane thought she heard him humming under his breath. Bill Joynson read her thoughts; the two of them were the last to leave. 'Bloody marvellous, isn't he?' Joynson said. 'Had them licking his hand again, like the vicar at a parish meeting. Pity it won't work this time.'

'Won't work? What do you mean? It's all settled.' Jane showed her notebook.

'Poor sweet little diplomat, you've got it written down, so you think it's true. I blew my top, didn't I? But I could have spared my breath; after last night's little number, Harvey's lost his authority.'

'Last night—you mean the King?'

'The King, hell. I mean the fruit, the bleeding red tomato. Delayed effect, but he won't recover, you see. And then we'll be in the cart—Prince, Lord High Chancellor, the bloody lot of us.'

Joynson stumped down the stairs groping in his pocket for the second half of last night's last cigar.

9.15 am

As Selkirk eased the car down the steep hill into Burford, she pointed to some chimneys above the trees in the valley.

'There we are,' she said. 'Lovely, isn't it?'

'Yes, pretty.' His hands felt sweaty on the wheel. This was either a ridiculous waste of time or a dangerous escape. Why had they acted so strangely at the hospital? With Coper it could have been jealousy, but what was she afraid of? The danger had not occurred to him then, but now he felt ludicrously ill-equipped in his starched collar and pin-stripe suit, Whitehall official playing private detective.

The wrought-iron gates were open. 'You can drop me here if you like,' she said. 'The walk will do me good.'

He pretended not to hear and drove on. She would have to do better than that. Trees, lawns, a tall ugly house in Cotswold stone. He parked the Sunbeam in front of the heavy oak doors. She was already out of the car, leaning through the window to shake his hand.

'Thank you *so* much, Mr. Selkirk, I'm most grateful.' Ignoring the farewell, he followed her up the steps and waited while she searched for her keys. She turned and said: 'Really, I'm quite all right.'

But he was ready. A drink, a bite to eat, a tour of the house—all too easily refused. 'I want to go to the lavatory,' he said.

'Oh—yes, of course.' Still clutching the Norfolk terrier, which was whining irritably, she fumbled in her bag. Her hands were shaking. 'How extraordinary! I seem to have lost my keys.'

'Don't be silly, Mrs. Coper. You know you haven't lost your keys.' He took the bag and handed her three Yale keys on a ring.

'Well, really, Mr. Selkirk, I don't see why—'

'Open the door.' The point of no return. Either he had made a complete fool of himself or there was something in the house.

'Who are you, anyway?' she said. 'Police?'

'M.I.5,' he said, and thought: Selkirk, you are mad.

She opened the door and he followed her in, hoping his terror did not show. If she could only hear his timid, civil-servant heart, pounding like a steam hammer! The house was silent, empty. He began to walk from room to room. Drawing-room—beer bottles, half-eaten sandwiches, cigarette stubs, yesterday's *Evening Standard*; dining-room —cigarette stubs, a blackboard, a map of Oxford; kitchen —twelve sliced loaves and a Sten gun.

As he ran upstairs he was vaguely aware that she had kept up a constant flow of exclamations of horror and surprise and the stupid little dog had followed them everywhere, yapping excitedly. He opened the door into a large bedroom. 'My room,' she explained. It was a love-nest, a fantasy room, decorated in varying shades of pink, the woodwork painted glossy white, the bedspread and curtains trimmed with lace. Everything that money could buy and taste would forbid was there. The rifles had been laid on newspaper to save the carpet.

Selkirk sank on to the corner of the bed. She sat beside him, and neither spoke for a full minute. The dog stood by the door, waiting for more fun.

'You knew,' he said finally.

'Yes,' she said.

'Who are they?'

'Friends of Barnett's, Movement people. He said they would be gone by this morning, so I wanted to clean up. The gardener and housekeeper were told to keep away till I came down. I didn't expect to find—rifles.'

'No, I doubt if you did. I think they left last night. They were in a hurry, because they thought that one of their number had telephoned the police. Tell me, Mrs. Coper, did you know what these people were doing?'

'No, only that it was very secret.'

'Why did you think your husband let me come with you?'

'Well, that worried me too. I thought then they might still be here, and it might be a trap—for you.'

'It didn't occur to you that I might be one of them?'

'No.'

'I see. Well, you certainly did your best to save me.' He laughed, but she did not share the joke. She sat with her head slumped forward, face buried in her hands, all polish gone. 'I suppose you have to report this?' The voice was a little girl's.

'Mrs. Coper, I shall have to, I don't have any choice. Let's just hope we can keep you out of a complicity charge.'

'Oh, it's not me I care about.' She was crying now; noisy sobs shook the loose-fitting silk dress. 'It's Barnett! I couldn't bear to see him ruined, I couldn't bear it! He's been so good to me, I love him!' As Selkirk started to make a gesture of sympathy her head fell against his shoulder. He could feel her breast against his arm; warm skin through the silk dress, her perfume in his nostrils. He was not often so near a woman and though frozen with embarrassment by her emotion, he found that undeniably, worryingly, something was stirring inside him. As she raised her face to plead with him again, he could easily have kissed her on the lips—it would have been just one more mad thing in an already mad situation, and he sensed it was what she intended—but instead he said: 'Come downstairs, I'll get you a brandy.'

11.30 am

After he had sacked the Home Secretary, Patrick Harvey walked into the garden of Number Ten for some air. It had been a bad quarter of an hour. Pallman, completely surprised, had almost wept. Then he had pulled the shreds of his pride about him and said that his doctor had ordered him total rest, and he had meant to resign anyway. His breath had been rich with alcohol, and the portly voice had quavered in self-pity. Harvey now felt slightly sick; but it had been necessary.

His wife was at the end of the garden clipping dead heads off the roses. She came across the grass towards him. The shallow basket under her arm was half-full of brown stalks and petals.

138

'The King is dead then? Bill Joynson told me.'

'Dead, yes. God knows how.'

'Then all this will stop, won't it? I mean the riots and sending the troops to Rhodesia, and David Thorganby resigning—it'll all have to stop?'

She had touched an exposed nerve. 'Helen, you don't follow these things, you don't understand. The King's death doesn't change any of that. Politics go on, you know. *Le roi est mort . . .*'

'Politics.' She repeated the word without any emphasis. 'Yes, I suppose so. I suppose they'll go on till you've ground yourself to bits.'

Harvey looked at his wife for a moment with fresh eyes. Neat auburn hair, unfashionable high-collared dress, warm colour still in her cheeks but a line of bitterness at each corner of the mouth. She doesn't speak her mind often enough, he thought; but then he was never there to listen. For a moment he wanted twenty years over again. But the neat black figure of the butler was crossing the lawn.

'Sir James Courthope on the telephone, sir.'

Harvey looked surprised. 'But I spoke to him less than an hour ago. All right, I'm coming. Don't worry, Helen, it'll turn out all right.'

But she did not meet his eyes. 'I must get back to the roses,' she said. 'They need doing every day.'

The sound of Courthope's voice was almost a comfort. Harvey was out of the shoals and reefs of private relations, back on the high seas of state affairs, where all you had to do was stand at the helm and steer straight and look as if you were in control. 'Yes, James, what is it?' he said.

'Since we spoke after your meeting, I have collected the Prince from Eton as you asked. He took the news very calmly. We are just about ready to leave Windsor for London. Of course he wants to see you as soon as possible. Could you come to the Palace at six this evening?'

'Yes, or earlier if he prefers. As I told you, Birchett is working on the constitutional details, but in an hour or so he should be ready to tell us exactly what has to be done.'

'There's one other thing the Prince asked me to say. I

139

told him the King had been going to broadcast this evening, and the Prince asked to see the script. Then he had the idea of making the broadcast himself, starting with a few introductory words of his own and then reading the King's own script. He is set on the idea, very keen indeed, and I haven't discouraged him. The script we worked out in Ravello is a strong appeal for national unity. I should have thought it was needed now even more than before.'

'I see.' Harvey thought fast. 'It's an excellent idea. But I ought to see the script first. When exactly was the King going to broadcast?'

'At five, and of course they're still holding the time open.'

'Can you get the text over to me?'

There was a slight pause. 'Yes, of course. If this hadn't happened, I'd have discussed it with you this morning. As soon as we get up to the Palace I'll send a messenger over with it.'

'Good. Is there anything else?'

'Nothing that can't wait till you come this evening. I don't want to add to your burdens.'

'Good-bye then.' Harvey had long ago invented his own visual telephone. He had the habit while he was talking of calling into his mind the physical image of the person at the other end of the line. This was easy with Courthope because of his striking good looks. Harvey had once been given the poems of Rupert Brooke as a school prize; Courthope despite his fifty years reminded him of the photograph in the frontispiece. As he turned away from the telephone Harvey remembered an incident of two or three years back. At the end of a state banquet in the Mansion House his official car had failed to appear, and Courthope had given him a lift home. A few days before, Courthope's wife, a pretty but foolish woman, had left him suddenly, finally, without explanation. Sitting beside Courthope in the car, Harvey had suddenly been sure that a dam was breaking; Courthope was going to talk about the broken marriage. But a pedestrian in the Strand had stepped suddenly from the pavement, Courthope had braked to avoid him, and the moment had passed.

Bill Joynson appeared in the doorway. He was in his braces, and his shirtsleeves were rolled up untidily. Harvey liked his staff to come neat and stay neat, but Joynson was privileged.

'Have you done the four o'clock statement yet?' asked Harvey.

'Yes, Birchett's got it. He wanted to make some changes, said he'd bring it back in an hour to clear with you. I'm having a hell of a time with the B.B.C. They've got the story from their man in Rome, who got it from the owners of the tanker. Trust Auntie to be first among the vultures. After a lot of argument they've agreed to hold it up, but they say what about their evening programmes—*The Jellybaby Show*, Part 36 of *Wuthering Heights*? All of it will be knocked to smithereens if the story's true. And what about the King's broadcast, which they've set for five? I think in fairness we'll have to tell them that's off.'

'No such thing. Get on to the Director-General from me and tell him to keep the five o'clock slot. The Prince will do it, but don't tell him that yet.'

Joynson looked at his master with admiration. 'You do manage to keep things moving. That should do a lot of good. Then there was another drama while you were in with Pallman. His Permanent Secretary rang from the Home Office and wanted to speak to him. I couldn't resist it, I told him his boss was getting the chop. Of course he went all stiff and formal, but I bet they're toasting you in Nescafé by now in the Home Office. Anyway, he asked me to tell you they've just had a report from the Chief Constable of Oxfordshire. The police paid a call on Coper's house down there and found it stiff with guns. In short, it looks as if the genial little folk who fixed the shooting in Oxford yesterday operated from Coper's stately home. The Chief Constable wanted to know if they could pull him in. The Home Office are asking the Attorney-General about his parliamentary immunity.'

'I see.' Harvey sat down heavily at his desk. He did not see. He felt that his mind was beginning to slow down. Was this good news, and if so how should it be used?

Joynson got there first. 'You can clobber the Movement
141

now, surely. Up to yesterday they've been a bunch of rowdy thugs making too much noise; a few bruises, police helmets in the gutter, that sort of thing. Lots of people thought they were going a bit far, but in a good cause. But Coper sitting down in his own house quietly planning to shoot his way to power, that's something else again, that's conspiracy. When that gets out he's finished.'

'Can they prove he was responsible? After all, he was hurt himself.' Harvey was still puzzled, not yet quite ready to believe that he had been wrong about Coper.

'That was a blind. They're still taking statements but they seem satisfied. I only heard part of the story, but that fancy wife of his gave him away. The full report should be over soon. It may be far bigger than we think.'

'Oh? In what way?'

'The tip-off about Coper's house came from Selkirk, Thorganby's P.S., and he, believe it or not, got it from Steele, the runaway guardsman found in Oxford last night. He went to visit him in hospital, God knows why. You needn't give me an O.B.E. yet, but it looks as if your Press Secretary may have been right for once.'

'What are you talking about?'

'It seems possible that Steele and Meredith, the guardsmen suspected of killing the R.S.M., were being held in Coper's house. In which case it was probably Coper's men who got them out of the barracks. Steele hasn't come round yet, but as soon as he does we shall have the truth.'

Harvey whistled. 'Now that *is* something I could use.'

'Of course the other twenty-three guardsmen are still missing. It's extraordinary that not one of them has turned up yet. Now if Coper was also responsible for that. . . . But that's carrying speculation rather far.'

'Yes. Well, thank you, Joynson. Be sure to tell me the minute anything new comes up.'

Joynson stood clumsily in the door. He had something else to say, but was for once at a loss. 'There's one more rather awkward thing. . . .'

Harvey looked at the gilt carriage clock on his desk: 11.30 already, and too much still to settle. 'Well, out with it.'

'Hutchinson of the *Express* rang. Was there anything in the story that you were on the verge of a breakdown and we had rushed in a specialist?'

'So you said I'd just been carted away screaming.'

'I pumped him for his source but he wouldn't say. Then I noticed on your programme for today: "3.30, Dr. Faith-Adams".'

'That's my regular six-monthly check-up. It was fixed at least a month ago. I've told them to put him off to next week. Who on earth has worked that up into a fairy tale?'

'We'll probably never know. Anyway I stamped hard, and I think I killed it. Hutchinson's not bad as they go.'

When Joynson had gone Harvey sat at his desk, forcing his thoughts into order. His fingers, set free to please themselves, tugged at a paper-clip until it was a straight line of metal. Yes, Joynson was right, the Movement had played into his hands. Parliament could meet next Tuesday. A short sharp Bill taking away Coper's immunity and declaring the Movement illegal—it could be through both houses within the week. Back in its own familiar territory, Harvey's mind relaxed. Almost as a therapeutic exercise he began to cover a large sheet of paper with the main heads of his speech on the Second Reading.

11.35 am

Mrs. Steele had been sleeping for three hours now in the room next to her son's. At 7.30 the doctor had told her the immediate danger was over and she had not been able to hold her eyes open any longer. They had offered her night-clothes but she preferred to sleep as she was in case she was needed. Her old black coat, bought ten years before at the Catholic jumble sale in Chenil Galleries, was folded on the chair by the bed, her worn shoes and voluminous bag placed neatly on the floor. She was curled on her side in the crumpled cotton dress, her long grey hair falling loose from the bun, and in the half-light coming from the curtained window you could see she had once been a beauty.

143

They tried to wake her gently but were forced to shake her by the shoulder before her eyes opened. She sat up quickly and said: 'What's happened?'

'Nothing, Mrs. Steele,' said the sister smiling, 'nothing has happened. Harry is gaining strength nicely, but I'm afraid we shall have to move you. The police want this room for another patient.'

The man from the C.I.D. came in. 'Sorry about this, Mrs. Steele. There's another gentleman in the hospital who has a few questions to answer, and we thought it would be easier if we did it in here. Then if Harry comes round we're not too far away.'

So they put her on a chair in the corridor while Harry was given an injection, and after a few minutes two uniformed policemen appeared with a fat, red-faced man in a wheel-chair followed by a woman in a yellow dress. The woman was dabbing at her eyes with a handkerchief and the man had a dressing over one eye. As they wheeled him into the room he said: 'And now I insist on speaking to my solicitors. Where the hell is the nearest telephone? I know nothing about all this balderdash and I advise you to remember there's still such a thing as parliamentary immunity.'

She closed her eyes and said a little prayer for Harry. Nothing much—it was hard to find the words—but it seemed to do some good, because shortly after that the sister bustled out of Harry's room and said: 'He's waking up. You can go in now, but don't overdo it—he's still very weak.'

One eye half open, the flicker of a smile, a whispered 'Hallo, Mum.' That was all she got, but it was enough. The doctor had said that even if he lived he might not be 'all there', and she had dreaded that more than anything; but now she knew it would not happen. Back in the corridor she wanted to laugh and shout, tell everybody, but there was no one about, so she sat saying 'Thank you, oh, thank you' and excitedly rearranging herself. For some reason she suddenly wanted to look her best.

The police went into Harry's room and the doctor into the other. The red-faced man made a terrible racket when

144

they changed his dressing, which surprised her because he did not look badly hurt and the doctor's hands were gentle—she knew that from watching him change Harry's bandages. Delicate, long-fingered hands with surprisingly pink palms. You could say what you liked about these African doctors, they were more gentle than the rest. Perhaps the red-faced gentleman wasn't too keen on the coloureds.

12.15 p.m.

Lord Thorganby sat at his desk in Eaton Place doing gloomy sums on the back of an envelope. To judge by the enormous post which had flowed through his letter-box at frequent intervals in the last twenty-four hours, his resignation had been welcomed by almost the whole British public except the tradesmen of the West End. These last were hastening to remind him politely of outstanding accounts, and he had been driven already to study for the second time in his life the arithmetic of living without the salary of a Cabinet Minister. The moor at Hallkirk—could Ralston persuade that American friend of his to take it again next year? Then there was the Turner. It had hung for twenty-five years above the sideboard at Eaton Place, two fishing boats fighting their way strenuously through a storm of yellow light. He had tried to sell it after the Labour victory of 1964 but the man from Agnew's had muttered about a similar painting of proved authenticity in one of the bedrooms at Petworth. Thorganby had been too proud to pursue the matter. His grandfather had certainly bought it as a Turner, and a Turner it must continue to be. He would try Sotheby's this time. That was one decision taken at least.

He got up heavily and went to the window. The scarlet and pink geraniums in the window-box were dusty and sprawling; they would soon be finished. London was a dismal place in mid-August. Elizabeth had been right, they should have caught that train to Scotland last night. There was nothing to keep him in London except a mound of unanswered letters. He saw the postman come round the corner for the third delivery that morning. By the time the batch of letters thudded softly through the letter-box he was back at his sums.

'Another special delivery; at least twenty more,' said his wife, bustling cheerfully into the room, a couple of smooth-haired dachshunds in her train. Lady Thorganby was better at facing turns of fortune than her husband. She drew on a fathomless reserve of brisk good sense. 'And here's one from Molly Downes. Scribbled on her knee at London Airport, she says, but she's always illegible anyway. "Many thanks for the lovely dinner . . . we both so much enjoyed ourselves," and so on. Ah, yes, I told you so. That girl of hers *is* in love again. She hardly touched her soufflé. A journalist, Molly says—rude, unsuitable, and Peter will throw a fit.'

Lady Thorganby began to flick cheerfully round the room with a duster. The two dachshunds climbed as of right on to the sofa. Flora the maid had been sent ahead to Scotland, and they were virtually camping in the London house. Lord Thorganby was beginning to think that his wife was set to make him deliberately uncomfortable until he agreed that they too should go north. Instant coffee for breakfast, and here she was quite unnecessarily messing up the papers on his desk. But he knew better than to start an argument, and his wife continued to dust and talk.

'There was a call for you while you were in the bath. A man from the *Daily Telegraph* asked if you had any comment on the latest Gallup Poll on Rhodesia. Fifty-six per cent now against the use of British troops. They will publish it tomorrow. I said you'd call back if you wanted to say anything.'

'Fifty-six per cent, did you say?' That was far more than in the last poll. If he had known the figure before yesterday's Cabinet he could have argued that the Newbury result meant nothing. Now it was too late.

Lady Thorganby moved in to the assault. 'Why don't you ring King's Cross, David, instead of sitting there moping? You know how difficult it is to get sleepers at short notice.'

Why not? There was no reason to stay in London. He

did not even know what reason there might ever have been. The end of his career, an anticlimax; an old man shuffling from the scene, by next week irrelevant and forgotten.

Over the languishing geraniums Lord Thorganby saw a taxi draw up outside the door and a tall man in a blue suit step out. His wife recognised the visitor first. 'Why, look, it's James Courthope. I'll go and let him in.' The dachshunds began to yap in unison.

'Courthope? What on earth can he want?'

Lady Thorganby paused in the middle of the room. Despite her dump figure, dull grey suit, frizzy hair, she could look militant when she chose. Even the duster was flourished as a banner.

'He must have come, David, because the King wants you to withdraw your resignation. And you will have to agree.

'But I thought you wanted—'

'I don't want you hanging about in London with nothing to do. But if the King appeals to you to go back into the Cabinet, of course you must go.'

'It's most unlikely, Elizabeth. Harvey would never . . .'

But the bell had rung and Lady Thorganby swept out to open it. Thorganby heard the polite greetings in the hall and his wife quelling the dogs as she showed Courthope into the study. Thoroughly confused, he shut his desk and went to join them. As he passed his wife in the hall she said: 'Don't ask him to stay to lunch. We've nothing but eggs.' When he entered the study Courthope was examining the backs of the eighteenth-century sermons which lined one side. The room smelt pleasantly of unread books. Courthope turned quickly and they shook hands. They had met often but did not know each other well. Courthope's grip was so firm as to be painful.

'I heard you were coming back from Italy today,' Thorganby said, and motioned Courthope to one of the brown leather arm-chairs which flanked the empty grate. 'How is the King?'

Courthope took a cigarette from his case and fitted it carefully into a holder. His voice was flat. 'I've come to tell you that the King is dead. His aeroplane exploded over the Mediterranean early this morning. An announcement is being made at four.'

'But you . . . ?' Lord Thorganby's mind, which did not work fast, was jammed on the thought that the elegant composed man before him did not look as if he had survived a plane crash hundreds of miles away a few hours before.

'The King had asked me to come on in advance.' Courthope lit his cigarette. 'Perhaps as time is short it would be better if I came to the point at once, and tried to answer your questions later. I realise that what I say will come as a shock to you. We do not yet know how the King died, whether by accident or foul play. We simply know that his plane blew up and came down in the sea and that there were no survivors. The Lord Chancellor is to hold an inquiry. But that is not why I came to see you. The King of course followed closely what has been happening here in the last few days. At Ravello I was the only person he could talk to freely, and I know what was in his mind. He came slowly to decide that Harvey had lost control of the situation and that a National Government was needed.'

'A National Government?' Thorganby was not really listening. Before his eyes was a picture of twisted wreckage bobbing about in a rough sea.

'Yes, a National Government, which would say a firm "no" to the U.N. and restore order and sound government at home. A temporary measure of course, until things had sorted themselves out. Yesterday, when he heard about your resignation on the radio, he decided to ask you to form such a government.'

'Me?' Thorganby realised that he was doing little but gape and ask questions. He rose to his feet and walked to the window, trying to grasp what lay behind his visitor's words. 'But there could have been no question of Harvey offering to resign. After all, he got his way in Cabinet yesterday.'

Courthope smiled—the smile that a schoolmaster reserves for the oldest, the stupidest, but the nicest boy in the class. 'David,' he said, 'you know, and the King knew, that in the last resort he had the power to compel Harvey to resign,

148

and if he wished, to ask you to form a government. A power not used for many years, but designed exactly for a situation like this. The King came to the conclusion that Harvey's politics were disastrous and opposed by the great majority of the people. So he felt bound to act as he did.'

'Act as he did?' Lord Thorganby visibly pulled himself together. He must stop behaving like a parrot to this man fifteen years his junior. 'Frankly, I find it hard to take in what you say. The King's death is in itself such a shock that the rest of your news hardly strikes home. I am most grateful to you for coming to tell me this, but now that the King is dead whatever he may have planned to do surely falls to the ground?'

'On the contrary, what he planned to do is more necessary than ever. The King, as you know, had arranged to broadcast this evening. The script, over which he took great care, travelled in my suitcase last night. He asked me to show it to you this morning. Here it is.' He produced a slim buff envelope from his inside pocket. 'I have already discussed this with the Prince and he has decided to deliver the speech himself, exactly as it is here, at the hour already fixed.'

'Are you saying that in the broadcast the Prince is going to announce a National Government?'

'Certainly.' Courthope spoke quickly and with precision, as thought he had rehearsed this part of the interview. 'The royal prerogative is now his, and naturally in this crisis he is guided by the conclusions which the King had come to. There is, however, one condition: you must first agree to form a government. No one else is politically possible. If you do not agree the whole plan falls. I therefore come to you, informally but on the new King's instructions, to ask if you will do as he wishes.'

Thorganby's surprise was now over. He became again the practised man of affairs. As he read through the script his experience led him quickly to the necessary questions. 'This will need a lot of thought and consultation. How long before I must give the Prince an answer?'

'The broadcast is set for five. You will understand why it cannot be postponed.'

'Yes, of course. Constable starts at dawn. Does Harvey know?'

'Not yet, but he will get an advance copy of the script just before the broadcast.'

'Surely he should be told at once.' Thorganby had no tenderness for Harvey but he did not believe in bending the rules.

Courthope hesitated. He straightened the handkerchief in his breast pocket. 'There is something else, which for Harvey's sake should be kept quiet, but you must know it. We heard yesterday at Ravello that Harvey is in a highly excited nervous state. I gather he had some sort of seizure last night, and a specialist has been called in today. Overwork, I'm sure, and he'll pull out of it; but it does mean that for the moment he can't really be treated as responsible for his actions.'

Thorganby thought of his last meeting with Harvey twenty-four hours before. They had shaken hands after the Cabinet, and Harvey had thanked him for the way he had put his case. Thorganby had stalked off in a huff; he had not liked the way Harvey handled the meeting. But the man had seemed entirely rational and in control of himself. On the other hand he was a highly-strung fellow, subject to sudden ups and downs: it would not be surprising if the strain had suddenly proved too much. Then he remembered something else about the Cabinet meeting and said: 'I'm not doubting in the least what you say, James, but of course I must be sure that there has been no misunderstanding.' He poured out two glasses of sherry from a decanter which stood on the table by the window and handed one to Courthope in his chair. 'At Cabinet yesterday Harvey read a telegram from the King which he interpreted as meaning that the King hoped he would press on with Constable.'

This time Courthope did not hesitate. It was clearly a question which he had foreseen. 'You put it very accurately. Harvey chose to *interpret* the telegram in that way. But if you remember the actual text the King simply urged that the Cabinet should make up its mind without more delay. I helped him draft the telegram. Although it would not have been right for him to say so, he hoped that you and

150

your colleagues would turn down Constable. In that case Harvey would have resigned, and he could have sent for you without using his prerogative of dismissal. Obviously that would have been simpler. When he heard of the Cabinet's decision, and then had new reports of unrest in the services and of Harvey's nervous state, he decided on the broadcast.'

Thorganby sipped his sherry. So Coper had been right after all. The King had been ready to use the last weapon, the ancient power and majesty of the Crown. And he, Thorganby, was the chosen instrument. An unintellectual but deeply felt sense of history had taken Thorganby into politics in the first place; now it filled him with half-formed feelings of pride and courage. But he was cautious and there were questions still to be answered. 'We have to be sure of the legal position,' he said. 'Have you talked to a good lawyer?'

Courthope noticed the 'we' and relaxed in his chair. 'Obviously I couldn't talk to anyone about the present line of thought, but there's plenty of material about the prerogative in the library at Windsor and the King asked me to look it up before we went to Ravello. There's no doubt about it. Legally the King has the power to appoint and dismiss Ministers. The constitutional text books say the power has "atrophied," "fallen into disuse," phrases like that, and most of them imply that it couldn't be used again. But those are only political judgments of the authors. The point is that the power has never been legally abolished.'

'But what about the House of Commons? Harvey spoke yesterday about calling Parliament back from recess.'

'That's not necessary, and can be countermanded. They're in recess till the end of October. That gives you more than two months of unfettered action; plenty of time to decide what you want to do after that. If things have gone well you could ask for a vote of confidence, and if they refuse it, advise the King to dissolve Parliament and hold an election. You might decide to give up your own title and sit in the Commons. There are many possibilities. But the first thing is to get a National Government going.'

An ice-cream van had parked at the end of the street.

151

The amplified music-box jingle upset Thorganby's train of thought, and he watched a ten-year-old sprint along the pavement outside, coin in hand. His excitement turned to indecision. All his life he had known that his abilities were not quite first-rate, and this had saved him from several follies. 'I shall have to think further before I give you an answer. I'm not at all sure I could find a strong enough Cabinet. Am I free to use everything you've told me in talking to the people I approach?'

'Of course, as long as they don't pass it on. And this may be a help in choosing allies.' Courthope stood, and put a white envelope on the table. 'I shall be waiting at the Palace for your answer. A message in writing would be best.'

'You shall have it by four.'

'Thank you.'

As Thorganby opened the study door Courthope turned to face him. 'You are very experienced, David, and you have a right to be cautious. But please think for a moment of the Prince. He's been called suddenly to the throne, he's inexperienced and uncertain, faced with a desperate crisis, exposed to a babble of conflicting opinions. He must have a guide he can trust. In the script he wrote yesterday the King in effect showed the Prince who that guide should be. I do not think you will tell him this afternoon that you refuse the task.'

After Courthope had left, Lord Thorganby opened the white envelope. It was a list of Cabinet posts typed out on crested notepaper of the Ravello Hotel, under the heading: *Possible composition of National Government.'*

'Prime Minister: The Earl of Thorganby (C)

Deputy Prime Minister and Leader of the House of Commons: Mr. Joe Wellsuch (Lab)

Minister of Defence: Mr. Michael Critten (C) . . .'

The list ran over the page. Thorganby read it carefully then carried it across the hall to the dining-room, where his wife was laying two places for lunch.

'Well?' she said. 'He stayed a long time.'

'Elizabeth, the King is dead, and they want me to be Prime Minister. Lunch must wait.'

His wife sat down so hard that the Hepplewhite chair cracked in protest. Lord Thorganby found the telephone directory and looked up 'W' for Wellsuch.

12.40 pm

Major Rackstraw looked around the room which had been his base for the last six months. Patches of damp showed through the wallpaper and at several points the flower pattern disappeared into white mould; knobs were missing from the chest of drawers and broken springs hung down beneath the bed. Through the open window he could see a string of barges floating downstream on the tide, passing under Tower Bridge. The broken panes had been fixed with brown sealing-tape.

He had kept the room in good order, installed a telephone, bought two easy-chairs for interviews. Papers had been kept in a filing cabinet, confidential material in a small safe behind the wardrobe. He had covered the damp patches with maps and covered the maps with coloured pins, to mark the positions of telephone boxes, police stations, anything that came into his head.

But now the place was littered with bottles, dog-ends, girlie magazines. Stale smoke hung in the air. Nine men sat around on the floor and the furniture, waiting for him to speak. Some were looking distinctly impatient.

'Sorry to keep you waiting, gentlemen,' he said. 'Everything's in order. I apologise for the change of plan. One of those small mishaps which happen in the best-planned engagements. I'm reliably informed that our friend Steele, even if he lives, will not have much of a memory for faces. For that we have Jake here to thank. The house in Burford is being searched, but they haven't got round to the farm yet. Provided you all kept your gloves on, there's nothing to incriminate any of us.'

'Where's these cases then?' someone said.

'The cases have been moved to King's Cross Left Luggage. I shall be giving each of you a numbered withdrawal ticket. All the money is in used notes and those who asked for

153

passports and plane tickets will find them in their cases. Hudson, your money is in Australian dollars as you requested. You asked for yours in gold, Winckelmann, and we've arranged that. We'll pick up the cases two or three at a time, then disperse. In case there are any complaints I shall be in the bar of the Great Northern Hotel. Any further questions?'

There were no further questions. A tug hooted in the river and the pub below was getting rid of its empty bottles. 'Good. In that case we'll RV under the clock at King's Cross at 14.30 hours. Hudson will dump the Ford and Moss the van.' He paused and looked once more round the room. The well-loved leader taking leave of his last command . . . A sad moment. 'Well, gentlemen, that completes our little operation. I think I can say it has been a total success; all our objectives have been achieved. It only remains for me to thank you and wish you luck. Dismiss.'

1 pm (2 pm, Italy)

In the early fifties Sir Basil Spence had designed a new Chancery for the Rome mission, to be built at Porta Pia, on the site where the original British Embassy had been blown up by the Zionists; but shifting municipal régimes in Rome and successive British balance of payments crises had ensured that never a brick was laid. So Sir Basil's drawings were now enshrined at the Royal Institute of British Architects and the mission continued to be housed in the Villa Wolkonsky, a large nineteenth-century mansion named after the mistress of Czar Alexander I. The villa, which overlooked the Basilica of St. John in the Lateran, had once been the German Embassy and its chief asset was a swimming-pool, presented by Hitler to his Ambassador to keep the man at his post during the summer.

Kemble heaved his pink frame off the Li-lo and into the cold blue water. The banks of flowers around the pool were shimmering in the heat, and the rest of the party —Anne, Lady Molly and her social secretary—had retreated to the shade, where a perspiring butler was putting the finishing touches to the buffet lunch. Cheese soufflé or tortellini alla crema, cold Galloway beef from the Montecatini herd or chicken pilaff, black grapes or pears á la Bourgignonne, gallons of Antinori rosé. . . . As he swam towards the shallow end with a rather basic breaststroke, head held nervously above the surface, Kemble selected his lunch and wondered why he ever lived in England.

Since they had come down to the pool the shadow cast by the King's death, looming ever more certain throughout the morning, had lifted slightly, but now the arrival of the Ambassador and Ralston, crumpled and weary-eyed from their long wait in Naples, brought the disaster back into their midst. With a pang of guilt Kemble remembered the housemaids ironing the black dresses in the Villa and his own exasperating search for a black tie in the Piazza Vittorio Emmanuele; composing his face, he tried to extract himself from the pool with dignity.

Ralston and Sir Peter swam together without speaking. They were followed by Raikes, the Head of Chancery. Raikes had been in charge all morning and looked as if he might disintegrate at any moment; his frantic backstroke was doubtless a release. Still grim-faced, the three climbed from the pool and the butler distributed apéritifs. Lady Molly broke the silence. 'For God's sake, you three, stop looking so funereal and tell us something.' She was well used to crises; Kemble's admiration for her increased at every turn.

The Ambassador waved a deferential hand at Ralston. 'Here's the man you'd better speak to, dear, he's the one who's kept us going this morning. I'm right out of my depth. Tell her, Dennis.' The shared ordeal had brought them to Christian-name terms.

Ralston accepted the compliment unsmilingly and turned to his hostess. His face was drawn, and Kemble was surprised how the man seemed reduced by his nakedness and disarranged hair. 'Lady Molly, there is almost no chance that the King is still alive. I and my men have just been examining some fragments of the wreckage brought by helicopter from the *Dalkeith*. The plane which exploded is the one I brought to Rome. The Navy are flying me out there this afternoon for confirmation but that is just a formality. The search goes on of course, but no survivors have been found.' He signalled to the butler for a second gin and tonic. 'I need hardly tell you what it means to me that this should have happened in a Herakles plane.'

Sir Peter cut in: 'He insists on taking the responsibility but it already looks as if there was another hand in this.'

'Whatever do you mean, dear?' Lady Molly was suspicious of dramatic statements.

'The Swanstar was sabotaged, for one thing.'

'It's not certain,' Ralston said.

'Damn nearly. Dennis here noticed it first and Stocks —he's the chief pilot—agrees. So someone wanted the King to change planes.'

'Or wanted a delay,' Ralston said. 'It could have been just that.'

'Could have been, could have been, but probably wasn't,' Sir Peter replied, and added with a smile: 'I never did meet a man so keen to grant the benefit of the doubt.' He turned back to his wife. 'But that's only the half of it, Molly—there's worse to come.'

'Let's have it then,' she said dryly.

'The crash, that wasn't caused by a mechanical fault either.'

'*May* not have been,' Ralston said.

Sir Peter looked exasperated. 'Surely you're not still asking us to believe that what happened to the Witch was an accident, Dennis. You yourself told me it is extremely rare for a plane to explode like that, to completely disintegrate before it hits the ground. And this is the first time a Witch has crashed, right?'

'True, but—'

'Stop blaming yourself, stop blaming Herakles, and face the truth; that plane was meant to explode. Now come and have some lunch.'

They walked over to the table and Lady Molly began to serve the tortellini. The ambassadorial appetite seemed to have survived the morning undiminished but Raikes and Ralston asked for small helpings; Kemble wondered what would happen to the left-overs.

They sat down under the parasols and Lady Molly said: 'But who would want to kill the King?'

Sir Peter was prevented by a mouthful of pasta from answering a question he had obviously been waiting for, and Ralston got there first. 'It is not at all clear, Lady Molly, that the King was murdered. Deliberately murdered, that is. If *both* planes were sabotaged—and no one can yet be certain that they were—then, I admit, it's possible the King was the target. But it's also possible, particularly if the damage to the Swanstar was an accident, that the King was the victim of an attempt with a different purpose.'

'What purpose?' Anne said.

'An attempt on me, and—unintentionally—your father. And on the plane itself.'

Lady Molly looked really incredulous. 'Kill Peter? And you, Mr. Ralston? Who would want to do that?'

Sir Peter swallowed the stubborn mouthful and waved his spoon at his wife. 'Silvestri,' he shouted, '—that's who.'

'Him!' Kemble exclaimed.

'Yes, him,' Sir Peter said. 'He was at the airport this morning, remarkably forewarned. Offered a Cavaliere to fly the King home. He's a Fascist, you know, no friend of ours, and quite unscrupulous. The country's full of them, people who've never forgotten the war, the communists have kept them on the boil . . .'

'Now just a minute, Peter,' said Lady Molly, 'calm down and explain yourself.' She had not seen her husband like this for many years. Where was the old caution, the hesitations and the measured phrases? If she had not known what the situation was she would have said he was enjoying himself. The morning had obviously been a strain; she wondered if he was all right.

Raikes intervened, speaking for the first time with nervous puzzlement. 'I must say, sir, I don't quite follow your drift. What exactly are you accusing Silvestri of?'

Before the Ambassador could reply Ralston was speaking, with the usual reasoning power and something like the old authority. 'Allow me to clarify things a bit. As you have already heard, the Witch could have been sabotaged, but in my view this could not have been done at Naples

157

Airport this morning. The plane was only there for a short time and the crew never left it. An act of sabotage—say, the planting of a bomb—could however have been carried out earlier, at Ciampino Airport, where, I confess, the plane was not as closely guarded as it might have been. Today the Witch was due to give a series of demonstration flights to some high-ranking officers and technicians of the Italian services. Now the aircraft business is a field of the most ruthless competition, Lady Molly, and I could tell you of practices by some of our competitors which you might find it hard to believe. Where a large government purchase is at stake, such as the one now contemplated for the Italian army, the competition is if possible even hotter. I have come across bribery, electronic eavesdropping, falsification of documents and on one occasion, in Saudi Arabia, we believe that the Herakles agent was murdered.' Ralston paused to sip his wine and nobody spoke. The water in the pool was still, no longer slopping at the sides.

'In these circumstances,' Ralston continued, 'sabotage does become a possibility. Someone may well have wished to ensure that those demonstration flights did not take place —or, possibly, that one of them ended in disaster. General Di Sarto and I were due to make the first run at six.'

'And you are competing here with the Silvestri Corporation?' Kemble said.

'Silvestri is only one among several firms who have a fairly equal chance of securing the contract. I would hesitate to point the finger.'

'So it's likely the Witch was sabotaged and possible that Silvestri did it.'

' "Likely" and "possible"—yes, that's about it. No more than that.'

The butler refilled their glasses from the straw-covered flask. The rest of the buffet was growing cold in the shade and flies were settling on the pears.

'What about this business in Naples then?' Raikes said.

Ralston's brow knotted. 'That is much more puzzling. Silvestri was there, and he is in thick with the Airport Commandant; also his movements around that time are a bit of a mystery. To put the best interpretation on it, he discovered on arrival at the airport that the Swanstar was damaged, saw the chance of a publicity coup, briefed the Commandant and tried to make his offer to fly the King look unrehearsed. If you want to take a blacker view, he deliberately caused the damage in the hope his plane would be used.'

'That's my bet,' said Sir Peter, wishing to recover the centre of the stage. 'I tell you, he was desperately anxious that the King fly in the Cavaliere, desperately. Of course, if he knew the Witch was sabotaged, that would explain it.'

'Without wishing to underrate Silvestri's capacity for villainy,' Ralston said, 'I still don't think he sabotaged the Swanstar.'

'Why?' Kemble said.

'Simply because the plane was very difficult to get at. The crew hover round it all the time, never let it out of their sight. Of course for one of them it would have been easy . . .'

'But that's preposterous,' said Lady Molly. 'It's the King's flight, they are picked men.'

'I agree it's improbable, the whole thing's improbable.' Suddenly Ralston looked tired, and Kemble glimpsed the self-control working behind the calm exterior.

It seemed a bad moment to add to the burdens of the day, but Kemble decided his contribution could wait no longer. 'Everybody seems to be ruling out one explanation: that Silvestri was after the King.'

'Oh, surely, that's quite out of court,' said Raikes, drawing on his ample reservoir of sporting metaphors.

'I doubt if he would go that far,' echoed the Ambassador, some of whose equilibrium had returned.

As usual it was Ralston who supplied the logical objection: 'How could he have foreseen the King would be travelling in the Witch?'

'I agree, he couldn't. He might have transferred his bomb from the Cavaliere to the Witch at the last moment. Or more likely it was in the King's luggage.'

Ralston smiled. 'The first of those suggestions implies connivance by my staff, the second by the King's. I think you're getting carried away, young man.'

'Well, there's one thing you should know,' Kemble said. 'We met Silvestri on our flight from London. He was returning from talks with Coper, the M.P., who makes components for the Cavaliere, and we all know what his views are. That man would go to any lengths to stop an operation against Rhodesia. I happen to have first-hand information that Coper is more or less deranged on the subject and takes a pretty light-hearted view of the constitution. If he thought it would serve his purposes he might have wanted to delay or stop the King returning. Assassination's hardly his line, but perhaps the plan misfired.'

Raikes said: 'In my opinion that's a wide.'

Ralston said: 'Silvestri's a businessman, he would never involve himself in that kind of thing.'

Sir Peter said: 'You've been too long in Fleet Street, my boy. Still, London should know about Silvestri's visit and that's interesting about Coper's firm. Raikes, you'd better go with Kemble and get a telegram off immediately while the rest of us have a coffee and try to forget about this business for a moment. All this speculation will get us nowhere. The Investigation Commission will be at work in Naples by this evening. Harvey's put the Lord Chancellor in charge; I knew him at Cambridge, he'll soon have the answer.'

As Raikes and Kemble rose to leave, the door to the pool opened and Longden, who had stood by in Chancery during the lunch-hour, arrived with a message for the Ambassador. 'Wing-Commander Stocks has just telephoned from Naples, sir, to say there's been another accident.'

'Oh no!' said Lady Molly. 'What is it this time?' Ralston and Sir Peter looked at the young Third Secretary with resignation. The day could bring no worse shocks.

'One of the King's Flight stewards, a sergeant, has been found dead. His neck was broken. He seems to have fallen from the roof of the terminal building, but they're wondering—'

'Yes,' Sir Peter said, 'I can imagine what they're wondering. Thank you, Longden.'

160

3 pm

'So that's how things stand, Alan. Wellsuch has agreed, and so has Hanckleigh for the Liberals. The Lord Chancellor said he would ring back. But we're strong enough already. Too many peers for modern taste, but at a time like this that won't matter. There'll be a great deal to do in the next few days and I'm counting on you to help me do them. Glad I remembered you were at Eton today. The spare room's free, you could move in here at once.'

Alan Selkirk sat back on the sofa, half-tired, wholly astonished. After the lurid excitements of the morning he had looked forward to a quiet gossipy lunch at Eton. Trumper's cook and his conversation were both prized by connoisseurs. But instead of chatting about the short-comings of his colleagues Trumper had shattered Selkirk with the news of the King's death. Then over the rack of lamb Betty had announced that Lord Thorganby was on the telephone. Would Selkirk please come at once to Eaton Place? Selkirk had thought that there must be a connection between the two events and as he urged the red Sunbeam up the M.4 had wondered what it was. Now he knew. 'But, sir, surely the King must have changed his views very suddenly? I thought—'

'Yes, so did I. But the point is, he did change them. I read the script myself and it is conclusive evidence.'

Selkirk thought of Coper's wild talk in this house two nights before. Thorganby had listened sympathetically then, and now it was coming true. He said: 'You've heard about Coper, sir? It looks as if he may have been pretty deeply involved in the shooting at Oxford yesterday. The police are questioning him in hospital.'

'Indeed? I didn't know that. I've often warned him against violence. You see I haven't put him in the list of Ministers.' Thorganby spoke as if Coper was an irrelevance. Selkirk thought his tone was unconvincingly off-hand. Coper speaking openly at dinner for a royal coup, Coper talking privately to Thorganby on this very sofa, Coper with rifles in his house. . . . And what about the script? The script was only evidence of the King's views if he himself had written or approved it. Could Courthope have had time to get in touch with Coper as soon as he heard of the King's death, concoct the script with him on the telephone and sell it to the Prince as genuine? Coper, Courthope, and possibly Thorganby—were they responding to events or making them? Selkirk tried to concentrate on what his employer was saying.

'. . . I'll write the letter of acceptance now and you can take it round to the Palace.' Thorganby sat down at the desk, which was still covered with bills. 'While I'm writing, would you look through these letters and see if there's anything that needs doing at once?'

Selkirk sorted the pile quickly. Before he had finished the telephone rang on the sofa by the door. When he lifted the receiver the line went dead while the caller put in sixpence, then a gravelly voice which he recognised asked to speak to Lord Thorganby. 'I think it's the C.G.S., sir, but he's calling from a public box.'

Lord Thorganby came to the telephone. 'Thorganby here. Ah yes, Roger, what can I do for you? . . . Yes, I'm afraid there's no doubt. Announcement at four, I believe. . . . Thank you very much, I felt I couldn't stay on. . . . No, no, your position is quite different, you certainly can't leave, it would be quite wrong, and in any case there have been later developments. . . . No, I'm sorry, I can't say more now. But as regards the big party tomorrow, the invitations may after all have to be cancelled. Do you follow me? . . . Yes, cancelled. . . . No, I really can't explain, but I promise to ring you again this evening—around seven, I hope. . . . Right, at your office. Good-bye and thank you.'

Replacing the receiver Thorganby said, more to himself than to Selkirk: 'Poor man. It will be no fun unscrambling Constable at eight hours' notice.' Thorganby returned smiling to his desk, sealed the envelope, addressed it 'Personal. H.M. The King' and handed it to Selkirk.

4 pm

Like figures in a Romantic painting, each one fixed in a
stylised position of respect or grief, they clustered round
the portable radio to hear the announcement that the
King was dead. 'God rest his soul,' said Sergeant Fairbrother
and removed his hat. The woman who had brought the
radio started to sob and ran back to her kitchen. The farm-
hands said nothing, and the tableau stayed as it was for
several seconds longer.

The cottage was on the high land about four miles out
of Burford on the Chipping Norton road and belonged
to the Coper farm. The old police Wolseley was parked on
a dirt track running in from the road along the cottage's
garden wall and leading to a wooden barn half hidden
by a clump of trees. C.I.D. had phoned from the Coper house
to say that since the Burford police were fully occupied,
would Witney send a couple of men to search the farm?
Sergeant Fairbrother considered the mission a waste of
time and had ordered the young constable to inspect the
barn while he stayed at the cottage.

Now the constable reappeared at the edge of the trees
beckoning with an exaggerated gesture and shouting something inaudible. Tacking carefully across the rock-hard
ruts, Sergeant Fairbrother took the Wolseley up to the
barn and they went inside. The constable showed what had
caught his attention: a loft floor patched with new planks
and a trap-door secured by a new padlock, tyre tracks on
the barn floor. Together they broke open the trap-door and
climbed into the loft, where they found twenty-three soldiers
sleeping in full battle order behind a wall of bales, snoring
some of them; lying in pools of vomit; and a sweet metallic
smell over everything. Sergeant Fairbrother recognised the
badge as that of the Grenadier Guards. Bending down he
started to shake a man by the shoulder, but he would not
wake.

4.10 pm

As Selkirk crossed the Palace yard in the bright sunshine he decided to walk back to Eaton Place. He was glad that the patrolling guardsmen and police did not react as he passed between them (still wearing his sports jacket) because he would not have known how to return a salute.

What a place! An impregnable fortress of protocol, where even the clocks seemed to clear their throats before striking. . . . As he walked through the gates in the high iron railings and out into the noisy, grubby, untidy world of ordinary mortals he was seized by a feeling of relief—the air seemed lighter, easier to breathe—and his step quickened.

The Prince—King, rather—was not surprisingly *incommunicado*. Selkirk had delivered the letter to Sir James Courthope, and he now reflected on his encounter with this little-known but powerful figure. A tall man, without an ounce of redundant flesh (nobody stays that thin without will-power) and still tanned from the holiday in Ravello, the brown skin emphasising the grey temples, the well-kept teeth, the brilliantly white stiff collar. And fashionably dressed; the traces of contemporary style were just sufficient, nicely judged, for a man of his age. The man was ridiculously good-looking, a caricature Englishman, the sort the British Travel Association liked to photograph against a background of clubland leather.

The manner fitted the looks, diffident but decisive. When Selkirk had handed him the letter he had said, looking at the sports jacket as if it were a genuinely curious object: 'You're Thorganby's Private Secretary, and this is his reply. Affirmative, I take it.'

'Yes, sir.'

Courthope's eyes were a pale shade of grey, with fair lashes. They were almost opaque, anything but a window on the soul—but now lit with a glimmer of satisfaction. 'Good. In that case we'll go ahead with the broadcast as it is. You can tell Lord Thorganby there is nothing to do now until after Harvey's audience at six, when we shall be in touch. I need hardly remind you of the need for absolute secrecy until then.'

It was easy to see how the man had got the job. Technological revolution or no, if you looked and talked like Sir James Courthope you could still do almost anything in England: cash cheques without a driving licence, walk past doormen, penetrate the concentric circles of the Establishment until you arrived at the heart. It would be hard for the new young monarch to resist advice from such a source. But what would the advice be? The anxiety which had nibbled at Selkirk's mind all that day took another large bite.

When he reached the house in Eaton Place he found a man on the doorstep about to press the bell.

'Mr. Selkirk? Pleased to meet you. I'm a friend of Jack Kemble's.'

Pale face and red hair; shiny suit over a dark blue button-down shirt and red tie. Scottish. 'Journalist' written all over him. Careful, Selkirk.

'Name's Hollis, Assistant Editor of the *Globe*.'

'Good afternoon, Mr. Hollis. What can I do for you? I'm afraid Lord Thorganby's not available at the moment.'

'No, it's you I came to see. I've heard from Jack Kemble in Rome. He thought you might be interested and said I would probably find you here.'

'I thought you people had dispensed with Kemble.'

'Yes, well, it was all rather unfortunate. Pressure of the moment. He did a daft thing, mind you—but I dare say in normal times we wouldn't have been quite so severe. Perhaps when this Rhodesia business is over . . .'

'And he's still in touch?'

'Yes. I doubt if it's brotherly love. After a time in this profession, Mr. Selkirk, it's hard to adopt an ordinary citizen's attitude to public events. The lad's not working for anyone else yet, he wants to know the truth and is hoping we will find it. Here's his telegram, sent this afternoon—you may like to read it. He was obliged to be somewhat cryptic.'

FUNNY GOINGS ON HERE STOP POSSIBLE SOMEONE CLIPPED

SWANS WINGS TOOK WITCHES BROOM STOP QUESTION IS
WHO STOP SUGGEST INVESTIGATE BARNETTS BUSINESS
VISITOR FROM ABROAD TUESDAY CONTACT SELKIRK CHEZ
THORGANBY YOURS AYE JACK

'Got a nice turn of phrase, hasn't he?' Hollis said.

Selkirk handed the telegram back and said: 'Mr. Hollis, I
think you and I had better take a turn round the square.'

Hollis smiled for the first time. 'I should enjoy that.'

They began to walk side by side, stepping off the pavement
now and then for a passing nanny and pram. Selkirk's face
was a picture of anxiety. 'Of course, you must realise—' he
began.

But Hollis held up a friendly hand and cut him short. 'I
know, you're in a delicate position. We all are. Kemble's the
guest of a British Ambassador, I work for a major national
newspaper—and whatever else the British Press may be, it's
highly cautious on the subject of royalty. We're miles away
from printing anything yet. So don't worry, I shan't let you
down, I've been in this game for years.' He offered a miniature
cigar and Selkirk, who never smoked, took one gratefully.
'Meanwhile I think we all have a responsibility to discover the
truth in this matter, don't you?'

'Kemble is suggesting sabotage.'

'He is indeed. There's nothing peculiar in that. Everyone's wondering the same thing and there's bound to be
speculation in all the Press tomorrow. But coming from
him, in view of where he is, the suggestion has a particular
interest.'

' "Barnett" is presumably Coper. Who was the business
visitor?'

'Silvestri, an aircraft manufacturer from Naples. Coper's
firm supplies them with components for a plane rather like
the Witch. Silvestri and Coper had a private meeting on
Tuesday morning and Silvestri flew back that night. We
talked to Coper's secretary in Wolverhampton—she was
quite free with the information—but I'm damned if I see
how we can take this any further. Why did Kemble want
me to talk to you?'

Selkirk considered revealing the conversation at Thorganby's dinner but decided against it. He had been confirmed in one preposterous suspicion that day; to try it again would be tempting fate. 'Kemble knows I've met Coper once or twice. I expect he thought I might have inside information.'

'And do you?'

'No. Of course the man's a fanatical extremist, just how much so is becoming clear with these discoveries at Burford. But from what I know it's simply a question of the Movement having more teeth than people believed. I saw Coper early this morning, and I seriously doubt if he deliberately planned to cause those casualties in Oxford. He may have overrated the opposition and thought he had to defend himself.'

Hollis turned the corners of his mouth down in a gesture of disbelief. 'They found rifles in his house, you know.'

'Yes, I know they found rifles'—Selkirk was glad to learn the police had kept his name out of it—'but they hadn't been used. And as for this other business, Coper's a patriot, he wouldn't try anything against the King. What good would it do him anyway?'

'Maybe the King supported Harvey.'

'Nobody knows what the King's views were.' Selkirk hoped the lie rang true. 'Tell me, how's that guardsman they found in Oxford—Steele?'

'Picking up, and he's started giving descriptions. It seems they sprung him from the barracks and were holding him at the house. He made a run for it in Oxford but they clobbered him before he could talk. I expect they thought he was finished.'

'He must have an iron skull. I'm glad he pulled through.'

'The police are looking for a man called Rackstraw, a cashiered major from the Paras—apparently he was running the show. We'll be getting a photograph tonight. There was a Frenchman, too, but he's giving a bit of trouble.'

They had reached the door of the house again and Selkirk signalled to Hollis to walk a little farther, out of the chauffeur's earshot. 'Now I have something to ask you, Mr. Hollis,' he said. 'Tell me what you know about Sir James Courthope.'

'The King's P.S.? Tory, standard model. Right of centre, I

would say. *Tribune* occasionally have a crack at him.
I expect the poor young heir is putty in his hands.'

"And as a man?'

'Fine war record, all that. His wife left him not long
ago—that was a bit of a black—and there were rumours.'

'What sort of rumours?'

'Oh the usual Fleet Street dirt. He was friendly with
that peer arrested in France, and there was something
about a soldier in Hyde Park. Nothing ever came of it.
Why do you ask?'

'Just curious.' Selkirk looked towards the house. 'Well,
I must go. Thank you for calling, and let me know if
Jack Kemble comes up with more.'

They shook hands and Selkirk went inside. The study was
empty and for what seemed a long time he sat with his
head in his hands, trying to shake the kaleidoscope into a
pattern. He could not think it out alone; he needed an ally. He
wished he had talked more freely to Hollis, who seemed
a sober sort of chap. He picked up the telephone and
called the *Globe*, but only ten minutes had passed and
Hollis had not come in yet. Selkirk left a message asking
Hollis to call at his flat on the way home. That would
be about midnight, he was told. No matter; Thorganby would
keep him late and in his present state sleep would not
be easy. . . .

'Ah, Alan. Glad to see you back. Message delivered
safely?'

Selkirk jumped at the sound of the familiar voice. 'Yes,
sir, I handed it personally to Sir James.' Lord Thorganby had
bathed and was wearing his best suit; the eyes in the
weathered face were glinting with an excitement which
Selkirk had not seen there before. He wished he could
share his master's enthusiasm for the new adventure.

Thorganby looked at his watch. 'We must get ready for
this broadcast. Warm the TV up, will you, and let me know
when it starts.'

4.50 pm

The Military Police Lieutenant put down the telephone and grinned at the bloodshot, half-closed eye watching him through the slit in the bandages.

'Got some good news for you, Steele.' He shouted the words slowly as if he were talking to a senile foreigner. Steele intended to say: 'All right, mate, I can hear you,' but it came out as an incomprehensible whisper. The officer leaned down and shouted again in his ear. 'That was Scotland Yard. The blood on your boot—it wasn't Reith's. So you're in the clear. Get that, did you? I'll say it again.'

And he said it again. Steele smiled to show that the message was received and looked around the room. The C.I.D. were reading *The Carpetbaggers*. Things were looking up. He closed his eye and drifted back to sleep, lulled by the choir of gnats singing in his head.

5 pm

In five million rooms the crash of the 'National Anthem' was followed by a silence, then an unfamiliar face on the screen, and a high, unformed, occasionally unsteady voice.

'At this hour today the King was to have spoken to you. You will have heard already that he died this morning over the Mediterranean. We do not yet know how or why. It is not for me to tell you what kind of man he was. Others will do this more eloquently than I can. I will only say that he put his duty to his subjects before everything else, and that today I, his successor, ask for strength to do the same.

'When he died the King was returning to England to speak to you about the crisis through which we are passing. Yesterday, during the last hours of his life, he wrote down what he intended to say to you, and I have decided to read his words to you this evening. Please remember as I speak that these are not my opinions but his, formed out of his experience and wisdom. On my

169

own account I will only say this: I accept the judgments handed down to me in these tragic circumstances and will act upon them.

'The King would have spoken to you as follows. I read from the actual script:

' "We in this country have all our lives taken political argument for granted. We are used to political parties which criticise and sometimes abuse each other. We are used to strong disagreements about policies and personalities. We have habitually accepted those things because they occur within a settled framework of democracy, law and order. We knew, or thought we knew, that controversy would not go beyond certain bounds, that the framework in which we all live would not be challenged. This has been our heritage.

' "But this time it is not so. Now, for the first time in our lives, political argument in this country has broken its natural bounds. Servants of the Crown are no longer obeying without question the orders of the Government. People are killing and being killed for their political opinions. How has this disaster come about? It has happened because the present Government has allowed itself to be persuaded into a policy of sending British troops to Rhodesia, a policy which is passionately opposed by a very large number of people —according to my information, by a majority of the country. I do not doubt the sincerity of those who believe this course to be right. Indeed I know them to be able and honest men. But they have pushed beyond the normal bounds of controversy, they are tearing the country apart. If they are allowed to persist in these policies we may well find that though they may not wish it they will finally destroy the framework of order which is the basis of British life and the envy of other lands. Already it is badly shaken. There are many countries in which the grenade, the rifle, the knuckle-duster are the ordinary way of expressing a political opinion; I do not think that any of us want Britain to become one of them. Yet in the last few days we have moved far along that path.

' "What in this situation is the duty of the Crown? In normal times the King stands above politics. He can warn and encourage his Ministers in private, but when they reach a decision he accepts it without demur. He does not take sides between political parties. He does not make controversial speeches. He leads a life largely made up of ceremony and formal routine.

' "But it was not always so. Before our political life settled down into the orderly framework which I have described, the King was at the centre of political life. It was the King who chose the Ministers, and dismissed them if they failed. This royal prerogative has not been used for more than a century; it has not been needed. But it still exists, it is still the law of the land, it is part of our constitution.

' "I have always believed that in an emergency, rather than see the country tear itself apart, or drift into some terrible disaster, it might be the duty of a King to use the old prerogatives. After long and anxious thought I have decided that such an emergency is now upon us. The Government has completely lost touch with the wishes of the people. It is no longer in control of events. It can no longer perform its basic task of keeping order. It is in fact no longer a government in any real sense. In moments of grave danger—in 1916, in 1931, and again in 1940—Britain has turned to National Governments, drawn from all major parties. History has shown this to be a sound instinct. I ask you to believe that the danger is equally grave today. This time, as I have explained, it falls to me, as your King, to give the lead.

' "I have therefore decided, using my royal prerogative, to require the immediate resignation of Mr. Harvey, and to establish a National Government, including representatives of all three parties. The task of this National Government will be to design and follow policies which will unite the nation. This must of course include abandoning the plan to invade Rhodesia. The National Government will be required to submit itself in the normal way to both Houses of Parliament when these resume their work in October.

' "The step which I am taking is a grave one. It is I believe justified by the danger through which the Kingdom is now passing. It can only succeed with the loyal help of you all, and I therefore ask you tonight for that help. I ask you to agree with me that only if we are no longer distracted by political strife, only if we are steady and united, can we hope to bring Britain safely out of the nightmare of these last weeks."

'Those were the words of the King, written by him yesterday at Ravello in Italy. I wish merely to add that in accordance with his wishes I am this evening sending for the Earl of Thorganby, whom I will ask to form a National Government. Good night.'

5.15 pm

'Good for him,' said Mrs. Kemble. 'That's just what those politicians deserved.'

'So back to the Middle Ages we go,' said Joe Hollis. 'What about Home Rule for Scotland while we're about it?'

'We've needed that for a long time,' said the Editor of the *Globe*. 'I tell you the country is crying out for leadership.'

'Extraordinary,' said Jane Richardson.

'This changes the whole picture,' said Ryder Bennett.

'You can say what you like, sir, I find it hard to believe the King would have used those words,' said Alan Selkirk.

'You're wrong, Alan,' said Lord Thorganby. 'That was the true voice of the nation. It always makes itself heard in the end, it's just that the manner was unusual.'

'My prayers are answered,' said Barnett Coper. 'Now you bobbies can do your worst.'

'I think he's quite right, don't you, Lieutenant?' said Mrs. Steele.

'Let's say I'm relieved, Mrs. Steele,' said the Lieutenant.

'Someone should tell him about the Stuarts,' said Sir Charles Melton.

'I shall resign,' said Hooper, knowing that he wouldn't.

'The British have gone mad,' said the Tanzanian delegate. 'For years they give away their empire without fuss, then they go mad.'

'Magnificent,' said Michael Critten.

'If I may say so, that was a masterful performance,' said Sir James Courthope, but the Prince did not reply.

'I shan't be able to look my African friends in the face,' said Anne Downes.

'I agree—it's a damn disgrace,' said Jack Kemble to his own surprise.

'It'll hit them for six,' said Raikes, not sure who he meant by 'them.'

'I thought it was rather fine,' said Lady Molly.

'You would,' said her husband. 'It's going to present some ticklish problems, I can tell you.'

'Operation completed,' said Major Rackstraw. 'We can take that flight to B.A. tomorrow.'

'We've run out of beer,' said Meredith.

Patrick Harvey said nothing.

As the drums rolled again for the National Anthem, he pressed the 'off' switch on the remote control. He sat in the green arm-chair and gazed at the spot of light in the centre of the screen until it disappeared, and did not notice his wife leave the study.

The broadcast had not come as a surprise. Not quite. The text had reached him by special messenger fifteen minutes before the Prince came on. As soon as he had read it he had telephoned Courthope, but his anger had exploded in vain against that chilly, well-prepared calm. Courthope had explained that he had not been at liberty to discuss the broadcast that morning because the Prince had not then formed his own view. He regretted the delay in sending the special messenger, but the final decision on the broadcast had only been taken a short time before. They were of course still expecting him at the Palace at six, and he might like to know in confidence that he would be offered the Garter.

Harvey had immediately summoned Joynson. A girl had explained that Mr. Joynson had gone out to buy a packet of cigars. Uncharacteristically Harvey had sworn at her, then told her to get the B.B.C. and the I.T.V. on the telephone. She had fussed unhappily over the unfamiliar buttons on the receiver, and the carriage clock on the desk, always kept

173

scrupulously to time, had struck five before the first call came through. Harvey had motioned the girl away and switched on the television; by the time it warmed up the Prince was already speaking. His wife had come in and stood silently behind him.

Somehow it had sounded worse, more definite and unchallengeable when spoken than on paper. Without moving from the arm-chair, Harvey rang again for Joynson, and this time he appeared, the band still on the cigar drooping unlit from his mouth.

Harvey pointed at the offending screen. 'You saw it?'

'Yes, in the other room, except for the first few words.'

'The King never wrote that script.'

Joynson took the cigar from his mouth and examined it for a few seconds as if surprised to find it there. 'Can you prove that?' he asked.

'No, of course not. It just rang false. It must have been Courthope. He's clever enough. He had time this morning to invent the script as soon as he heard the King was dead, and sell it to Thorganby and the Prince as genuine.'

'He must have worked quickly. A crazy chance to take. And what was his motive?'

'I don't know—political, I suppose. He's a buttoned-up sort of man. Anything might be going on beneath that surface. Anyway, he's the only one who could have done it.'

'Look here, sir.' Joynson had never called the Prime Minister 'sir' before. He sat down heavily on the desk, knocking sideways the signed photograph of Mr. Macmillan. 'You've got no proof of this, no evidence at all, you can't even suggest a plausible motive. At this moment every voter in the country's crying his eyes out in front of the telly. By tonight there'll be no Kleenex left in the Kingdom. It was the best soap-opera since *Oliver Twist*. If you start claiming it was a hoax they'll be up here in droves to tear you limb from limb. Or they'll say you've gone mad, and there's enough saying that already.'

Harvey looked at the shapeless tweeded hulk of his Press Secretary with disgust. 'So you want me to give in?'

'Of course I don't.' Joynson jabbed at an ashtray. 'I'd give my pension to have it different. But you've no choice.'

'We'll see about that.' Harvey was carried along by his anger. He pressed a button on the desk. 'Get me the Lord Chancellor, the Leader of the Opposition and the Foreign Secretary in that order. But first bring in that last police report from Oxford.'

Ten minutes later Harvey was making the last of the three calls.

'. . . So you see, Ryder, it's quite clear that the so-called mass defection from the Grenadiers was in fact a mass kidnapping. The mutiny at Chelsea was not genuine, nor was the riot at Oxford. There was a conspiracy behind them all and Coper led the conspiracy. All we need now is a link between Courthope and Coper. . . . Yes, I tried this out on the Lord Chancellor, but he wasn't interested. Said it was speculation; said if asked he would have to admit that the King's constitutional argument was sound; said he thought his own office should in a sense be above politics. I asked him point-blank if that meant he would serve under Thorganby and he said he's already given his word. Think of the trouble I took over that man this morning. . . . What's that? Garrigan? Yes, I've just tracked him down. Sounded very upset. Said he'd called a Shadow Cabinet for tonight. He hadn't been approached and wouldn't serve under Thorganby, but he knew Wellsuch had accepted and probably two or three others on his side. Said he couldn't stop them. I asked him to come with me to the Palace, but he wouldn't. . . . So there we are, Ryder, it's check but I hope not checkmate. I must go to the Palace now. I'll try and talk the Prince out of it. In any case I shall tell him it's far too late to countermand Constable now, that the operation's virtually started and must go ahead tomorrow as planned if there's not to be total confusion. . . . Thorganby did *what*? . . . Countermanded? But that's outrageous! What authority did he have? . . . I see, I see. . . . I never expected to hear you say that. You've changed. You used to be the bravest of us all. Oh well, it's late. I must go. Good-bye.'

Harvey turned away from the desk. His face, then his body seemed to sag as the anger left him. He did not look directly at Joynson. 'The Foreign Secretary agrees with you. And the C.G.S. has suspended Constable already, after talking to Thorganby.' Then, in a final outburst: 'You really all believe the King wrote that rubbish?'

'It simply doesn't matter since 5.15 what the old King did or didn't do,' said Joynson. 'The new King has put his seal on it now, and that's that.'

Harvey almost collided with his wife outside the study; she carried a clothes-brush. She said: 'I've telephoned Blackheath and warned them to air the flat. The cases should be packed by the time you get back from the Palace.' She sounded neither happy nor unhappy. Harvey hoped for some kind of comforting gesture but she hurried away down the landing.

5.45 pm (6.45 pm, Italy)

WEDNESDAY

Villa Wolkonsky,
Via Conte Rosso 25,
Rome.

Dearest Alan,

Well here we are in Rome. V. hot and Jack's a hopeless tanner, but lovely food etc. Often think if the poor old taxpayer could see this he might have something to say!

Isn't it awful about the King? Everyone here's in a frightful flap, as you can imagine. Mad rush for black dresses, then the F.O. said no mourning. Was rather disappointed. It's just that he was so good and it's so sad, one felt like making a gesture. I expect a lot of you back there are wondering if it was an accident. Daddy's sealed my lips of course (only he could do it!) but—well, it didn't look much like an accident, did it?

We've just been listening to the Prince. Quite a speech. Daddy was flabbergasted—apparently no one *knew* the King thought like that. He doesn't believe the King would have made the speech just as it was, says it puts Harvey in an impossible position. So I suppose we'll now see a battle royal between No. 10 and the Palace. (Has this ever happened before? I see what you mean about the British constitution.) I hope Harvey sticks to his guns, but it's going to be horribly difficult for him, isn't it, on a jingoistic issue with everyone so starry-eyed about the Monarchy and fed up with politicians?

Poor Alan, I can guess what you think about it all. I really had no idea you civil servants worried so much about these things. I thought you were all supposed to be impartial and in the end they made you like that whether you wanted to be or not. Suspect most of them are, and you're the exception. You've always looked after the underdog, haven't you? I remember you would never let anyone bully me and when we had to go to those ghastly teen-age dances you were always abandoning some glamour-pot to get me off the wall.

What else? Oh yes, Ralston's here. You were quite right (again!) to tick me off for being rude to him—he's nice. He's been such a help to daddy in all this business and really they hardly know each other. Of course he's terribly upset that it should have happened in his plane, and you can see he's determined to get to the bottom of it. If it *wasn't* an accident, and he finds out who was responsible, I shudder to think what he will do. I'm sure he's the sort of man who once he sets his mind on something, always, always does it. Has a sort of quiet intensity about him which is rather terrifying—no, it's more than that, it's a sort of *dispassionate passion*. Very muddled! I'd never make a psychoanalyst, that's why they kept me on field-mice at Oxford. Oh, I found out one thing. He was married years ago, and lost his wife (polio, Mummy thinks) three months after the wedding. Perhaps that explains it—Herakles Aviation a wife-substitute etc. But fancy having a great empire like that and no one to do it all *for*. Really I do feel sorry for him.

Must fly. Jack's taking me to supper with some American friend—job hunting, I suspect.

Take care of yourself. It was lovely to see you again after all this time. Will be back in the autumn. Till then,

lots of love,

Anne.

P.S. Remember the underdogs!

7 pm

As she took the tonic out of the refrigerator Jane Richardson wondered what had come over Alan Selkirk. She had known him off and on for three years. They had served on an interdepartmental committee together, something to do with the International Wool Agreement, and this had led to lunchtime sandwiches at the Tate (once) and the National Film Theatre (twice). Then nothing more, except that they nodded and smiled when they passed each other in the street, till suddenly he had telephoned that afternoon to ask if she had been on duty the night before and invited himself for a drink.

The flat was in a filthy mess; she hadn't had time to clean it that day. Ashtrays overflowing from the night's vigil, and an unmade bed next door. But men never noticed these things, and in any case Alan Selkirk seemed to have a great deal on his mind.

She glanced at the mirror on her way back to the sitting-room. She was definitely putting on weight though still the plump side of fat. She looked closer. What a healthy, ordinary face she had. Unexciting brown hair, eyes ditto, and now a few lines sketching themselves in odd places. 'Kindly but shrewd' someone had once said of her eyes. The same someone had said she always looked as if she had just come in out of the rain. She was never sure if it had been a compliment. Did Alan Selkirk like outdoor-looking career girls with moderate tennis and moderate degrees?

As she put his drink on a little cork mat in front of the sofa Selkirk leant forward, hands on knees, in a gesture she remembered. His hair was getting thin. 'Look, Jane,' he said. 'You heard the Prince's broadcast?'

'Yes, I slipped away from the department and listened up here.'

'Well, I've a feeling it was bogus.'

'Bogus? But—'

'I know it's crazy, but then so's everything else just now.' He returned for a moment to his formal civil-servant

178

manner. 'You must forgive me if I don't tell you everything I know. I can't prove much, and it might conceivably be dangerous for you to know it. But I have a suspicion that either Courthope or Coper had a sudden brainwave this morning, and between them they invented that broadcast and foisted it on the Prince.'

'But that's fantastic.' Jane found that she was enjoying herself. This was better than the International Wool Agreement.

'Fantastic, certainly. But I want to establish how Courthope spent this morning. The point is, did he have long enough to cook the whole thing up? And when did he talk to Coper, who's in hospital in Oxford? It couldn't have been in the second half of the morning because by that time Coper wasn't available for private conversations. It must have been early, perhaps very early. I know that by soon after eight Courthope knew the King was dead. But how long had he known it? When did he first hear there were no survivors?'

Jane thought hard. 'I'm afraid you've gone wrong somewhere, Alan. Sir James Courthope didn't hear that till long after nine.'

'Nine! That can't be right. You must have muddled the times.'

Jane was nettled. No need for him to speak in that tone just because his theory was crumbling. She might be a girl, but she was still a Foreign Service Officer of ten years' standing, painfully trained in accuracy and clear thought.

'There were three messages,' she said slowly. 'The first said contact had been lost. The second said the tanker had reported an explosion in the air. I passed the two messages to Courthope at Windsor as well as to Number Ten, both early on. I forget the exact times, it was a great rush. But of course neither of these messages came anywhere near proving that the King was dead. The explosion might have been something else, or the King might have survived it. The hard news came in a message from the *Dalkeith*. I remember the time of that: 0825. It said it was the Witch which had exploded, and there were no survivors.'

'And you passed that to Courthope at once?'

'No, I didn't, that's the point. Ryder Bennett told me to show it first to the P.M. So I went down to the park door and handed it to him when he arrived. Then there was the meeting of Ministers in Ryder Bennett's room, which I went to. That went on till about 9.20. Then the P.M. left, saying he would ring Courthope. So Courthope could not possibly have known there were no survivors till about 9.30.'

'But he could have heard about the *Dalkeith* message from somewhere else. The signal would have come first to the Navy Department. He could have got it from them. Or Ryder Bennett could have phoned him while you were down at the park door.'

'No, Alan, it's no good. The Navy Department were under strict instructions from Ryder Bennett to pass anything about the King to me alone. And Ryder Bennett definitely relied on the P.M. to deal with Courthope. If he'd already spoken to him, he would have said. Besides, Courthope wouldn't have gone to collect the Prince without authority from the P.M., and I'm sure he didn't get that till 9.30.'

Selkirk looked at her as if he was going over her words again in his head, then said: 'Good God.'

'What do you mean, "Good God"?'

'Don't you see what this means?'

'Yes, of course. It means that Courthope had precious little time to have his brainwave, contact Coper and work out all the skulduggery you've credited to him.'

'No, no, no!' Selkirk banged down his glass. The gin and tonic spilled and overflowing the mat, fixed quietly on the polished surface of the table, 'It means something far worse. Look. Courthope went down to Eton between eight and nine, told the Prince the King was dead, and took him away. Took him away *"to begin his reign."* Those were the words he used. No "ifs" and "buts"; the King was dead, he said so well before nine o'clock. Now you tell me he couldn't have had that knowledge till nine-thirty. Either someone has the times wrong or Courthope knew in advance that the King was going to die.'

'Alan, you're running away with yourself. Courthope's

far too grand to be a madman or a crook. Someone's been pulling your leg.'

Selkirk did not seem to hear her laughter. 'Wait,' he said, 'I've just thought of something else. What the hell was he doing at Windsor at all?' He jumped up as he said this, and for a moment Jane thought he was going to grab her in his excitement. 'I should have thought of that before. His excuse for coming home ahead of the King, for not travelling in the plane that blew up, must have been that he had work to do: had to fix up the broadcast, or see Harvey, that sort of thing. But anything like that would have to be done in London. Then off he goes, not to Buckingham Palace, but to Windsor. That only makes sense if for some reason he wanted to be within five minutes of the Prince at Eton. Can you think of any other explanation?'

Jane was over by the window, looking down on her favourite view. The plane trees in the park carried their evening load of starlings and the angry jabber reached her over the noise of traffic. 'No,' she said, 'I can't. I must say it all looks rather odd.' Then she remembered something else. 'I was told to send a box of the latest telegrams over to the Palace at midnight so that Courthope could look at them when he got in. First thing this morning they rang from the Palace to say that he'd unexpectedly changed his plans and gone to Windsor, but didn't want the telegrams sent on.'

Selkirk moved quickly to the door and for a moment Jane thought he was not even going to say good-bye. Then he came back and kissed her clumsily on the cheek. 'Sorry about the lunacy,' he said, 'and keep it all to yourself.' She was too astonished to reply.

As he descended the painted halls of the Foreign Office, Selkirk remembered that he had left his Sunbeam outside Thorganby's house in Eaton Place. For some days now because of the demonstrations the police had forbidden parking in the neighbourhood of Whitehall. He found a taxi in Birdcage Walk. On the short drive he tried once again to bring his thoughts to order. It all rested on Trumper of course. But Trumper was a bit of a muddler. Could he be trusted to have got the time right? To a sleepy schoolmaster a clock striking eight was not all that different

181

from a clock striking nine. The first thing to do was to check Trumper's recollection. He could telephone Eton from Thorganby's study.

'Quiet tonight, guv'nor,' said the taxi driver. 'Perhaps we'll get some peace from now on with this National Government. My missus always said the old King would fix things up somehow. And so he has, poor man, in a manner o' speaking.'

8.30 pm (9.30 pm, Italy)

'I've heard a lot of theories today about what happened to that plane, but that one is the most darn stupid.'

Barry Tucker, Well-Dressed Bachelor and International Man from Boston, Massachusetts, *Washington Post* Correspondent in Rome and Assistant Correspondent of *The Times*, wiped the last traces of grilled *spigola* from his plate with a lump of bread, leaned back and repeated: 'Without doubt, the most darn stupid.' He had once worked for *Time-Life* in London and Kemble had been a fruitful contact. But it had been a purely working relationship, long since lapsed, and to Tucker this soliciting of his hospitality, the assumption of comradeship in the cheery phone call from the Embassy, seemed a typical piece of limey cheek. With the possible exception of *The Times* he considered the British Press inexcusably frivolous; likewise Kemble.

'Why so stupid?' Kemble said.

'Listen,' Tucker said, 'you are asking me to believe that Silvestri or one of the other aircraft corporations sabotaged the Witch to clinch the deal with the Italian Army. Well, to start with, those boys may be ruthless but they don't take unnecessary risks. They would never try a thing like that for a contract this size. As a proportion of their annual sales, it's peanuts.'

Anne leaned forward to interrupt. She disliked this man, with his studiously masculine manner and tales of high life in *Cinecittà*. 'Perhaps that's true for the American firms,' she said, 'but what about Silvestri? He's not so big, it might mean more to him.'

'You can rule Silvestri out,' Tucker said, 'and I'll tell you why. Two weeks ago Bethel, my boss—he's *The Times* Correspondent here—was wined and dined by General Di Sarto, who told him the Army have decided to buy the Dutch plane, the Fokker 284. We were not allowed to quote the source but obviously it was a deliberate leak. Our contact in the Ministry refused to deny it, and we think a provisional contract with Fokker may have been signed already. The Minister's in the General's pocket, his consent is just a formality.'

'Why don't they announce it then?' Anne said.

'These things take time in Italy, especially with a Coalition Government. There's a heck of a lot of hoops to go through: technical committees, official committees, Ministerial committees, the parties—the Christian Democrats may not like this one, they have a strong pro-American faction—and it might need Cabinet approval. It happens all the time, executive action running ahead of the legislature. It's the only way to get things done. The General was trying to be helpful, warning off the other firms before they mount too big a sales drive. North America got the message; they cut back on their effort at the Air Show.'

'*The Times* didn't print the story,' Kemble said.

'No, damn their eyes, they decided it was a rumour. Makes you wonder what correspondents are for. They checked the story with Herakles in London, who said that they had heard differently from a higher source. Apparently Ralston still thinks he has a chance, so to save hard feelings, the General's going on with the game. But Silvestri's sources are better—he knows he's licked.'

'Are you sure?' Kemble said.

'Bethel checked with old man Silvestri himself and he confirmed the Fokker deal. That good enough for you?'

They finished up the second bottle of Frascati and walked to Santa Maria in Trastevere. Anne gasped at the beauty of the square—it never failed to surprise her—but Kemble smoked and stared at the cobbles, lost in thought. The fountain splashed and glittered in the floodlights, Lambrettas and Vespas yapped at their heels, Anne was offered a tour of the city by a youth in a white suit. Tucker shepherded them across the piazza to a café in the corner and ordered three coffees.

Kemble emerged from his reverie. 'That's very interesting, what you say, Barry.'

'It's on the house,' Tucker said, smiling at Anne.

'It takes us back to square one.'

'Meaning?'

'Meaning that if the Witch wasn't got at for commercial reasons, someone was after the King.'

Tucker nodded, head, shoulders and all; all his mental steps were illustrated by a physical gesture. 'That's the way I figure it—but who? and why?'

'Tell me more about Silvestri. Is he only in the aircraft business?'

'Hell, no, he's got a finger in every pie—electronics, computers, refrigerators, steel. He's big in pipe, supplied a lot of it for the Trieste-Lvov gas pipeline, and he was in the consortium laying that pipe from Zambia to Tanzania.'

'Zambia-Tanzania? That was dropped, wasn't it?'

'Yes, too difficult to build. They had to go through some really hairy country and the schedule slipped, E.N.I. ran out of cash and tried to screw the World Bank for a bigger ante. But the Bank wouldn't have it, said that since the Multiracial Settlement the Zambians could get all the oil they needed through Rhodesia. So the project was dropped. They're still fighting about the compensation.'

Anne watched as Kemble leaned forward, taut. Dog scents rabbit. 'That must have hit Silvestri pretty hard.' Trying to keep the drama out of his voice.

'It did,' said Tucker. 'He was all tooled up to make miles of the stuff. There was talk that he would be swallowed up by I.R.I. but they baled him out with a share of the Russian pipeline.'

'Which is now finished.'

'Right.'

'So the best thing that could happen to Silvestri now is for the whites to win in Rhodesia. If that frontier is closed again, the Zambians will want oil from Tanzania. The King was opposed to the Rhodesian whites—'

Tucker threw back his head and roared with laughter.

"Oh that's great!' he cried and after another guffaw: 'Great!' As the laughter subsided to a chuckle he shook his head in elaborately feigned wonderment at Kemble and treated them to a further cadence of 'greats.'

'What's so funny?' Anne said.

Tucker banged the little iron table with the flat of his hand. 'Anne, you're a lucky girl; you are dating the second Ian Fleming, no less.' Again he howled with glee, then suddenly switched off the mirth and looked at Kemble with something approaching venom. 'You British kill me. The baddy's always got to be a foreigner, hasn't he? Wogs, wops, dagoes, Yanks, against the clean-limbed cricketing gent; Bulldog Drummond *contra mundum*. Come on, Jack, grow up. The party's over, it's a fairy-tale. I don't know who killed your King, but I tell you this—it wasn't poor old momma-loving, social-climbing Silvestri.'

Anne was pale with rage but Kemble smiled as the old Cromwellian quote came to mind. 'Barry, friend,' he said, 'I beseech you in the bowels of Christ, think it possible you may be mistaken.'

9.10 pm

Meredith reached for the receiver, but Rackstraw said: 'Wait, I'll take it.' Only one person knew this number. Meredith should not be asked to keep too many secrets.

Rackstraw carried the telephone into the far corner of the room, watched it ring for a moment then lifted the receiver. 'Yes? . . . Oh, it's you. How did you know I was here? . . . He told you, did he? What do you want then? Make it snappy.'

He stood listening for half a minute, then swore and said: 'So he's on to it, the clever little monkey. . . . The same one that found the house, yes. Well, we shall have to do something about it, won't we? Got his address? . . . Hold it, I'll get that down. . . . Selkirk, Flat 20, Darwin Court, Bramham Gardens. . . . Good. We'll take care of him. Thank you, Louise.'

Rackstraw slammed the phone back on to the table and

swore again. 'Once you start you're never finished,' he said.

'Who's Louise?' Meredith said.

'Never you mind. Get your shoes on, we've got work to do.'

10 pm (11 pm, Italy)

Sir Peter Downes placed the report in the safe, closed the door and twirled the combination. So the preliminary finding of the Italian authorities was sabotage—to the Swanstar by the steward, to the Witch by persons unknown. There was still nothing to connect the two events other than the law of probability. The only piece of new evidence was the unidentified Carabiniere car seen to leave the airport shortly after take-off (no officer of the Naples force was known to wear an eye-patch). Silvestri was the chief suspect, now under interrogation; but his motive? A mystery. Pray that the man doesn't come to tomorrow's reception! That would be very awkward. He pulled a sheet from the top of the pad and scribbled a minute in the red Biro which is the prerogative of Heads of Mission. 'H.O.C., if Silvestri comes tomorrow, keep him in a corner, P.D. Copy to C.C. for inf.'

He slipped the minute in the top of the 'out' folder and rose wearily from the desk, poured himself a neat whisky from the decanter and dropped on to the leather sofa in the centre of the cavernous study. A sudden thunderstorm was rattling the french windows, rain pounding on the leaves outside. It had turned quite cold.

He thought of the Prince's speech: extraordinary, shattering, brave. Good thing or bad thing? From habit his mind evaded the moral judgment and fell to calculating the chances of success. The late-night Italian news had included a telephoned dispatch from their London correspondent; it looked as if Thorganby would get his Cabinet. The F.O. would be in turmoil, Under-Secretaries cancelling their dinners, telegrams flying about. But here was he, alone in his study with no one to talk to. He had hoped Ralston would

186

be back by now for a late-night chat, but he was still out. The energy of the man! An hour after climbing from a Navy helicopter he was in black tie, immaculate as ever, and off to dine with his agent. That's the way industrial empires are built (or the way Ambassadors think they are built). In spite of everything Ralston was still going after the army contract and a new Witch had been flown out to Ciampino. His man had arrived with the blueprints that afternoon, a burly ex-copper called Blenkinsop, and was in the connecting bedroom, safely under hatches.

In the whole of that long day Sir Peter had only once caught a glimpse of his companion's internal anguish. When the officer from the *Dalkeith* had shown them the specimens of the wreckage Ralston had fingered the pieces of charred metal as if they were the remains of a person he loved, and suddenly covered his face with his hands. The man was obviously still tormented by guilt. He should see the Italians' report—that would help to set his mind at rest; but now it would have to wait till tomorrow. . . .

Gulping sadly at his whisky, Sir Peter wondered how it had been in the Witch. Had there been any warning, a few seconds for the realisation of death before the white-hot blast scattered them into the void? He might have been in the plane himself. The narrow escape from death brought home the futility of his life: the pointless parties, people like automatons, the endless debilitating effort not to give offence. Really, once you had got your 'K,' there was not much to keep you in the job.

He put down the glass and climbed the stairs to bed.

When Kemble and Anne came in twenty minutes later they were told the Ambassador was unavailable. Kemble decided a report on his conversation with Tucker could keep until the morning.

12 Midnight, August 6th

Extract from the Diary of Alan Selkirk

 . . . No one at Eaton Place. T. must have gone over to No. 10. Let myself in, called Trumper. Trumper positive on times, i.e. Courthope telephoned him just after 8 a.m., collected Prince before 9. No doubt there. As I came out of T.'s study Courthope was standing in hall. Very polite, had heard nothing. T. had given him key, asked him to call after dinner. T.'s Cabinet now formed: 5 Labour, 2 Lib., rest Tories. Some dead wood, esp. Labour trade unionists, but will see him through.

Now what? Harvey's caved in, Constable cancelled, Parliament in recess. Predictable demonstrations at Palace and No. 10, but nothing police couldn't control, streets now quiet. General reaction is calm acceptance. Man in Street discovers he lives in a monarchy and likes it. (Perhaps he knew it all along, only dons and politicians thought otherwise.)

But:

(a) King's death unexplained. Kemble suggests sabotage.

(b) Coper at centre of conspiracy. Responsible for Chelsea mutiny, Oxford shooting. Could/would his people have killed H.M.?

(c) Courthope and broadcast. No link so far between Courthope and Coper, but Courthope's actions this a.m. v. suspicious. Ditto sudden change in H.M.'s views. Hollis says Courthope right-wing and ? queer. Will ask him more if he turns up tonight.

I can't *prove* anything out of this. I was too definite in Jane's flat. But must pass it on to someone who can make proper inquiries ? Harvey. I don't know him, and anyway he has no authority now. ? Thorganby. Yes. At times I thought he might be involved with Coper, but certainly wd. have nothing to do with killing King. So have written to tell him what I know and suspect.

And also in same letter resigned. Don't want to seem priggish but the going is now definitely too rough. What wd. Anne say? Funny, her face keeps stopping me think. But she'd approve.

So now. What will become of me?

Selkirk closed the diary, read through his letter of resignation once again, stretched, then leaned his elbows on the desk, rubbing his eyes. He looked at his watch:

12.15. Hollis should be here any moment. It would be good to test these theories against some good Scottish common sense.

The cuckoo bell chimed in the hall and he went to the door, but instead of Hollis he found two strangers, one holding a revolver. 'Are you looking for me?' he said, and was pleased with the steadiness of his voice.

'Your name Selkirk?' asked the older one.

'That's right.'

'Then turn round, put your hands above your head and let's go back inside. We have things to discuss.'

Selkirk did as he was told. They stood him up against a wall and the older man put the barrel of the revolver under his chin. The young one looked about the flat, then came back and said: 'No one here.'

'Good. Now, Mr. Selkirk, we can get down to business. A short while ago a friend of ours heard you talking to a Mr. Trumper at Eton, and he didn't like what he heard. Perhaps you would like to tell us what you were trying to prove and who else you've discussed it with? That's all we need to know.'

Selkirk had always been a stickler for accuracy, and even now found time for a split-second satisfaction at being proved right before turning to the problem of how to stay alive. Clearly they would kill him as soon as they thought they knew enough; he must stall them till Hollis came. 'I don't know what you're talking about,' he said, whereupon the revolver was jabbed hard into the soft patch below his jawbone, choking him, forcing his head back against the wall. His scalp crawled in anticipation of the bullet.

'Hey, Major!' The young one had found his diary. 'Take a look at this.'

The gun was removed and Selkirk straightened his head. So this was the famous Major; and the other, of course, was Meredith. The wavy hair was now black but the pinched, hostile face was the same as the one in that day's *Times*.

Meredith took the gun and Rackstraw read the diary in silence, then opened the resignation letter and read that too.

'Well, well, quite the little Sherlock Holmes, aren't we? Let's see, several names here. Hollis and Trumper, we know about them, then there's this Kemble, and "Jane." Let's start with Jane, shall we?'

Rackstraw took the gun and replaced it under Selkirk's chin. 'Come on, who is she?'

Selkirk stared at the vacuous eyes, too big for their sockets, above the uneven moustache (too mediocre, surely, to be the face of death?) and said nothing.

'Silent hero, eh? We'll soon see about that.'

So they cuffed him about a bit, and played Russian roulette with the barrel in his mouth, and kicked him in the groin; but still he did not speak. He was waiting for the bell and thinking: 'This is impossible, it can't end now, here in this ordinary little room with two total strangers.' But the cuckoo chimes did not come, and they held his head against the gas fire, and then he knew he could not go on and if Hollis came they would kill him too, but someone, surely someone, would guess the truth, Jane Richardson would guess. . . .

As his hair began to singe he shook them off and struggled to his feet shouting: 'Help! Help! Help!' He had reached the door before Meredith brought him down. They scrabbled together across the lino, Selkirk's shouts getting weaker as Meredith thrust a flick-knife between his ribs, again and again, until they lay like exhausted lovers, Meredith panting on top, Selkirk dead beneath.

Rackstraw put the diary and the letter in his pocket and they ran down the stairs, passing a man with red hair. When they reached the Earl's Court Road Meredith said: 'What about those others?'

'We'll leave it as it is,' Rackstraw said. 'I've had enough. They'll probably never guess without mastermind back there, and even if they do, we'll be out of the country.'

Later Rackstraw decided to keep the letter and the last few pages of the diary, and sewed them into the lining of his suitcase. There was always the chance that after this was over some powerful people might decide he was safer dead; but if he put these papers in a bank, 'to be delivered to the appropriate authorities in the event of my death,' that would be some protection.

Thursday, August 7th

3 am (9 pm, Wednesday, New York)

Sir Charles Melton had come to the conclusion that for this, the most difficult meeting of his career, he should model himself on his Soviet colleague. He marched silently into the Security Council chamber with Hooper and three others of his staff in a close phalanx behind him. He refused to talk to journalists or even to his friendly American neighbour at the Council table. He sat impassive through three angry African speeches. The moderates were gloomy, the extremists cheerful. The news from London had revived all the old underlying suspicions of Britain which he had spent the last four years trying to kill.

Finally his turn came to speak. He read tonelessly and verbatim from the paper before him.

'His Majesty's Government in the United Kingdom have reviewed their attitude towards the resolution passed by the Security Council on Tuesday, August 5th. This resolution called for military action by United Kingdom forces in Rhodesia. In the opinion of His Majesty's present Government this resolution is illegal on two grounds. First, it constitutes an interference in the domestic affairs of a member state, contrary to the provisions of Article 2 (7) of the Charter. Second, it invokes the use of military force although the conciliatory procedures provided for in Article 33 of the Charter have not been exhausted. For these reasons, His Majesty's Government have instructed me to withdraw the support given by their predecessors to this resolution, and to inform the Council that they are not prepared to employ United Kingdom forces to carry out its terms.

'I am further instructed to state that His Majesty's Government propose in the near future to call a conference in London to which legitimate representatives of the various communities in Rhodesia will be invited. They are confident that this procedure offers the best hope of restoring the peaceful co-operation between races on which the future of Rhodesia must necessarily depend.

'In these circumstances His Majesty's Government consider that no useful purpose can be served by further discussion in the Security Council of the use of armed force, and they have instructed me not to participate in any such discussion. Thank you, Mr. President.'

Melton collected his papers together, zipped his neat black bag, stood up in a moment of complete silence and walked out of the chamber, followed by the phalanx. The doors swung to behind him but he could hear the pandemonium erupt within. He walked quickly along the corridor and down the stairs, stepped into the waiting Rolls-Royce. He ordered Leon to drive to the Mission's office, but as the car began to draw away, the door opened and Spriggs, the *New Statesman* correspondent, scrambled in. He had been running. 'Phew! You moved fast, Sir Charles. Well, are you going to resign?'

Melton tried to sound annoyed. 'Resign? Of course not. When you're in the front line you don't resign. That's a luxury for politicians to play with.'

'But it's nonsense, all that stuff about a conference. The South Africans will be in Rhodesia by tomorrow night. You know that as well as I do.'

'You journalists have to know all the answers, if you didn't you'd be fired. I don't know about the South Africans. But I do know the old King was an honest man, Thorganby's an honest man; we could be in worse hands.'

Spriggs looked at the man beside him in real astonishment. 'But it'll end in disaster, it's bound to,' he said.

'When you're as old as I am you'll know you don't know for certain how anything will end. And please don't smoke in my motor-car.'

Spriggs jumped out at the next red light. The official Humber carrying Hooper and the two First Secretaries almost knocked him down. He swore at their tail-lights and felt better.

3.30 am (4.30 am, Italy)

'Don't go back to sleep. You can't stay here, someone's bound to find us. Don't go back to sleep don't go back to sleep I shan't stop until you get up don't go back to sleep. . . .'

'Shut up. I'm going.' Kemble hauled himself upright, swung his feet off the bed, then paused, face buried in hands, exhausted by the effort. 'Oh dear,' he said, 'oh dear.' The lees of cheap Frascati lingered in his throat, movements which stretched or folded his sunburned skin were agony. His voice sounded like the hinge of the château door in a Hammer film. 'It's all right for you, born in Djakarta, lugged around the tropics in your cradle. Me, I'm English. Haven't the F.O. heard of air-conditioning?'

'Daddy doesn't approve of it.'

'I tell you heat like this weakens a man's moral fibre, and that's not all. All that crap about sex in hot climates. . . .'

'Drinking *Sambucca* half the night doesn't help.'

A joke or a challenge? Kemble peered at the form curled beside him, brown all over with patches of white. 'You're a wonderful understanding woman,' he said.

'So they tell me. Here's your dressing-gown.'

'I'll stay for another half-hour.'

'You will go, now.'

He staggered to his feet and fumbled for the sleeves in the bundle of Paisley-patterned silk, then kissed her on the ear, hoping to buy a delay. 'Have a good day at the office, darling,' she said. He slapped her bottom and left.

The corridor was pitch black, without landmarks. He spread his hands to find a wall and crept cautiously along it. He would have to find his room from memory. A floor-board creaked, then another. The slower he put his foot down, the longer the creak; swift, decisive movement would be safer. He took three rapid paces forwards and his hand crashed against a door handle. In the same instant the door flew open and he was pinned to the floor, one arm held in a tight grip behind his back, a naked foot on his neck. Blinding torchlight in his face, then darkness again.

'Sorry, sir. Thought you was an intruder. Can't be too careful, you know.' It was Ralston's valet.

Kemble picked himself off the floor. 'That's all right, Blenkinsop. Glad to know you're on the *qui vive*. I was just looking for the . . .'

'Second on the right, sir.'

'Thank you.'

Kemble pulled the chain with particular vigour.

6.35 am

Lift out of order. Two men, running down the stairs, faces averted, difficult to see in the half-light. No answer at the door; cuckoo chimes echoing in the empty flat. Something familiar somewhere, something disturbing . . .

Suddenly Hollis was awake, ripping off the sleeping mask, prising the plugs from his ears. Now he knew who the men were. Sleep had been a solvent, releasing the half-glimpsed faces from his subconscious and fusing them into the police photographs on page 3 of the first edition.

He pulled together his orange kimono pyjamas, a typically absurd present from his actress sister, and telephoned Selkirk's flat. The line was dead. Guilt and foreknowledge of disaster pressed like a weight upon his stomach. He phoned the police and began to dress.

10.15 am (11.15 am, Italy)

'*Nel nome del governo e del popolo italiano spero che questa nostra settima Mostra Aeronautica di Roma, mentre rafforza non solo i rapporti tecnologici e commerciali, ma anche la cooperazione intelletuale e spirituale tra i paesi industrializzati, possa fornire un aiuto prezioso alla prosperità dei paesi in via di sviluppo, alla ricerca della pace e al benessere di tutti i popoli del mondo.*'

Intoxicated by the Ciceronian symmetry of this final

sentence the Minister for Trade and Industry stood smiling into the television lights and whirring cameras. He would have liked to have gone on all morning, but the Air Show must be opened and the Prime Minister, whose turn it was next, was not noted for brevity. Panicked technicians set about transferring the microphones to the centre of the table as the applause continued. Yes, it had been a good speech, fulfilling the four main requirements: building up from a dull technical subject into sentiments of universal application, offending no one, containing no expression of opinion, and committing the speaker to no action whatever. That sort of thing took practice.

The Rome Air Show was in the *Palazzo dei Congressi* at E.U.R. (*Esposizione Universale di Roma*—a bleak, angular complex of halls begun by Mussolini on the edge of the city for a World Fair which never was). The exhibits in the *Palazzo* consisted of models, documents and photographs; the aircraft were on view at Ciampino Airport a few miles away. The rubbernecks went to the airport, the business was done in the *Palazzo*. On the first floor were offices occupied by the principal exhibitors and buying delegations, and a conference room, scene of the opening speeches. Every seat in the room was taken, Ambassadors and other dignitaries to the front, *fritto misto* to the back, and a crowd of bored officials standing round the edge. The suction fans in the ceiling worked to extract the rising waves of hot air and cigarette smoke, but fought a losing battle.

The Minister for Trade and Industry finally sat, adjusting his mohair suit for the zoom lenses.

The simultaneous translation, which had lost several lengths on an earlier technical passage, limped in to the finish. '. . . will give a precious help to the prosperity of the less-developed countries, to the search for peace and the welfare of all the peoples in the world.' The girl's tired voice could not transmit the Minister's enthusiasm for his words. She could have come from anywhere between Lucerne and Chicago. Kemble lifted the earphones from his head and stretched his neck. An army of invisible gnomes had attached weights to his eyelids; will-power alone would never keep them up.

195

A hand on his sleeve. Brown and well-manicured, with tufts of black hair on the back of the fingers: a familiar hand.

'Mr. Kemble, I would like a word with you if you have a moment.'

'Oh, it's you. All right, if you like.'

The office had an illuminated sign in the window —'SILVESTRI S.P.A.'—which looked as if it had been made to fit the space and used for several years. A fan was going in the corner and a secretary in an imitation Pucci blouse was prodding spasmodically at an Olivetti portable. The secretary was dismissed, the fan switched off, cigarettes offered and lit.

'How is Lady Molly?'

'She's all right.'

'And Sir Peter?'

'He's fine too.'

'Good, good.' He had aged since Tuesday night, looked tired and ill at ease. His shirt had been worn the day before, and he was pulling at his cigarette as if it was a matter of vital importance that the smoke reached the very bottom of his lungs. 'It must have been a shock, this business of the King.'

'A shock, yes, it was.'

'Mr. Kemble, there are people who think I was responsible for that accident.'

'Are there really?'

'I see you know.'

'I wouldn't have thought—'

'I do not wish to know what you think. The humiliation to me of submitting to these questions is unimportant. They have to be asked, the truth must be known. I merely inform you that I was not responsible, and that even if I had wished to do such a disgraceful thing, it was quite impossible.'

'The Ambassador is puzzled by your movements at the airport.'

'It is true, I did not leave the airport, I arranged a small pretence with the Commandant, a distant relative of mine, which I hoped would assist the King to select the Cavaliere. It was foolish and unnecessary, but the fact remains that

196

if the King had used my plane he would now be safe in England.'

'England's not so safe with your friend Coper on the loose.'

'My journey to Wolverhampton was strictly business, as I told you. All these things will be clear in time—I do not wish to discuss them now.'

'What *do* you wish to discuss?'

Silvestri extinguished his cigarette and paced about the room, then twirled the blades of the fan with his finger. When he turned to face Kemble, his expression had changed to that of a man who is about to make a difficult request and is not sure how it will be received. 'I am about to make a difficult request, Mr. Kemble, and I'm not sure how you will receive it.'

'Try me.'

'We are not exactly friends, are we? Nor even old acquaintances. Yet on the two occasions we have met I have formed a distinct impression of you. You have, I would say, small regard for the feelings of others or for the finer points of etiquette. Like all good journalists, you also have a strong wish to see the truth exposed. I am hoping that taken together these two characteristics will permit you to commit a small indiscretion in the interests of the truth. The fact that I might derive some benefit thereby would, I am convinced, play no part in your motives. If you did it at all you would do it for your own reasons. So yes, I think I will try you.'

Kemble laughed. You had to hand it to the man. 'Your English is perfect, Mr. Silvestri,' he said. 'Where did you learn it?'

Pouncing on the first hint of co-operation, Silvestri drew up a chair and reached again for the onyx cigarette box. 'The London School of Economics, a long time ago. It was the best period of my youth. But we must keep to the subject, we have little time.' He ensured that the office door was closed and returned to his chair. 'Kemble, you know it has been suggested that the Witch was sabotaged by a commercial competitor?'

'Yes.'

'And that I am suspect because I am competing with Ralston for a contract with the Italian Army?'

'Yes.'

'Well, that is rubbish. The contract will go to Fokker, I have known it for some time. The correspondence files in our head office will prove that we reduced our sales drive in this direction some months ago. But if I were able to show to you that Ralston knows this too, and is here on some other business in which I have no concern, that would help, would it not?'

Kemble's appetite was whetted. He knew that sly, greedy look had come across his face which other men get when they see a pretty girl. 'Yes, Silvestri, I suppose it would,' he said quietly.

'Well, here are a few facts; see if you come to the same conclusion as I do. There is a big South African delegation here, unusually big. They say they have come to buy civil aircraft, but none of the firms exhibiting that type of aircraft has yet been approached. In my opinion they are looking for missiles, ground-to-air and ground-to-ground; that would give them the superiority they need over the other African states. Because of the U.N. ban they cannot buy the arms they want except from illegal private dealers. But if they could buy the *know-how* they could make the things themselves, the way they are now making spares for their air force.'

'But wouldn't the ban cover that too?'

'Indeed it would. But such a sale could be easily concealed.'

'And what makes you think that this is what they're after in Rome?'

'They tried to get it from me. As you may know, my company has been making control mechanisms for the E.L.D.O. rockets and supplied the electronic equipment for last year's Spanish-Italian satellite. Last week I was approached in confidence by the Air Attaché of the South African Embassy and asked if I would be prepared to discuss the sale of some of our manufacturing data with three members of their delegation. Of course, I refused and reported the matter to my government. And in case your suspicious mind is still at work, I am able to tell you that I discovered enough of their requirements to know that my company could not meet them, but another company could.'

'And which is that?'

'Herakles.'

'Good God, you're not suggesting—'

'I'm suggesting nothing. I am giving you facts and leaving you to judge, remember? You can take my word for it, what the South Africans need is mostly to be found in the Icarus, the tactical missile developed for the British Army by Herakles.'

'The production order was cancelled.'

'That's right, and poor old Ralston had to hawk his rocket around the Middle East. It was an expensive failure.'

The speeches were over and the conference room was disgorging a flood of distressed humanity into the comparative cool of the corridor. Kemble saw the Italian Prime Minister pass the office window on his way to a tour of the exhibits. He was followed by an agitated Sir Peter Downes, who appeared to be looking for his chauffeur. The Embassy reception would already have started, Lady Molly would be holding the fort.

'This is all very interesting, Silvestri, but if you want me to believe that Herakles are flogging secrets to South Africa, you'll have to produce more facts than that.'

'Wait, I have three more: one, the South African delegation is leaving tonight.'

'What?'

'Yes, they are booked on a flight to Cape Town this evening. Which means they have got what they wanted, or given up. It seems a bit early to have given up. Two, Ralston dined with them last night.'

'He dined with his agent.'

'And three members of the South African delegation, no one else present. They had a private room at a trattoria in Trastevere.'

'Can you prove that?'

'Yes. Three, Ralston is keeping a large metal trunk, said to contain blueprints, under guard in his suite at the Villa Wolkonsky.'

'How the hell did you know that?'

199

'I thought you would ask. It embarrasses me to tell you, but the issue is too grave for me to be coy about it. One of Sir Peter's footmen is the nephew of my housekeeper, they come from the same village in Puglia. For some time I have been kept informed of Embassy gossip.'

Kemble looked at Silvestri with new respect; the play-boy exterior was deceptive. 'And you think the trunk contains the blueprints of the Icarus missile?'

Silvestri's confidence had returned and he decided to risk a harder approach. 'What do you think? I suppose he told you they were drawings of the Witch. But that wouldn't need guarding—there are no secrets about that plane. Any one of a dozen manufacturers could copy it tomorrow and Ralston knows it. Besides, why would he bring the blueprints to Rome? Sometimes I think you British will believe anything.'

Now it was Kemble's turn to be disconcerted, and to pace about the room. 'But Ralston could go to prison for this. Why would he risk that?'

'Money?'

'He has plenty.'

'Yes, but has Herakles? They've made a loss for the last two years and the shares are dropping.'

'What do you want me to do?'

'Look in the trunk.'

'You don't want much, do you? I'll have to think about it.'

They shook hands and Silvestri showed Kemble to the door. 'Yes, think about it,' he said. 'I wouldn't like you to take an unnecessary risk.' But he knew that Kemble's curiosity would get the better of him, and so did Kemble.

What neither knew was that a small appliance in Silvestri's telephone had transmitted their conversation to the office of the South African delegation.

11 am

Lord Thorganby was back in the Lord President's office in Whitehall, at his old desk under the antlers and the heavily varnished portrait of Peel. He had had a friendly enough word on the telephone with Harvey the night before, and agreed not to move into the offices of Number Ten till Friday.

Things were going well, he thought; indeed the first hours had been much easier than he had expected. Some of the Cabinet were inexperienced, but old Wellsuch had done well to bring in four Labour men with him. They would all meet for the first time that afternoon. Birchett would be over before long to settle the agenda. Meanwhile the boxes were beginning to flow in; Thorganby had kept the Foreign Office in his own hands for the moment, hoping at the back of his mind that Ryder Bennett would agee to take it back again after a decent interval.

He rang the buzzer. A trim woman of fifty with rinsed blue hair and an orange tweed skirt trotted in. Miss Delloway had served as Assistant Private Secretary for twelve years now and Thorganby was her fifth Lord President.

'Ah, Ethel. No sign of Alan Selkirk yet?'

'No, sir. I've just rung his flat again, but there's no answer. The exchange say the number's out of order. I rang Lady Thorganby too, in case he'd gone to Eaton Place, but she hasn't seen him. Normally he's so punctual, sir, I can't think what's happened to him.'

'I expect he'll turn up. It's a confusing morning for us all.' In fact Lord Thorganby had never felt less confused. 'Has that telegram from New York come over yet?'

'Yes, sir, here's the advance copy.'

Thorganby read the telegram approvingly. Steady chap, Melton, not too long-winded, no complaints about his instructions. There would be the usual hullabaloo at U.N.O. of course, but it would die down. The important thing was to get the constitutional conference going. Marlborough House, he thought, and do it in style. The King should come and open it. Thorganby had a pleasing vision of sun on the helmets of the Household Cavalry as the King arrived at the portico, loyal sun-tanned white Rhodesians, smiling chiefs in dazzling robes, a banquet, a fine imperial occasion under the chandeliers. . . . Meanwhile the F.O. were drafting a telegram to keep the South Africans in hand.

Thorganby wrote on a sheet of blue crested paper: 'Following Personal for Sir Charles Melton from Prime Minister. Well done. You have my full confidence in your difficult task.'

'Get this sent at once, will you, Ethel?'

As Ethel Delloway passed Selkirk's empty desk in the anteroom, she noticed an envelope lying on it addressed in a neat italic hand: 'Alan Selkirk Esq. Personal and Urgent. By hand.'

11.10 am (12.10 pm, Italy)

Kemble closed the door of Silvestri's office and walked towards the lifts. The corridor was now empty. In the office two doors down, a hand pressed the 'stop' switch on a tape recorder and a voice said in French: 'You had better get after him, but wait till the lift arrives.'

A rattle of chains in the lift-shaft, and the aluminium doors hissed open. Kemble stepped inside. So many buttons, and no Italian to help him out. SST, ST, T, 1, 2, 3—what was the word for 'ground floor'? When in doubt go back to Kennedy's Latin Primer. His finger settled on button 'T'. The doors trundled towards each other, closed on a suède shoe and went into reverse. The man jabbed at the 'T' again and stood with his back to Kemble, watching a girl run down the corridor. The doors closed before she could make it.

Exhibition halls need high ceilings, so their ground floors are apt to be some way below their first. The *Palazzo dei Congressi* conformed to the rule and had a slow lift into the bargain. Poidatz, who had used the lift several times, knew he had fifteen seconds. Long enough: he braced his hand for the karate chop. He should have had the advantage of surprise, but Kemble had seen the eye-patch and whatever his other deficiencies, his mental reactions were quick. Training should still have decided the issue, but sometimes an amateur's first move can be so reckless, so stupid by the ordinary rules, that the pro is caught on the hop. By the time Poidatz's hand had started its backward arc Kemble's head was travelling horizontally with great velocity at the small of his back. The right reaction would have been to sidestep the battering-ram and let it smash against the lift doors, then break it with a rabbit-punch; but Poidatz did not have time and was flung again the doors himself. The impact left him dazed, emptied his lungs of wind, but he turned and as Kemble charged a second time aimed a kick between his legs. Again he was a fraction too late; the kick missed its mark and Kemble's head bored into his stomach, slamming him back against the doors. The lights flickered, then revived, the lift lurched in the shaft with a hollow booming of aluminium. As Poidatz's hands closed on his neck Kemble did a thing he had seen on the telly—jerked his head upwards with maximum force. It worked. His skull caught Poidatz on the chin and brought him to the floor of the lift. The eye-patch was off, the scar bright red, the teeth clenched with pain. Kemble kicked at the head with all his force; blood flowed from the nose and mouth; he kicked again and the eyes closed; he was still kicking when the doors opened.

Still convinced he was in danger, Kemble ran like a madman across the polished marble floor of the entrance lobby. But the Frenchman lay unnoticed on the floor of the lift and the doors closed on his outstretched fingers.

Through the glass doors, down the steps. White heat bouncing off the white stone. Lady Molly's Morris still where he left it, P.V.C. scorching his legs through the thin trousers, but it starts, it starts. White stone colonnades and green glass office blocks; danger at every window; much too public, this modern suburb, too many open spaces. 'Get me out of here, must get out.' Reaction sets in, he begins to call on his maker. 'Jesus Christ, don't let them kill me.' But he waits at the traffic light and turns right, as he should, on the Cristoforo Colombo and takes the dual carriageway to Rome and gradually gets a grip of himself.

By the time they found Poidatz, Kemble was half a mile away.

11.20 am

Letter from Jane Richardson, Foreign Office, to Alan Selkirk, delivered by hand to his office and opened by Lord Thorganby at 11.20 a.m.

Dear Alan,

I'm so glad you took me into your confidence yesterday. I was slow to take it in, and you dashed off before I made much sense, leaving me with a sleepless night to look forward to!

I hope you won't mind, but I've butted in on your private sleuthing and tried to fill in one of the blanks. It occurred to me that Courthope might have done something at London Airport when he arrived on Tuesday night which explained his going to Windsor instead of London. The airport duty officer that night was a man called Lavering; a bit young, but I've always found him helpful when we've been on duty the same nights. So I've just rung him at his home number. Of course he was in bed—I'd forgotten he would be catching up on lost sleep. But his wife woke him up, then I woke him up even more, poor man. This is what he said.

C. called a private London number as soon as he arrived. 126-7145. Lavering scribbled it in a notebook. Lavering overheard him say something to this number about a change of plan. Then C. spoke to the King and to Perkins in Ravello in Lavering's presence. Lavering didn't understand all he said, but he's quite clear that C. was advising H.M. to come back earlier than planned, and that H.M. agreed. After that C. told Lavering he was going to Windsor, not B.P. Finally he spoke to the P.M.

What do you make of this? It looks very much as if the change of plan came as a result of that first private call. I looked up the number, thinking it might be Coper's—though of course you'd said he was in Oxford. It was ex-Directory. On an off-chance I got hold of the list of Cabinet Ministers' numbers we're issued with. Surprise, surprise. *C. spoke to Michael Critten from the airport that night.*

204

Over to you again—unless I can be of any more help. Shouldn't you talk to Harvey? Or I can, if you like. I know his daughter quite well. Women have their uses, you know.

See you soon,
Jane R.

11.30 am (12.30 pm, Italy)

'General and Mrs. Di Sarto.' Anxious to terminate his brief moment of responsibility for the star guest, the butler passed the General to Lady Molly as if he were a tray of fine china. Longden hovered in the background (it often seemed to Longden that he spent most of his working life hovering). The General kissed Lady Molly's hand: '*Ambasciatrice.*'

'*Buon giorno, Signor Generale.*' The General began to speak at length about the King's death, and Lady Molly simultaneously explained why the party was still being held. Sir Peter came to her aid and ushered the General to where Ralston was standing. Drinks appeared and Raikes toiled to translate the jocular courtesies. The queue of guests waiting to be received was as long as ever.

A mile to the west Kemble had reached the Arch of Constantine. The pock-marked arches of the Colosseum loomed above the little Morris. He was off course but not yet lost. Weaving through the log-jam of long green buses, he followed the yellow signs to San Giovanni.

'My, this is really something, isn't it?' Anne stood on the terrace as Barry Tucker admired the garden.

'Yes,' she said, 'it is pretty. Shall we take a walk?'

They went down the steps and the noise of the party faded behind them. The air was full of summer smells and the sound of splashing fountains as they strolled away under the umbrella pines.

Kemble inched the Morris across the Piazza S. Giovanni.

Thirty yards behind him a white Fiat 124 was trying to close the gap. In the passenger seat Poidatz was easing his bruised fingers round the trigger of an automatic pistol. An articulated tram was bearing down on Kemble's starboard bow, playing chicken Roman style. Kemble put the Morris into second gear and lurched forward, exposing his flank. Thin sheet steel of B.M.C. versus a bumper of solid iron. . . . But the tram-driver had seen the CD plates and had his licence to think of; the tram ground to a halt, bell clanging, hydraulic brakes pumping in protest. The Morris continued forward and the tram closed in behind it, trapping the Fiat.

'. . . This aqueduct is in *fine* shape.'

'Yes, we're very proud of it. Our Ministry of Works patched it up.'

'Can we see this Roman tomb you people have here?'

'Of course. It's over there.' Barry Tucker's thirst for knowledge was only equalled by Anne's thirst for another gin. They were peering into the dark recesses of the colombarium when the Morris jerked to a stop in front of the Chancery building.

'Jack!' Tie loose, jacket torn, hair all over the place. He was limping. 'Where on earth have you been?'

'Never mind. Explain later. I want you to come with me, we have a job to do. Sorry, Barry.'

'*Avanti*, my friends,' Tucker said. 'Never let it be said that Barry Tucker stood in the way of true love.' Silly ass, thought Kemble as he led Anne towards the villa.

'What's all this about?' she said.

'We're going to search Ralston's room, we'll never get a better chance than this.'

'You must be out of your mind.'

'No, but lucky to be alive. Someone who wanted me to know told me what's in Ralston's luggage, and someone who didn't tried to kill me. That's enough to make me want to know.'

'But how will you do it? What about that thug?'

'I rely on your charms to lure the good Blenkinsop from his post. Now listen carefully . . .'

They crossed a gravel space littered with black limousines and arrived at the front door of the Residence. The party had reached that awkward stage where the early arrivals are leaving and the late arrivals are coming. The Ambassador's chauffeur helped the American Minister's wife from her Lincoln Continental, then turned to read the car-ticket numbers of departing guests into a microphone. The doorway and the hall behind were crowded with a two-way traffic of refugees from the Tower of Babel; an Italian admiral was signing the book; Longden was hovering.

They went upstairs and Kemble shut himself in Anne's bedroom. Anne went to the upstairs drawing-room, locked the connecting door to her mother's study and put the key in her bag, then took the key from the other door. She crossed the landing and knocked at the door of Ralston's suite. After a pause Blenkinsop appeared in shirt-sleeves holding a bottle of beer. He was wearing a shoulder holster. Anne explained that Ralston was asking for him in the upstairs drawing-room. Blenkinsop had strict instructions not to leave his quarters, but this was the Ambassador's daughter and the room where Ralston was waiting was just across the way. It looked all right, so he put on his jacket and followed her across the landing. When they reached the drawing-room they found that Ralston had mysteriously disappeared. Anne said she would go and look for him. She closed the drawing-room door and locked it, then ran back to the suite.

Kemble was already there, opening cupboards, looking under the beds. Blenkinsop had made his base in an arm-chair by the window. The chair was surrounded by bottles and half-eaten sandwiches; a copy of the *Daily Express* was lying across the arm. Close to the chair was a sofa set at an angle across the corner of the room and behind it they found the trunk. It was locked.

Kemble cursed and heaved at the lid. It would not budge. He tried kicking at the catches but they held. In desperation they searched for a heavy object. Blenkinsop was pounding on the drawing-room door. Anne disappeared to her parents' bedroom and returned with Sir Peter's golf clubs. Kemble took the putter and began to swing at the lock of the trunk. Whang, whang, whang, whang. The putter rose and fell, the blows reverberated down the staircase. Anne stood by the door and listened to Blenkinsop shouting, and pleaded with Kemble to stop. Then the lock gave, springs and pieces of twisted brass falling softly to the carpet.

Anne came back to the corner of the room and together they lifted the lid. There were no documents inside, but a man, wrapped in a cocoon of blankets to protect him from the sides of the trunk. His eyes were half-open and his pale features immobile, but he was breathing evenly. It was the King.

11.38 a.m.

'Thank you, Superintendent. You did quite right to bring the papers straight to me. Does his mother know yet?'

'No, sir.'

'I'll tell her myself. If it's not irregular I'd like to see the man Hollis's statement when it's typed out.'

'Very good, sir.' As the tightly buttoned Superintendent left the room Lord Thorganby tried to concentrate his thoughts for a moment on Alan Selkirk. Only thirty minutes since the police had telephoned to say he had been murdered, and already his image was blurring. A nice chap, cheerful and obliging. A good man to have around, reliable, quick but calm, and for one of his years and generation exceptionally sound in judgment.

But someone had wanted him dead. Thorganby smoothed out the three papers before him and read them through again carefully. Selkirk's letter of resignation and a fragment of his diary, both found on a Major Rackstraw, Coper's chief henchman, arrested at London Airport that morning and identified by the journalist Hollis as the probable killer of Selkirk. Then Jane Richardson's letter, brought in from Selkirk's desk by Miss Delloway as soon as she heard of the murder, and reluctantly opened by Thorganby.

Lord Thorganby frowned and puzzled. He did not like detective stories. All his life he had heard tales of villainy and corruption in high places; ninety-nine per cent had

been false. He could think of a dozen reasons why Courthope should choose to spend the night at Windsor. The
argument about times was over-elaborate and confusing.
Selkirk had got a bee in his bonnet, that was the sum of it.

But someone had had him killed to silence the buzzing
of that bee. There seemed little doubt of that. Not Critten,
not Courthope, of course, but someone. The thing had to
be cleared up, and quickly, before the Press got at it.

'Miss Delloway, would you please ask the Minister of
Defence and Sir James Courthope to come over here as
quickly as possible on a personal matter?'

11.50 am (12.50 pm, Italy)

Ambassador, Head of Chancery and Third Secretary boggled
at the contents of the trunk, trying not to believe what they
saw. Sir Peter recovered first. 'He's still alive?' he said.

'Yes,' said Kemble, 'he's breathing. They must have
been injecting him with something.'

'We must see he's all right, that's the first thing.' In
Sir Peter's mind appeared a composite image of all the
flaps and crises of his diplomatic life. How had he ever
allowed himself to be flummoxed by such trivia? As he
stared down at the gaunt familiar face (here! in this
bedroom!) he found to his surprise that he was equal to
the moment. Forgotten muscles began to work, and he was
once again the resolute young ensign.

'Longden, get Doctor Baldi here as quick as you can.
Don't tell him who it is, just say a British V.I.P., but tell
him what he has to treat. If he doesn't know about this
kind of thing he must find a specialist as quick as he can.
If Baldi's out, any of the Embassy panel will do. Then
get the Blue Sisters to reserve a private ward and have
their resident doctor standing by. Don't tell them anything
more. Then phone for an ambulance. Off you go, quick.'

Still scribbling his mental list, Longden ran for the door.

'Oh, Longden.'

'Yes, sir.'

'One other thing. Before you start phoning, get McInnes

and one of his men to report to me here, at the double.' The military phrase seemed appropriate. 'There's a rifle in Registry, they'd better load it and bring it with them.'

'Surely you're not going to shoot it out with Ralston here?' Kemble said.

'No. McInnes can take care of Blenkinsop. With the fellow already locked in the drawing-room it shouldn't be too difficult. Still, he may be armed.'

'He is,' Anne said. 'A pistol strapped to his chest.'

Sir Peter was undeterred. 'McInnes was at Alamein, he's handled worse than that.'

'What about Ralston?' Kemble said.

'Ralston, yes. Something a little more elaborate for him, I think. He'll run for it as soon as he knows. Raikes, I want the Embassy gates closed immediately. No one is to leave the grounds until I say. Tell them to expect Ralston down there —they'll recognise him by now. When he comes they're to lock him up in the Admin. building. They can use what force they like, but not more than they need. They can get the *Celere* to help them.' (The *Celere* were detachments of mobile riot police posted by the Italian Government at the gates of the bigger foreign Embassies.) 'If he shoots they can shoot back. On second thoughts, you'd better go down there yourself and fix it up. We'll give you five minutes, then Kemble here will go down to the ballroom and tell Ralston that the game is up. He won't do that until we've take care of Blenkinsop and put the King under armed guard in here. I suppose there's just a chance Ralston might go berserk, in which case we should be prepared. Anne, you stand at the head of the stairs and let us know if he comes up. But I doubt if he will—he's bound to bolt, there's nothing else he can do. If he does, let him go; it's better if we nab him at the gate. Don't want to endanger our guests, and the less of a spectacle the better. They'll all be selling their personal accounts to the Press tomorrow. I can see what *Lo Specchio* will make of it if they have a chance.'

Two minutes later McInnes arrived exhaling beer fumes and carrying an ancient .303. They shouted to Blenkinsop through the door to drop his gun and when they heard it clatter to the floor, they cocked the rifle and charged. Sir

Peter took a deep breath and shut his eyes. But Blenkinsop offered no resistance. It turned out later he knew nothing. He had been Ralston's security man since leaving the Force and had often been asked to guard an item of his master's baggage. When they showed him what was in the trunk he fainted.

The crowd in the ballroom had thinned to about a hundred. The caviare was finished and people were starting on the sausage rolls. Ralston was talking to Lady Molly when Kemble took him by the arm.

'A word in your ear, Mr. Ralston.'

Ralston followed Kemble to the corner of the room, looking over his shoulder at Lady Molly. The look said: 'This young man is too ignorant to realise he can tell me anything in front of you, bear with me while I humour him.' Aloud he said: 'What is it, Kemble?'

'I've just had a look at your blueprints. Very interesting documents.'

To Kemble's astonishment this produced no reaction whatever. Ralston looked at the floor, frowning with thought. A new problem had come up. Unexpected, but like all problems it would have a logical solution. The first essential was to verify the facts: 'You opened the trunk?' he said.

'I did. With a golf club. Hard work.'

'Where's Blenkinsop?'

'Flat on his back. We're looking for smelling salts.'

'I'd better get up there. Those blueprints are valuable.'

'I shouldn't bother. Sir Peter's there, and others. They're armed. And it's not the blueprints they're worried about, as you well know.'

'I have no idea what you're talking about. I must see Sir Peter at once.'

They walked out into the marble entrance hall. As Ralston reached the foot of the stairs he seemed to change his mind and ran through the front door, pulling his car keys from his pocket. Kemble watched the black Hertz Fiat disappear down the curving drive. 'You didn't sign the book,' he shouted.

When Raikes had first arrived at the gate it had taken him

some time to get anyone to listen to him. A first-class theatrical row was in progress between the guards and two men in a white Fiat 124 who evidently thought they had been asked to the party. With great reluctance the argument was finally abandoned, the *Celere* jeep was driven inside the Embassy grounds and the gates were closed at his command. The men in the white Fiat stayed outside. Raikes said he would deal with their problem later and hoped they would then go away; but clearly they had not given up the struggle. One of them wore an eye-patch, he noticed. Unpleasant-looking chap.

He glanced at his watch. It had taken four minutes to complete his preparations. The gates were secured with a padlock and chain. The *Celere* jeep was parked at right angles across it, the crew holding their weapons at the ready. Two black Mercedes, packed with irritated guests from the German Embassy, had pulled in to the side of the drive. Raikes had positioned himself just inside the door of the Administration building.

The Fiat squealed to a halt, back wheels sliding sideways. Ralston rapped the high-pitched horn. Nobody moved except Raikes, who left the shelter of the building and approached the car. Ralston wound down the window and said: 'What's going on? I have to get back to the Air Show. Let's have these gates open, Raikes.'

'I'm afraid we can't do that,' Raikes said. 'Please get out of that car and follow me in here.'

Ralston raised his right hand to the level of the open window, and Raikes saw that it held a little black gun. 'Don't be silly, Raikes. Let's have those gates open, there's a good fellow.'

Raikes stood his ground. All said and done, he was a brave man. At his signal the crew began to dismount from the *Celere* jeep.

'You're outnumbered, Ralston, it's no good,' he said.

Eyes popping, the Germans watched the show from the two Mercedes. Raikes looked at Ralston. Ralston looked at the white Fiat.

'Outnumbered? I wouldn't be so sure of that.'

One of the *Celere* had reached Ralston's car and was resting a Beretta submachine gun on the open window. The others were surrounding the car at an indolent walk, spacing themselves at five-yard intervals. Suddenly the white Fiat did a three-cornered turn and accelerated down the street. Ralston watched it disappear round the corner, replaced his gun in the glove compartment and followed Raikes into the Administration building.

12 Noon

Michael Critten was already in a rage. He took his stand in front of the ugly pink marble fireplace and glowered across the room at the Prime Minister. Sir James Courthope sat quiet and stiff in the chair by Lord Thorganby's desk.

'I don't understand you, David.' In this sort of mood Critten looked like an outsize inflatable rubber toy. 'I'm up to my eyes in work. Constable's only half unscrambled, all the brass in the Ministry flapping like old women, and you call me here to ask if I had a private telephone conversation the night before last with James Courthope. And all this just because a couple of damnfool civil servants have been writing crazy letters.'

'The difficulty is,' said Thorganby, 'that one of the damnfool civil servants is now in the mortuary with fourteen stab-wounds.'

Critten glanced at Courthope, seemed about to say more, but checked himself. Courthope did not meet his look.

Thorganby shuffled together the papers on his desk. He was embarrassed, not sure how to proceed. He fidgeted with the silver inkstand. 'The first two documents which you have just read were found by the police on one of the two men who are now accused of my Private Secretary's murder,' he said. 'So of course the police will follow up the matters mentioned in the documents in case they are connected with the murder. I thought it right to tell you both this as soon as possible.'

Courthope was wholly preoccupied by a small stain on

213

the carpet, but Critten returned to the attack. 'This is preposterous. You're the Prime Minister, you can tell the police to get the hell out. Tell 'em not to waste their time and ours.' Critten's voice was explosive. His massive frame lurched from the fireplace, and he planted both fists on the red morocco of Thorganby's desk, waiting for an answer.

Courthope spoke for the first time. He looked at neither of the others, but out of the window across Whitehall. As usual his voice was controlled and flat. 'Of course Lord Thorganby can't call the police off unless he's satisfied there's nothing in Selkirk's insinuations. But that shouldn't be difficult. Take the first point. I decided to go to Windsor the night before last because I wanted to talk to Trumper first thing in the morning about the Prince's studies. A decision on this was long overdue, and there would just have been time to deal with it before . . .'

Courthope tailed off as the telephone on the desk buzzed. Now it was Thorganby's turn to be exasperated. This encounter was difficult enough without interruptions. 'I told you not to put through any calls.'

'It's the Ambassador calling from Rome, sir. He says it's urgent and very important. Won't talk to anyone but you.'

'All right, put him on.' Thorganby cupped his hand round the mouthpiece. 'James, you'd better listen on the extension in the next room. It's bound to be something about the crash.'

Sir James Courthope went into the anteroom, sat at Selkirk's desk by the window and lifted the receiver.

12.06 pm (1.06 pm, Italy)

Sir Peter sat at his desk and waited for the call to Downing Street. In a few moments his Embassy would be a bedlam of police and doctors, journalists hammering at the gates. Now was the time to tell the Prime Minister, with a quick calm phone call, followed by a confirming telegram. 'Put it in cipher and make it Emergency, Personal for the P.M.,' he said to Longden. 'All the world will know pretty soon, but a short delay may be useful to London. Anyway it's not

214

our business to announce it. As soon as I've spoken to Downing Street get me the Lord Chancellor in Naples.'

Longden was everywhere, making notes, passing orders, holding two phones at once. He had removed his tie—a sartorial innovation which seemed justified by the occasion —and his shirt was clinging to his ribs. Sir Peter made a mental note to thank the boy afterwards, but now there was still too much to be done. 'And Julian,'—the unexpected use of his Christian name brought shafts of sunlight to Longden's heart—'as soon as we can we should prepare a written record of Ralston's movements while he was with us. Everything he did, everything he said, any message he sent or received, and so on. I'd like you to co-ordinate it.'

'I'll have it ready by tonight, sir.' Longden found another space on his crowded memo pad. 'There was one rather peculiar message yesterday which I handled myself. Came in just after five, our time. Phoned from London, but the caller didn't leave a name. Ralston was still on the *Dalkeith*, so it was passed to me.'

'You spoke to the chap?'

'No, I just took the message from the telephonists afterwards.'

'And what did it say?'

' "The fish have bitten." I assumed it referred to some business deal, but it could be anything.'

'Indeed it could. The man must have collaborators somewhere. He couldn't have done it alone.' Sir Peter picked up the telephone. In the ground-floor exchange expert hands adjusted the disposition of plugs and switches. 'Ah, Amy. Any news of the call to Downing Street?'

'It should be through any second, sir.'

Amy headed the Ambassador's fan club. Of all the Embassy staff, H.E. was the only one who consistently recognised her voice and then succeeded in attaching a name to it.

'Good. Tell me, Amy, are you the one that took the message for Mr. Ralston yesterday—the one about the fish?'

'You mean the message from Buckingham Palace, sir. Yes, that was me.'

Sir Peter twitched in his seat as if he had received a small electric shock. He looked inquiringly at Longden. 'You didn't tell Mr. Longden it was from the Palace.'

'No, sir, I didn't think it was necessary. The caller said there was no need to give any details—Mr. Ralston would know who the message was from.'

'So how do *you* know where the call came from?'

'London called back the Palace exchange after they connected us up.'

'You're sure of this? I want you to be sure, Amy, because I'm about to repeat to the Prime Minister what you have just told me.'

'Yes, sir, positive. But someone can always check with the Palace, can't they?'

'Yes, I suppose they can.'

'Your call to Downing Street, sir.'

Sir Peter transferred the receiver to his left hand and dried his palm on the blotter.

12.15 pm

Thorganby put down the telephone and said: 'They've found the King. He's alive. Ralston is under arrest.'

Critten glared from the fireplace. He looked harassed but full of fight, like a bull after five minutes in the ring. Instinctively his fist closed round the brass poker.

'How the bloody hell . . . ?' he started, then changed his mind. With surprising agility he launched his big body across the room to the door which led to the anteroom, and flung it open. The room was empty. On Miss Delloway's desk, which was wedged in a corner by the far door, stood a cup of steaming coffee. As Thorganby followed Critten into the room, the other door opened and Miss Delloway appeared. She was flushed and carried a glass of water. 'Oh, I'm sorry, sir,' she said, 'I thought you were still on the telephone. Sir James was listening on Alan's extension in here and then he asked if I could get him a glass of water. He looked terrible, white as a ghost. I wonder where . . .'

Thorganby and Critten stood by the window looking

216

down. Four or five people had already gathered round an object on the pavement below. The Lord President's office was only four floors up, but four floors were enough.

Critten's anger had gone. 'So he was wet, like all his kind,' he said.

Thorganby told Miss Delloway to ring for an ambulance. Then he called Scotland Yard on Selkirk's telephone. Neither man spoke while they waited for the police.

Tuesday, August 19th

SECRET
P.M'S EYES ONLY

Office of the Paymaster-General,
AUGUST 19   *Downing Street, S.W.1.*

Attempted Coup d'Etat *between August 4th and August 7th*

The following is a summary interim report, as requested by you, on the facts so far established by the Police, Security Services, the Italian authorities and the British Investigation Commission in Naples. Draft appendices are available giving further statements made by the principal protagonists, unfinished lines of inquiry, etc., but I have assumed you will not wish to see these until they are complete.

Objective
The objective of the conspiracy was to frustrate Operation Constable and ensure that by August 9th, the time fixed for the South African invasion of Rhodesia, the United Kingdom, being the only country equipped and prepared to intervene by force, was in the hands of a Government opposed to such intervention. This was to be achieved by abducting and later murdering the King.

Note: The conspirators correctly assumed that the existing Government under your leadership would approve Operation Constable and that this decision would be backed by the King.

Conspirators
The principal conspirators were Ralston, Courthope and Critten. We are satisfied that Coper was not involved. I deal later with the role of his wife. Lord Thorganby and Silvestri, the Italian aircraft manufacturer, are likewise innocent.

Motives

(a) *Ralston* headed the conspiracy. He appears to have acted throughout for purely financial reasons. His dedication to Herakles Aviation amounted to a monomania. The firm was in serious financial straits which could not much longer be concealed from the Board of Trade or from shareholders. At a meeting in Lisbon last December South African Intelligence offered him the sum of £6 million, to be channelled through Swiss banks, in return for attaining the political objective described above.

(b) *Critten* has admitted to very strong racial views, of which Ralston was aware. These views were sufficient to lead him to join the conspiracy when approached. Once recruited, he appears to have been the most belligerent of the conspirators. He is also the only one who has confessed with reservations and is prepared to defend his views. This aggressive tendency is increasing. He is already under psychiatric treatment and there seems to be some question of his fitness to plead in court. According to my latest information he may be suffering from a tumour on the brain.

(c) *Courthope* was a homosexual. In 1972 an incident in Hyde Park involving a corporal in the Irish Guards had been brought to the attention of Critten as Minister of Defence. On Critten's instructions the incident was given no publicity. Critten later used it to draw Courthope into the conspiracy.

Note: An important characteristic of the conspiracy was that all the three chief conspirators intended that their part in it should never be known. They expected to retain their position even after the crisis.

Method

The conspiracy fell into two distinct parts.

A. It was first necessary to prepare the country psychologically for the revival of the royal prerogative, by creating the greatest possible public disorder and confusion. For this purpose a subversive organisation was created which carried out the following tasks on August 4th and 5th:

(i) the mutiny at Chelsea Barracks, provoked by Meredith,

a member of the organisation who joined the Guards
Division six months earlier for this specific purpose, and
the murder of Sergeant-Major Reith by the same;

(ii) the abduction of Meredith (and, accidentally, a
second guardsman, Steele) from Chelsea guardroom;

(iii) the capture and detention of 23 guardsmen, and the
theft of their equipment;

(iv) the explosion at Rhodesia House;

(v) the violence during Coper's meeting at Oxford;

(vi) the incident at the B.B.C. during your broadcast.

Note: (iii) was achieved by the use of a new gas,
TDB2 (Tetraflurodichlorobromopropane), stolen from Porton
Down in April (viz. my report at the time).

This organisation was set up by Ralston and Critten
together. To head it Critten recruited Rackstraw, an ex-major
of the Parachute Regiment, who thereafter received his
orders direct from Ralston. By offering large sums of money,
Rackstraw was able to recruit ten others; but so far only
Rackstraw and Meredith have been apprehended. For
special tasks Ralston found Poidatz, an ex-member of the
O.A.S., contacted through Mrs. Coper. Mrs. Coper also
arranged without her husband's knowledge for their house in
Oxfordshire to be used as a headquarters. A lady of French
origin and expensive tastes, she had long been an associate of
Ralston, who in 1970 and again last year had paid substantial
debts which she had not wished to admit to her husband.
Ralston and Critten accepted this arrangement, reckoning
rightly that if the organisation was discovered, suspicion
would fall on Coper. In fact Coper and the Movement knew
nothing of the conspiracy.

B. The main conspiracy involved kidnapping and secretly
holding the King for a period of days, during which
time it would appear that he was dead. The King's return
from Ravello to London early on August 6th was the
opportunity for which they had planned. Critten had
suborned a Sergeant Smith of the King's Flight to damage
the hydraulic system of the Swanstar, on which he was
serving as a steward, as soon as the plane arrived at Naples.
(It is now established that Sergeant Smith's death the
next day could not have been accidental. His neck was

220

broken by a blow similar to that suffered by L/Cpl. Evans at Chelsea. Interpol say that Poidatz was the likely killer in both cases.)

Courthope, who had contrived to travel home in advance, had already impressed on the King by telephone from London Airport the need for his immediate return. Ralston offered the Witch to replace the damaged Swanstar. The offer of an Italian plane, the Silvestri Cavaliere, for the same purpose, was not foreseen by the conspirators; but Ralston managed to get his own offer accepted and later made use of Silvestri's offer to divert suspicion from himself. The Witch was carrying a bomb of unknown power placed there by Poidatz, who after the Oxford incident had been flown to Italy hidden in the plane's tail. Just before take-off the Witch paused in darkness at the start of the runway. (Courthope by persuading the King to advance the time of his departure had ensured that it would take place while the airport was still dark.) This was the moment at which the King was removed from the plane. A gas was released in the plane which rendered the King and his party instantly unconscious while the pilot and navigator were protected by masks. The navigator dropped the King from the plane at the start of the runway and Poidatz drove him from the airport in a stolen Italian police car. According to Critten's statement the pilot and navigator had been instructed to fly the remainder of the King's staff to a disused landing strip near Nice, where they would be given fresh orders. They remained ignorant of the bomb planted on the plane until it exploded, killing them and their passengers.

Poidatz took the King to an address in Naples where Ralston's Italian agent was waiting. They began the six-hourly injections of sodium amytal and glucose-saline to keep the King under sedation, and transferred him to a ventilated metal trunk, of a type corresponding to the one which Ralston had led the Embassy to expect. The agent took the trunk to Rome and delivered it locked to Blenkinsop, Ralston's bodyguard, who was ignorant of the contents. Ralston's own room had been selected as the least probable and therefore safest hiding-place. Ralston continued to inject the King himself.

221

Meanwhile Poidatz returned to Naples Airport and dispatched Sergeant Smith. It is thought that the murder was carried out on the personal orders of Ralston, who doubted the Sergeant's ability to hold the Lord Chancellor at bay.

In the U.K. the Prince was persuaded to broadcast on the basis of a false draft prepared in Ravello by Courthope.

The same night (August 6th) Ralston met the South Africans at a secret rendezvous in Rome and made arrangements for the transfer to Herakles of £6m., payable in six equal instalments over a period of 2 years.

Those are the main points. If you wish them amplified orally, I am of course available.

B.S.R.

Harvey closed the brown folder and waved it appreciatively at his Paymaster-General. 'Thank you very much, Bernard. But there's one big point you haven't explained.'

'Fire away,' said the Paymaster-General. 'I'm afraid it's very condensed.'

'You say they were going to kill the King in the end. Obviously they couldn't have kept him prisoner indefinitely, and they'd have lost their necks if he'd returned to the throne. I see that. But why on earth didn't they kill him at once, simply let him blow up in the plane? That trunk business in Rome was very risky.'

'Yes it was, and they had some argument about it beforehand. But they couldn't be sure the plot would work as smoothly as it did. The Prince might have refused to act, you might have refused to resign, Thorganby might have refused to serve. There were plenty of hazards. So they decided to keep the King as a hostage. If the plot had crumbled in the early stages they would have used him as a bargaining weapon, his safety against theirs. The King alive in the trunk was their insurance policy. If everything went well the insurance policy would have been quietly cancelled, and an unknown corpse found in some Roman slum.'

'Charming,' said Harvey. 'Of course Thorganby's Government couldn't have lasted long. But I suppose that wasn't necessary. It would have lasted long enough for the South

222

Africans to have moved into Rhodesia. And once they were in we'd have needed more than Constable to get them out.'

'Exactly. As it was the South Africans were flummoxed. They didn't react quickly enough to the plot's failure, and we managed to get Constable in first.'

'By a whisker, thank God. But there's one other thing I don't understand. Courthope messed up the timing on the Wednesday morning. Why did he ring up Trumper before he could have known the King was dead?'

'That was their big mistake. But it was understandable, really. Critten realised rather late in the day that there was a serious risk that you or someone else would get to the Prince first. He was so keen that Courthope should be there first that when they spoke on the telephone on Tuesday night he persuaded Courthope to jump the gun. Then, as you know, Thorganby's P.S. was bright enough to spot the discrepancy in the timing. Courthope heard him telephoning to Eton from Thorganby's study and, through Louise Coper, got the others to kill him.'

'Yes. I owe a lot to that young man, and the other two. They're getting their George Medal this morning. Only one's on his feet to collect it, but I gather the mothers are there.'

'A gong well earned.'

'Not much thanks to you, Bernard. It's a poor reflection on the Security Services when the nation is saved by three young amateur detectives. Will you have another sherry?'

'No, thanks. I'm taking my boy to Lord's.'

'You saw the tape as you came in?'

'No, what was on it?'

'Ian Smith has accepted our formula for his Cabinet, six White, five Black, an African to have the Ministry of Justice.'

'Does that mean we've got a permanent settlement?'

Harvey laughed. 'Permanent? That's a word I don't know. It means that with luck we can keep both the U.N. and the South Africans quiet for a year or two.'

They had expected pomp and ceremony but it had all been very informal. After the Investiture the King had said a few words to each of them. Mrs. Kemble and Mrs. Steele had

223

dabbed at their eyes once or twice but Mrs. Selkirk had kept her composure, standing slightly apart from the others and dressed in black for her son. Kemble had made the King laugh, and that had relaxed the atmosphere; but afterwards none of them could remember what the joke had been.

Kemble helped the three widows into the back of the official Humber, and sat beside the driver. There was a big crowd at the gates, several hundred people cheering, flash-bulbs, TV cameras and microphones. Kemble got out and said a few words for all of them and held up his medal for the cameras, then the police cleared a way for the car.

They decided to go back to Mrs. Steele's for a celebration and to give Harry his medal. No one was sure if Mrs. Selkirk would want to come, but she said she would.

The street was crowded with well-wishers and more Press. Someone had found them Union Jacks, saved since the Coronation. Kemble handled things again, making a little speech and lining them up for the photographers, then they all crowded into Harry's bedroom and Mrs. Steele made a cup of tea.

Kemble said: 'Here you are, Harry mate, compliments of His Majesty', and tried to pin the thing on his pyjamas. Everyone laughed at that, and there were a few more tears.

'Here, Mum, you keep it,' Steele said, grinning through his bandages. There was a crate of beer under his bed and he and Kemble both had a bottle while the ladies drank tea. Anne Downes arrived in a taxi and the mood was gay as one by one they described the scene at the Palace, trying to remember every word that the King had said. Then there was a sudden silence and Anne said what they were all thinking. 'It's so cruel that Alan isn't here, and so brave of you to come, Mrs. Selkirk.'

'It was my duty to come,' Mrs. Selkirk said. 'Alan would have wanted it; he had a keen sense of duty.'

'More than any of us,' Kemble said. 'They owe it to him more than to any of us.'

'He simply did what plenty of others would have done. His father was the same age, you know, when he died in the Normandy landings.'

'But that was different,' said Mrs. Steele. 'That was a war.'

224